SHE MADE IT MATTER

Chiara Talluto

Don't turn back. Begin anew.

Copyright
ALL RIGHTS RESERVED

Praises

An inherently entertaining and deftly crafted novel from first page to last, "She Made It Matter" showcases author Chiara Talluto's genuine flair for originality, memorable characters, and a thoroughly reader engaging story with an ultimate message of hope and redemption. While especially and unreservedly recommended for community library Contemporary General Fiction collections, it should be noted for personal reading lists that "She Made It Matter" is also readily available in a digital book format (Kindle, $4.99). ~~Reviewed by *Midwest Book Review*

...I would recommend "She Made It Matter" to any readers interested in realistic stories of self-discovery, recovery, and emotional healing. Chiara Talluto has written a compelling story that displays that hope and inner peace can be found, even through the most unconventional journeys. ~~Reviewed by Deanna Francis with *Windy City Reviews*

... So many of us are dealing with some level of pain or addiction, or ghosts from our past, that we crave stories of those who can rise from the ashes. "She Made It Matter" is such a story. I liked getting to know Amanda and witnessing the changes in her perspective and personality as the story unfolded. I also liked journeying into her painful past, with its secrets and heartaches, and watching her fight her way out of her veil of darkness. ~~Reviewed by Susan Miura, author of *Surviving Carmelita*

... Author Chiara Talluto works wonders in this relatively short but totally jam-packed work, which transcends the boundaries of women's fiction and/or inspirational fiction and gives a fully-rounded and highly realistic literary drama. ... ~~Reviewed by K.C. Finn with *Readers' Favorite*

Dedication

To you,

To the addicted, the selfish, the ashamed, the righteous, the rebellious, the sinner, the sinned by, the forgiver, and to the forgiven.

You are worthy, you are loved, and you are cherished. YOU ARE FREE. Make your life right. Make your life matter.

Part I: THAT WAS THEN — GOING HOME

"A time before, a time no more. This ground is bumpy and pebbled with scars."

Musical Inspiration for this Section

"Home" by Daughtry

"It's Your Life" by Francesca Battistelli

Chapter 1

April, 2000. Chicago, IL.

J oshua Lenger rolled his head on the pillow and glanced at his younger
sister, Amanda, sitting on a chair across from his bed. He studied
her, marveling at how his once scrawny, freckled-nosed thin-lipped
sibling had blossomed into a beautiful young woman.

With laboring breath Josh whispered, "I have to tell you
something."

Amanda stopped her nervous foot-tapping and leaned closer to
him. "Don't talk, just rest."

"I—I need to tell you something. Whatever you do in life, make it
right; make it matter. I mean it. Everything. Make it all matter."

Joshua stiffened as thundering bolts of pain shot through his body.
Here it comes. Wide-eyed, he tried focusing on the slow-rotating ceiling
fan and then exhaled.

Above the bedframe, a flat green line ran across the screen as an
uninterrupted beeping sounded. Joshua's breathing ceased; his body
deflating like a laundered sheet flowing over a mattress.

The beeping halted. *He's gone.* She caressed his yellowed face,
destroyed from the chemo during the last nine months. All of Josh's
silky, charcoal-colored hair had fallen out. At twenty-eight, four years
her senior, he resembled an old man, crinkled by the weight of life's
burdens and a debilitating illness. Moving her fingers, she grazed her
beloved brother's swollen purple lips; *they still feel warm.*

There was scratching at the windowsill. Amanda noticed a young robin struggling to grab the ledge. After a couple of failed attempts, it flew away, perhaps taking Josh's soul along for the ride.

A year of suffering big brother. You can rest, it's over.

Two nurses rushed into the room. Amanda stepped out of their way. With a numbing realization of what had just transpired, she collected her jacket and purse and headed out the door.

Pausing mid-step, Amanda turned. "6:43. Time of death was 6:43 p.m."

Chapter 2

Gripping the steering wheel a little longer than necessary, Amanda checked her reflection in the rearview mirror. Her stringy ponytail was listless, dull, and in need of a wash. Peeling a mint from its wrapper, she popped it in her mouth to conceal a vinegar–tasting breath overpowering her senses.

She grabbed her green duffel bag, a bottle of soda, and opened the door, leaving the keys in the ignition. Abandoning the rusted, 1989 burgundy-colored Cutlass Supreme wasn't something Amanda had planned to do, but the plates were long expired, the muffler dangled thanks to a coat hanger, and the heater and radio hadn't worked in several months. Thieves would strip it, or it would be towed. Either way, she was done with it.

Hoisting the bag over her shoulders, Amanda began walking four blocks west on Adams Street toward Union Station. It was Wednesday night, close to eight-thirty and the stars were out gleaming brightly above the buildings. Most of the shops in the financial district of downtown Chicago were closed with the exception of a few restaurants.

Amanda's stomach rumbled as she passed a diner; the smell of grilled meat and onions permeated the air. Moving on, she hiked over a bridge above the Chicago River. The wind slapped at her face, disheveling her hair. She lifted the collar of her fleece jacket. It was April, but the temperature felt more like a thirty-degree February in the Windy City.

Slipping through the automated doors of the train station, Amanda took the escalator to the lower-level, coffee and popcorn teased her nostrils. She passed a bar noticing drunken investors and techies swapping the day's conquests and discussing the latest online tools. They stopped talking, watching as her thin frame bustled by.

Behind the glass of the Amtrak ticket counter, an elderly black agent read the evening paper.

She approached the counter. "Hi. When is the next train to Mount Pleasant, Iowa?"

The Amtrak agent pressed some keys. "Tomorrow at two."

Amanda had no place to stay. She didn't have any girlfriends, only loser ex-boyfriends. Her apartment lease had expired and she never renewed it, so the landlord kicked her out. She had no job, losing it while staying with her brother at the hospital. And now no car, ditching it thinking she'd be able to take an Amtrak to Iowa within the hour.

I'm so stupid. What the hell am I supposed to do for the rest of the evening?

The agent peered over her glasses. "What will it be? I don't have all night. We close at nine-thirty."

Amanda cursed. "Sorry. Make it a one way ticket, please." *I'll worry about a place to stay when I get there.*

"That'll be thirty-eight dollars."

She gave the woman the exact amount and grabbed the ticket from the window slot. "Thanks."

Putting the ticket in her duffel bag, Amanda made a quick stop at a restroom and took the escalator up to Adams Street. She didn't want to stay in the station at the moment. The doors locked at eleven. Later, she'd sneak in past security and try to lay-low in a corner somewhere.

There weren't many options to choose unless she got a hotel in the city. *Forget that!* Amanda needed the three hundred and fifty dollars she had to last until she made it to her destination. She'd promised Joshua she'd go to Iowa and settle things with their mother.

The wind cut at Amanda's face. *I could go back to the car? Sleep in it for the night?* She spotted an inexpensive eatery she'd been to once before, east of Wacker Drive, on the left side of the street. *No use. The car may already be gone. Besides, I'm starving.* She hadn't eaten anything since the night before when Joshua's condition had changed for the worst.

Inside Louie's Pub and Grub, an older woman with lavender-colored hair approached her, smacking her lips and popping bubbles. "Table for one, girly?"

Amanda surveyed the noisy dining area. The place was dark with a gray haze in the air. There were several tables occupied. She gazed over at the bar; a few patrons were watching a reality show on a flat screen.

"Can I eat at the bar?" *I really shouldn't because bars get me in trouble but I don't want to sit at a table by myself, either. To hell with it!*

"Whatever you want, darling," the lady remarked as she headed to the bar area, her musk-scented perfume trailing behind.

Hopping on a wobbly stool at the corner of the bar, Amanda placed her duffel bag on an empty stool next to her, besides a man dressed in business attire.

The bartender strolled over to her. He was good-looking; athletic with blondish hair and a thinly-groomed goatee. "Hi, what can I get for you?"

Amanda removed her jacket noticing a hand-written sign on the wall displaying the evening's beer specials. "I'll have a Miller Light and a menu, please."

"You got it."

The businessman grinned; she caught him staring at her. His shaven head glistened under dangling, pear-colored lights bulbs. He cradled a mixed drink in his hand, the one with a shiny wedding band on his finger. "You don't like Bud Light?"

"Excuse me?"

"You asked for a Miller Light."

The man was nice-looking; had green-eyes, was in his early forties, maybe. He wore a dark-blue suit that was nicely fitted.

Amanda shrugged. "It doesn't matter to me."

He scooched closer, "Doesn't matter, eh? People argue about beer and to you it doesn't matter."

"I'm not a connoisseur. I just wanted something cold."

"Okay, I'll let you slide this time."

Menu in hand, she forced her attention to the list of options as the liquor bottles on the shelves teased her. She decided on a chicken salad wrap with potato chips.

Amanda drained her beer. The nine-thirty news was on. *Less than three hours ago...* She stared at the commercials, anything to distract herself from thinking of her brother.

The man in the suit held out his hand to her. "I'm Gregg, by the way."

"Amanda."

"Nice to meet you. Are you from around here?"

Amanda picked at the label on her bottle, contemplating whether to tell this man that she'd lived in Chicago for the past ten years and was on her way out of town. She hesitated. "Oh, um, passing through. I leave tomorrow afternoon. You?"

"Here on business, from Seattle."

"Nice, do you like Chicago so far?"

"I do, but it's a little lonely when you're here on business."

The bartender stopped by. "You want another beer? Your food should be ready shortly."

"Yes, I mean no. Say, how much for a shot of whiskey?"

"$5.00."

"Oh." *Damn, I could have two shots at Davey's for the price of one.*

"Here let me, Chris," Gregg waved a twenty at the bartender. "You can refill mine so the pretty lady won't have to drink alone."

"That's awfully nice of you. Gee, thanks."

"My pleasure. May I join you?" Gregg pointed to the stool next to her.

"Okay." *I could use a stronger cocktail and a bit of friendly conversation after all this crap.* Moving the duffel bag between them, she dropped it to the floor on the other side, and Gregg slid over.

When their drinks arrived, he offered up a toast. "To company."

"Right, to company." *Here's to you, big brother.*

When her food came, Amanda picked at it while they chatted about sports, weather and his business. He even mentioned his children, six-year-old twin boys.

"I hate being away from them," he admitted, sharing wallet-sized photos of two bright-eyed, blond-haired grinning boys dressed in fancy black suits.

"They're cute," she replied, putting a chip in her mouth.

"Thank you. Unfortunately, their mom doesn't let me see them that often. I travel a lot and we've been separated for four months. Getting ready for a divorce."

"I'm sorry to hear that," Amanda shook her head.

"It happens. Are you married? Have kids?"

"No, none of the above."

"Real nice," the man beamed, revealing straight white teeth. "You're very pretty."

Amanda blushed; feeling the heat of the whiskey. "You are very kind, Gregg."

The bartender came and took Amanda's plate. Looking at her watch, she realized it was ten-thirty. She signaled for the check. *I got to get to the station before it closes and before I order anymore drinks.*

You're leaving so soon?" Gregg leaned closer to her. She caught a whiff of bourbon on his breath.

"Um, yes," she fumbled through her wallet.

He tapped her arm. "Would you like to hang out with me tonight?"

Amanda was startled by his forwardness. *He's nice but I don't think so.* "Are you asking what I think you're asking?"

The man backed away. "I don't know, what do you think?"

Guilt briefly tugged at her conscience. *What would Joshua say?* She had become easy with men. Her experience held true. How many times had her big brother rescued her when she was drunk, fighting off guys looking for a good time? Amanda longed for companionship because there was a constant emptiness in her heart. Alcohol helped. *Another drink might help me to forget my brother is really gone. No, I can't. I have to go.*

Amanda crossed her arms. "It's a good thing you're not a mind reader. Where are you staying?"

"At the Wentworth Hotel."

"I know where that is. I'll hang out for a little while."

Gregg snapped his fingers. "Hey, we can get a little bottle, kind of a nightcap. I saw a convenience store down the street."

"Alright." *I can use some more toothpaste and extra clean underwear for the trip.*

The restaurant was closing. Chris was checking out two patrons at the other end of the bar. Amanda gathered money and placed it on top of the bill. Gregg did the same.

Scooting off the bar stool, Amanda reached for her bag, but Gregg snatched it first. "Here, let me."

"Thank you."

Standing next him, the man wasn't much taller than her 5'5" frame, but bulkier, like he worked out.

When they exited the restaurant, the wind had tapered off and what remained was cold, damp, air. *The train station's closed. This is my only option.*

They strolled in silence for a half-a-block. When they arrived at the store, Gregg opened the door for her. "After you."

"I just need to get a few things. Let's meet at the registers?"

"Sure."

As they parted to opposite aisles, Amanda paused and watched after Gregg. Her brother had passed away a few hours earlier, and here she was already planning to bed a stranger. *Josh is gone. What am I doing?* Staring at an empty aisle, she tapped the mobile phone inside her back pocket as she often did, anticipating a call from him.

Someone bumped into her. "Oh, pardon me," Amanda replied, moving out of the way. *Get a grip.*

She picked up toothpaste, gum and a five-pack of white bikini undies. When she approached the only cashier, Gregg was already there with a bottle of bourbon and a six-pack of Coke.

He chuckled, "I like your choice of underwear."

She couldn't hide the package with all the other items she was holding. "Shut up," she snorted.

They each paid for their purchases and left. Outside, Gregg paused. "I've never done this before."

"Done what?"

He winked at her. "This."

Amanda groaned. Was she actually considering sleeping with this man? *This isn't right.* Tomorrow was a new beginning for her. Tonight would be the same old, same old. She was desperately seeking companionship and Gregg looked like he was in the same situation. *What's one night anyway?*

He laughed, "We're one-night stand virgins."

Amanda grabbed his arm, looking at the passing pedestrians. "Oh my God! Not so loud. What are you doing?"

"Trying to calm my nerves."

"Geez, that makes two of us."

When they arrived at the hotel, Gregg held the door for Amanda. This was a newly renovated hotel. Formerly the Sheraton, it reopened a year ago as the Wentworth. Never having been inside, she examined the interior design; it smelled like a floral shop.

Rich cherry furniture graced the entrance. A glass table with thick, bronzed legs held a large vase full of fresh cut wildflowers and roses.

"This is gorgeous."

"Yes, it is! Come with me." Gregg guided her to the elevator doors. They traveled up to the seventh floor and walked to room 7102. He waved his key card over a slot, heard a click and pushed open the door.

Gregg flicked on the lights. As they moved through the short hallway, she observed a bathroom to the left and a closet directly across. Straight ahead and to the left again was a king-size bed with a beige comforter covered in brown and gold-striped pillows. A flat screen television sat on top of an oak dresser across from the bed. Farther along in the corner was a desk with a hanging lamp hovering over a closed laptop and a few stacks of papers shoved underneath it.

"Lovely," Amanda put her bag on the floor and walked to the window. She peeled back the sheer drapes, looking at cars and taxis below.

Gregg removed his suit jacket and tie, arranged the bottle of bourbon and soda on the dresser, and grabbed the ice bucket. "I'll be right back."

Amanda opened the closet, slid off her jacket and hung it up besides two neatly pressed business suits. She hauled the extra suitcase stand from inside the closet and put it up against the wall in the hallway, placing her duffel bag on top along with her purchases.

Amanda was getting her toothpaste and toothbrush when Gregg sauntered in.

"Make yourself comfortable," he whispered, sliding past her, their bodies touching briefly.

Tiny, prickly goosebumps broke out on her arms. Shaking it off, she asked. "May I take a shower?"

"Of course. I'll make us a couple of drinks."

"Thanks."

Amanda grabbed her toiletries and entered the bathroom, placing them on the counter. Gregg had a razor, shaving cream, deodorant and cologne occupying the space. Amanda moved them aside, but not before picking up his cologne and smelling it—hints of citrus and baby powder. A shiver ran down her spine. She stared at her reflection in the mirror. Her face looked pale in the bright lights and taking down her hair, it limply hugged her neckline.

She removed her clothing and got in the tub. She lathered up with the hotel's liquid soap and shampoo. *It feels great to wash away the image of my brother's dead body.*

The room was steamed up, so she wiped the mirror with a washcloth. She ran a comb through her wet hair and applied lotion all over her body. Putting on undergarments, Amanda slid into a white, fluffy robe that hung behind the door.

Gregg was lying on the bed, sipping his drink and watching a basketball game.

"Your drink is on the dresser."

"Great. Thank you."

"Relax, I'm going to change. Turn the channel if you like," Gregg said while removing his wedding ring.

The ring is off now.

Sitting at the edge of the bed with drink in hand, Amanda retied the belt around her robe. *A nervous reflex I guess.* Idly flipping through channels, she paused long enough to take a few sips of bourbon, feeling the burn coating her throat. *Better.*

A few minutes later, Gregg emerged wearing black boxer shorts and a white tank-top. He hopped on the bed and pushed the comforter away from their feet.

"Snuggle up to me," he said, smoothing the sheets.

Amanda hesitated. *What am I doing here?* Taking a long drink, she placed the half-empty glass on the dresser and joined Gregg.

"Comfortable?"

"Yes."

Gregg stroked her arms. "You are really gorgeous."

Amanda's face reddened, feeling the moment; she tried to give herself permission to relax. They kissed, gentle and awkwardly at first, and then fast and desperate, a desperation of two different longings. *I think I can do this. I'm being cared for, right?*

He peeled open her robe, kissing her neck and caressing her breasts through her bra. Amanda pressed against his chest, noticing a small tattoo; a green rattlesnake encircled his right pec. She ran her fingers across it, having seen a similar tattoo before.

"You like it?" He took off his undershirt.

"Yeah, I do."

"I got it in the Marines. Several buddies and I have the same tattoo. We also purchased these silly pendant necklaces. I don't even wear the damn chain; it's supposed to be a sign of brotherhood."

Amanda pushed away from him. "Where were you?"

"Shit, I've been all over the damn Middle East. Spent time in Germany too. I got this 'tat', about five years ago. Why do you ask?"

"My brother had been in Germany a few times. He had a similar tattoo."

Gregg inched closer. "You're kidding? What's his name?"

"Joshua ... Josh ... Lenger." Saying his name made Amanda tremble. *This is wrong. I have to stop now.*

"I think I remember him, tall guy, wavy hair, very health conscience."

Amanda nodded.

"You're his sister? What a small world! Where is he now?"

There was no denying the realization; Joshua was dead. Amanda placed her hands over her face.

Gregg reached over, "What's wrong?" She backed away. He shifted, giving her space.

Amanda composed herself. "Gregg, I'm sorry." She closed her robe and got off the bed. "I can't do this. I have to go."

"Wait, did I do something wrong?"

She went to her bag, looking for clothing. "I really need to go." *I'm so stupid!*

Gregg grabbed her shoulders and spun her around. "What just happened? Whatever I did, I'm sorry. I don't understand."

She lifted her head and met his eyes. "My brother died *today*. He was at the Veterans Administration Hospital."

"Oh my God! Why the hell didn't you tell me?"

Amanda put her head down and whispered, "What am I supposed to say to a stranger at a bar? I'm leaving town tomorrow because my brother made me promise to find our mother in Iowa to tell her he's dead."

Gregg moved a strand of hair from her face. "What did he die from?"

Still in shock, denial, or stupidity, she couldn't decide, she uttered, "Leukemia."

"I'm so sorry. Please don't leave."

Amanda looked up. "He was my only family. I'm all alone now."

He embraced her. "Not tonight, you're not alone."

Weary from her sudden loss, Amanda dropped her clothes on the floor and fell into the man's arms. He carried her to the bed, all expectations gone, and held her under the covers as she cried until she couldn't anymore.

Chapter 3

A persistent ringing woke Amanda. She lunged for the culprit—the telephone.

"Yes?" she mumbled, mouth dry.

"Hello, this is your wake up call, the time is—"

Amanda slammed the receiver, laid back down and massaged her sticky eyes lids. She was alone in bed. Her head instantly popped up, remembering Gregg's room and the Wentworth Hotel.

Cautiously, she lifted the covers, relieved to see her undergarments still looking like new. Her eyes darted to the bottle on the dresser; a quarter of the bottle was empty. *Oh, no! What happened?*

A minute later, Gregg walked out from the bathroom wearing a pair of blue boxers and a fresh white undershirt.

"Hi."

"Hey."

"How did you sleep?"

"Good, I think. What happened last night?"

Gregg snuggled in her neck. "Technically, nothing. It's okay. I enjoyed falling asleep next to you."

"I'm sorry."

He put his finger to her lips. "Shh, it's all right. I'm really sorry about your brother. I want you to know, I did have a nice time just the same." Amanda sighed. "I gotta go. I have a lot of meetings today. I should be done by two, we can—"

"My train leaves at two."

Gregg grabbed a pair of socks and put them on. "Do you have to go today?"

Amanda sat up. "The ticket's paid for. I need to get this over with."

He rubbed his chin. "I understand. Tell you what?" He grabbed a piece of stationery and a pen and wrote his number down. "Stay as long as you want. Call me sometime. I'd like to keep in touch."

"Thanks." She accepted the paper, memorizing the number just as a yearning swept through her body; she wished they'd made love last night even though it wouldn't have been the wisest thing to do. The moment passed, and so did the desire.

Gregg adjusted his tie, "If you change your mind and want to stay one more night, we can finish what we tried to start."

Exhaling, Amanda felt tormented. "I shouldn't."

She scooted off the bed and went up to him; they kissed, lingering a little. Gregg let her go, putting the extra keycard on the dresser next to their empty glasses. He picked up his briefcase and left.

She watched him, hugging her body, aware of a bursting desire within her. Amanda didn't have time to dwell on her feelings, though. After washing her face and dressing, a pair of blue jeans and a long-sleeve jersey, she repacked her stuff. It was eight o'clock. A pounding headache began so she took two aspirins from Gregg's pill box, washing them down with lukewarm water.

Amanda considered her next step, temptation tugging at her heart. She could cancel her train reservation, stay one night and leave the following day, or, she could continue as planned.

Amanda liked Gregg, but he had materialized at the wrong time. She wasn't good at relationships. Nothing ever lasted, anyway. It would be sex and good times, nothing more. Leaving was the right thing to do.

Taking another piece of stationery and a pen from the desk, Amanda scribbled.

Gregg,

I need to fulfill my brother's wishes and close another chapter in my life. You're a great guy. It was nice meeting you, despite the circumstances. I truly wish we had met when things weren't so messy for me. Thank you for being there. Safe travels to Seattle. XOXO, Amanda Lenger

Folding the paper in half, Amanda placed it under the bottle of liquor next to the extra keycard. Her head still pounded. *I shouldn't.* But then she did—shooting back half-a-glass of liquid fire. She steadied herself as her throat burned and her empty stomach gurgled from the alcohol rush.

Going to the bathroom sink, Amanda added a partial glass of water and tightened the cap. *He won't notice.* One final look around to make sure all was in place, she lifted her duffel over her shoulder and marched out of the door and then exited the hotel.

After a brisk walk, Amanda found an empty bench in the train station. She checked her money and telephoned a local hotel in Mount Pleasant to reserve an overnight stay. With a few hours to spare, she watched morning commuters. *God knows I should have stayed in Gregg's room a little while longer. No, no. The temptation to finish off his liquor is just too much for me to handle. I need time to plan what to do when I get to Iowa.*

It had been ten years since Amanda last saw Louise. *Is Mother even alive?* All she had to show for it was an address on a piece of paper that her brother had given her. *How did Joshua get this address, anyway?*

Amanda needed a reconciliation of some kind, but another part of her didn't want any relationship with the woman. *Why didn't Mom come looking for us?* She remembered the time when she brought up that same question to Josh.

It was the end of September. Three weeks had passed since escaping Des Moines due to Louise's instability and her brother didn't want them being in a toxic environment anymore. Amanda and Joshua had found a hostel in Chicago on the corner of Congress Parkway and Wabash. The hostel was designed for travelers, mostly young adults, in dormitory-style accommodations. It was also cheap, only thirty-dollars a day for the both of them. Amanda had stayed in a female section, rooming with three other women, while Joshua bunked in the male area, rooming with two other guys.

For the time being, Amanda wasn't attending high school. Josh had been working on paperwork with a friend back home to get her records secretly transferred to Chicago.

During the day, they roamed the city looking for an apartment they could afford while Joshua filled out job applications. They were sitting on the lawn in Grant Park one afternoon, tired and hungry, she remembered.

"Josh?"

He stretched, his face creased with stress. "Don't worry, I'll find a job. Soon we'll be eating more than canned food."

Amanda shook her head. "No, it's not that."

"So the hostel isn't the best. Do you think I like it?"

She touched his arm. "Will you just stop?"

Joshua sighed; the corners of his eyes were dark and puffy. He was carrying a heavy burden; getting them a place to live, finding a job and taking care of his younger sister. Amanda felt sorry for her brother because he didn't need the pressure.

"Why hasn't Mom come looking for us?"

"Nobody knows where we are except for Burt, and he's getting your school stuff in order."

Amanda recalled shaking her fists in frustration. "It's as if we've disappeared."

Her brother glared at her. "Well, kind of. I for one don't want to go back. Seeing Mom drunk and with all kinds of men parading in the house, no thanks."

"We could have helped her? I want Mom to be the way she used to be."

"HELP? She doesn't want help. Mom doesn't want us anymore, remember what she called us—'pieces of shit'."

"What happened to her, Joshua? Why did she change so drastically?"

Joshua looked away, "I don't know. She changed when Dad died. Maybe she couldn't handle it. Or she didn't want to handle it. All I can think is she was a coward."

A couple of cyclists rode past them.

Amanda wrung her hands. "I hate her."

Her brother nudged her. "I want to hate her too. But we shouldn't. Don't lower yourself to her level. You have to be strong. You're fourteen and have your whole life ahead of you. Don't worry; I'll always be here with you, no matter what."

Amanda jabbed him. "No matter what? Even when you get married and have a family of your own, you won't disown me?"

Josh poked her back. "Yes, no matter what."

Even with her brother's comforting words, thoughts of betrayal and abandonment from their mother still churned inside her stomach.

They were quiet for a bit; just people-watching. With their financial situation weighing on her mind, she asked, "How are we going to live? This is a lot of responsibility for you."

He patted her cheek affectionately. "We'll be fine, you and me. I promise."

"Fine, huh?"

"That's right." Joshua stood up. "Want some ice cream?"

"Now, this early?"

He raised his arms in the air. "Why not? You *do* like ice cream."

Amanda squinted at brother's face. "I'm not ten anymore."

"I know. But ice cream is awesome at any age."

Joshua began walking; Amanda followed behind. He would make everything right for them. He had to.

At one-thirty-five, Amanda climbed the stairs of the California Zephyr, traveling to Iowa. She put her bag in the overhead and slumped in the seat next to the window.

A woman stood on the platform holding hands with her young daughter. Amanda cringed at the loving image before her eyes. She recalled when Louise had held her in that way. They were in line for a Ferris wheel ride at the Iowa State Fair. Raising her eyes, she watched her mother and father whispering and giggling. They were in love. They had all been happy, and Amanda had never felt more secure than that time standing in a crowd with her parents.

Amanda's brown eyes welled up; she grabbed a napkin from her jacket pocket. *I'm such an idiot.* The mother and daughter were gone and so was the warm memory.

At exactly two, the train pulled out of the station; it would be a four-hour trip. Amanda uncapped a small bottle of whiskey and took a sip, glancing around. She'd bought it on clearance at the pharmacy in the train station. *What am I going to say to Mom? How will she react when she sees me?*

She took another sip. Her body shook with disgust. The liquor was bitter, but it relaxed her nerves. *What if Momma's reaction isn't inviting, what should I do?* A few more sips. Amanda capped the bottle. *Okay, stop. I have to make this last four hours.*

She rested against the back of the seat. *I have to quit overanalyzing and get this done.* The future was an unknown for Amanda. She'd have to start over somewhere. Going back to Chicago was not something she looked forward to because it would just be a painful reminder of Joshua's death.

Chapter 4

The train chugged along; Amanda could no longer make out the Chicago skyscrapers. Questions crammed her brain. *After Mount Pleasant, where to? Where will I live? Can I make it on my own?*

Joshua often reminded her not to rush things. She remembered him saying, "If one lived fast, death would come just as quickly. However, if you savored life and all the crazy moments it gives you, then it will be harder to forget the things that matter."

In the final days, her beloved brother was convinced he was the victor over such a diminishing affliction as leukemia. Unfortunately, the damning disease had slowly and painfully consumed him.

Shaking her head, she noticed her reflection in the glass. Her face had an orange tinge from the lighting. Ten years had gone by since leaving their mother's home. Now, twenty-four-years-old, living like a runaway, and losing her brother, had aged her.

Forget was what Amanda wanted to do. *Everything—my childhood, my mom and my brother, I want a big eraser to wipe this board clean.*

Her thoughts were distracted by two teenage boys fighting over a video game a few rows ahead. Their mother, sitting across from them and eating chocolates, kept shushing them, but they weren't listening. Amanda stretched her thin, jean-covered legs across the seat. The chocolate-eating woman triggered an argument she'd had with Josh last year over his leukemia diagnosis.

"Look at you acting all 'Positive Patty'," Amanda huffed. "You've been diagnosed with cancer for God's sake! You will die and I'll be all alone!"

"'Life's like a box of chocolates, you never know what you're going to get.'"

"Seriously?" she barked back, covering her head with her hands. "Stop with the stupid Forest Gump quotes!"

Joshua reached across the table filling her plate with macaroni and cheese, their third straight night of the boxed dinner. "Don't play with your hair. Eat."

"No," Amanda replied, pushing her dish away.

They sat at a white plastic patio table they had bought at a garage sale. They'd placed it in their tiny, two-bedroom one-bath apartment located on the north side of the city. It was shoddy, but it was what they could afford at the time. The El stop was a block away, and every time a train passed, their six-flat building shook.

Her brother growled. "Sometimes we need to accept—"

Amanda was unable to hear the rest of what he said because a train thundered down the tracks. He crinkled his forehead. "Understand? Now eat your food before it gets cold."

Straightening up in her seat, Amanda wondered why she never asked Joshua about that conversation afterward. Her brother was organized and protective of her. With him gone, she worried about her future. Barely receiving a two-year college education, she hoped to return to school when time and money permitted to earn a Bachelor's Degree in Business Management.

In the meantime, Amanda had held several jobs during their ten years in Chicago. She had been a hotel reservationist, an administrative assistant, and recently a salesperson at a boutique. It was temporary, but it helped pay the bills. With little money in her pocket, she needed to find a job soon.

Luckily for them, Joshua had great insurance and all of his medical bills had been paid by the military because he had done three, six-month tours in both Afghanistan and Iraq, then being stationed at a camp in Germany. During those tours, Amanda struggled emotionally. Loneliness and dread consumed her thoughts with not having a parental figure around. But she was not entirely alone; there were the constant male suitors and alcohol who kept her company. Feelings of being lonely were bearable, only just.

Each time her brother returned, the superficial relationships ended, even though she continued to drink secretly. It was an unbreakable habit—like a security blanket. Her mother, Louise, had become a pro at it and Amanda had fallen into the same shoes.

Amanda had been grateful for her brother's protection. There would be no one to care for her or get her out of any predicaments now.

Peering over at the two teenagers, she noticed they had finally calmed down; the younger one looked like he'd be dozing soon. With the little liquor bottle empty, *that didn't last long*, sleep seemed like a good idea. Amanda closed her eyes as Iowa drew closer.

Chapter 5

It was summer and the air was still, stale and so sticky that loose granules of rock stuck to Amanda's sweaty body. She has been playing in the sandbox with her brother. They were at a nearby park; Louise took pictures of them with her Polaroid. Their mother was constantly taking pictures and putting them in albums to show their father. He drove a truck and was out of state most of the week.

"Mommy, Mommy, look what we're building, an 'astle'," four-year-old Amanda squealed.

"Castle, Amanda. Not 'astle'." Joshua corrected her.

Their mother beamed, pointing the camera in their direction. "That's great, honey, smile, kids." She and Josh stuck out their tongues, making funny faces.

Louise oohed and ahhed. "Awesome, wait, now hold that pose."

Afterwards, they went to the Dairy Queen and enjoyed a double scoop of vanilla ice cream, while pouring over dozens of photos, laughing and making up stories to tell their father when he returned home. Amanda had been so happy.

Little did they know, three years later, their bubbly family life would burst by a freak car accident, killing their father, John.

It happened on a bright spring day, a Tuesday, in the middle of the afternoon. Amanda and Joshua had gotten off the bus and were skipping up the driveway. Usually, the garage door was open and Louise would be sitting on a lawn chair reading a book, waiting for them. On that day, the garage door was closed, and they were greeted by wailing from inside the house.

Sprinting through the front door, they found their mother cradling the phone, curled up on the floor, shaking and sobbing. After a long while, she told them what had happened.

John had been in Fargo, North Dakota. In the Midwest, heavy snowstorms were causing all sorts of havoc. Her father was traveling north when a semi-truck swerved into oncoming traffic and slammed into his truck. He died instantly.

Their father's passing impacted all of them. Joshua was hurting the most. He adored their dad; always tried acting cool like him. When the boy stopped eating and drinking for a couple of weeks, their mother rushed him to the emergency room because he became too weak.

Seeing Joshua plummet made Amanda sink into a deep sorrow. Every room in the house, every sport's telecast, every Jazz song on the radio, and even the tools in the garage were constant reminders of a man who swooped into their lives occasionally while his overpowering presence remained long after he'd leave for work.

Her memories flashed forward a few more years. Amanda was fourteen and Joshua eighteen. It was her brother's high school graduation and they were getting ready for the long-anticipated event. Louise was sprawled on the living room couch in a dead sleep with two empty liquor bottles on the coffee table.

Joshua approached Amanda, "Let's go."

"Wait, what about Mom?"

"She isn't coming."

Amanda folded her arms over her chest and stared at her older brother. "Wake her up now."

"She's drunk, passed out on the couch."

Her eyes grew moist. "But why won't you try?"

Looking handsome in his tan suit, white shirt, and blue tie he had bought at the local thrift store with money he had earned working part-time at Pete's Pizza Palace, Joshua pulled her through the hallway and into the kitchen. "You're the only one I care about. Don't you want to see me get my diploma?"

Amanda quivered. Of course she wanted to be there for her brother's big day, but with her mother missing out, it had made her see the dysfunctional home she was living in.

"Okay."

The next scene was a little blurry in Amanda's mind. It was August, two months later. Des Moines was experiencing one of its hottest summers. The windows were open in their apartment; a thick warm haze shrouded their tight living quarters. Amanda was draped on the bed with earbuds firmly lodged in her ears, music blasting.

Joshua suddenly bolted through her bedroom door. "It's time," he yelled.

Amanda yanked the earplugs out. "What?"

"We're leaving."

"Right now?"

He grabbed her left arm, "Yes."

Amanda squirmed, "I'm afraid. I don't think we should."

"Trust me, I'll take care of you. If we don't get out of here, we never will. Do you understand what I'm saying here?"

There was banging and glass shattering in the kitchen. With panic coursing through her, Amanda gathered her belongings. Fifteen minutes later, she finished filling up a small black garbage bag and met Josh outside her bedroom. They tiptoed through the corridor to the front door when they were stopped by Louise's raspy voice.

"Where the hell are you two going?"

They froze and faced her. Her house dress was torn and she had the beginnings of a bruise under her left eye.

Joshua pulled his shoulders back. "Out of here, Ma, away from you."

Louise cackled, "Pieces-of-shit, kids."

Ray, her boyfriend, approached them and burped loudly. "Let them go. They'll be back. Oh, and pick me up some soda from wherever you're going."

"I should have never born you two," their mother wheezed, "nothing but trouble, both of you. Get out!"

A distressed Amanda couldn't move. Her mother's harsh words sunk into her like quicksand.

Josh glared at Louise, "Look's like you're getting your wish, Ma."

And with that, he opened the door, dragging his younger sibling behind him.

Chapter 6

"Next stop, Mount Pleasant Station."

Amanda stirred, peering out the window at the red glow of the Iowa sky. *Time to face Mom.* It was almost six as the train coasted into a deserted station; unlike the noisy congested Union Station in downtown Chicago.

There were less than nine thousand people in this small, blue-collar town; manufacturing was their leading means of support. The biggest county attraction was the annual Old Thresher's Reunion, an educational but fun gathering held in August which included demonstrations of antique farming equipment. A hundred thousand spectators came out to see the old engines. *Why would Mom, so active and outgoing when she was younger, want to live in this quiet town rather than stay in Des Moines where we'd grown up?*

The train eased to a halt. Amanda grabbed her duffel bag and filed out with the rest of the passengers.

"The station will be closing in forty-five minutes."

Hurrying inside the train station, she stopped and leaned against the wall, dropping the bag at her feet. From inside her back pocket, Amanda nervously removed a torn yellow piece of paper with an address scribbled in red ink (Mom's home address), and a gray envelope with a P.O. Box written on the outside with a brand new silver key inside it.

Two weeks earlier, Joshua had given these items to his sister hoping she'd finally reconcile with Louise. He had found the information thanks to a military friend's aunt in Des Moines, Iowa. The aunt knew of their mother and where she'd moved to because they had both lived in the same trailer park.

"You have to go and set things right with her, for me and for you."

"This sucks. I don't want to go alone," she complained, frustration burning inside her.

"Amanda." He coughed as he passed her the envelope with the key inside it. "It took me a long time to find Mom again, she moves around a lot. I wish I had the information before. Unfortunately, I can't go. You see the condition I'm in? Please understand that you don't need her in your life. You'll be okay. I've made sure of it."

She opened the small envelope. "What am I supposed to do with this stupid key?"

Joshua's voice became hoarse. "First, visit Mom, then go to this post office and get to the lockbox."

Amanda threw the envelope on the bed. "I hate her. She abandoned us. You want me to visit her and do what? I'll spit in her face, that's what."

Her brother's coughing became worse and Amanda rushed out of the room to fetch him some water.

She offered him a paper cup. "I'm sorry for upsetting you."

"Thanks." He took a long sip. "Sis, you have to do this. I won't be here much longer."

"Quit now! Don't say anything more." Stomping to the window, Amanda focused on the neighboring building's rooftop air-conditioning units. She needed desperately to stop the explosion of anger bubbling inside her.

Her brother's cough lessened as he said, "I can't change my situation. My time is up. You'll prosper, I know you will. I hated Mom for what she did to us but I've forgiven her now and so should you. Do it for me, please."

Amanda hugged her arms. The reality of her circumstance was staring her in the face. Her beloved brother was leaving this world; taking the easy way out. She couldn't deny him this last request.

Amanda slipped into a white taxi waiting to take her to her destination. A wave of uncertainty overcame her. *Why did I agree to do this? I'm not strong enough. I need another drink to calm me down.* Sober at the moment, she vowed to follow her brother's instructions. There were many unknowns she'd have to face and get through.

She pictured her mom wearing the same house dress, the one she last saw her in. Her hair would be in disarray and she might be a little heavier. Louise hadn't been into a healthy lifestyle after their father died. Beer and whiskey became her new diet.

Amanda saw herself marching up to Louise and looking her straight in the eye.

"Hi Momma, remember me? ... Amanda, your daughter."

"I live in Chicago now."

"Where's Joshua, you ask? Wow, great question. He passed away, Mom. Yep, he had cancer. It's just me now."

Amanda imagined her mom's shocked look, the same look she had when they found out their father died. Then, Louise might cry, or not. She wasn't sure. Maybe they'd hug and her mother would say, "I've missed you. I'm sorry. I blew it." And, all would return back to normal. *Maybe?*

After driving forty minutes, passing rolling farmlands where crops were starting to come into season, she arrived at the Grand Heritage Trailer Park.

Small trailers and larger ones were neatly aligned in parallel rows reminding her of trucks parked for the night at a roadside truck stop. Some trailers were decorated with festive lights, their door stoops brightened by geranium-filled flowerpots. Other homes were plain, lacking warmth and a home-like feel to them.

The taxi inched along as both she and the driver scanned the mailboxes for 513A32 Windsor. There was a bend in the road, following the street sign, the driver veered left.

Moving slowly, Amanda got a sick feeling in the pit of her stomach. Kids were playing ball outside one trailer; they stopped to stare as the taxi cruised on by. Amanda spied an old medium-sized tan trailer with the matching address.

"Stop here." They were half a block away. "Keep the car running, please."

Amanda debated whether she should get out when the door to the trailer opened. A wrinkled-looking woman wearing a haggard, red polka-dot housedress walked onto the porch with a cigarette hanging from her mouth. *My mother!* She stared through the glass of the taxicab. *It can't be?* Louise had aged tremendously in just ten years.

With a cold demeanor, she tossed a black bag into an open garbage container next to the stair railing. Louise had never been a pretty woman, but she had several admiring features which Amanda recalled from childhood. A simple beauty: clear-skinned, friendly green eyes; ponytailed, flaxen-colored hair; casually dressed in jeans and t-shirts; and always smelling like lemons and baby powder. Later though, when Amanda was older, her mom resorted to dressing in shapeless, boxy dresses, spending most days smoking and drinking, especially after losing her job of fifteen years as a bakery production operator.

Louise squinted over at the taxi, taking a long drag. Amanda crouched in the seat hoping not to be noticed.

Her driver, an African-American older gentleman, looked over his shoulder. "Miss, you want to continue waiting?"

A teenaged boy slowly biked past, gaping at Amanda in the taxi. They made eye contact. He had a brown-blond crew cut.

Standing on the porch, Louise took another drag and threw the butt onto the pavement, while talking to the boy as he rode by. Amanda watched her mom go back inside the house.

Looking down at the piece of paper, Amanda crumpled it. "We can go now. Please take me to my motel." She provided the cab driver the address. *This isn't Momma. Sorry Joshua.*

"As you wish."

Her stomach growled. "Is there a convenience store or a restaurant around here?"

"Yes, near your motel. Check with the front desk."

"Great."

Amanda hadn't wanted to stay overnight in Iowa, but at this point what was there to do? She hadn't planned her trip out very well, and she repeatedly cursed herself for not getting a connecting ticket earlier or a round trip ticket back to Chicago. But then again, she didn't want to go back to the Windy City, either. For now Amanda was stuck in this town. She clasped her hands together. *Stay focused. Think.*

As the taxi drove out of the trailer park, Amanda watched the same farms pass her by. *If I had gotten out of the cab would Mom have remembered me?*

The driver peeked through the rearview mirror. "Are you in some kind of trouble?"

Amanda laughed. "Trouble? No sir, I'm not."

He pointed his finger at her. "You don't look like a troublemaker." She smiled for the first time that day.

The taxi approached the motel; the driver shifted the car into Park and turned to face her. "Young lady, whatever your problem is, I suggest you face it straight on. You'll never get closure. Life is cruel, but forgiveness is freeing."

Amanda's shoulders sagged, "Thank you. I appreciate your kind words."

It was not quite dark, but from under the overhead streetlamp shining through the front window, the man's face glowed. "May God be with you."

She squinted at the meter as the cabby pressed a button, the amount changed to zero.

"What are you doing?"

He waved her off. "Go."

Amanda reached for the door handle, shocked by the kindness of the driver. "Thank you, again."

As the cab sped away, Amanda spotted the convenience store next to the motel and walked over to it. There, she picked up a pint of whiskey. *Just in case.*

Entering the motel, she approached the check-in counter. A medium-framed woman dressed in a slightly frayed black vest over a tight, white blouse, was hunched over the keyboard of a desk computer. Straightening up, she greeted her. "Welcome to the *W*. I'm Danielle. How may I help you?"

"I have a reservation under Amanda Lenger."

She tapped at some keys. "Here we go. One night, non-smoking, queen-sized bed?"

"Yes."

Amanda studied the clerk who could have been a couple of years younger than herself; she had pale skin and crooked front teeth. Catching a whiff of Cheetos or chips on her breath, Amanda glanced down, spotting a small bag under the counter. Her stomach growled again.

Danielle punched more keys. "That will be $55.00, on a credit card?"

"Is cash okay?"

"You'll have to pay it up front."

Amanda rummaged through her purse and pulled out the money. Her fingers grazed the envelope with the key her brother had given her to the lockbox. *I better not forget to go here tomorrow.*

Danielle gave her a keycard and a receipt. "Room 229. Go through the hall, turn right and take the elevator to the second floor."

"Perfect, is there a place to ear nearby?"

The clerk smiled, retrieving a menu from a drawer. "There's a pizza joint and they have sandwiches."

Amanda flipped through the menu, already knowing what she wanted. "Do they deliver?"

"Yes."

"Great, may I use your phone to place an order?"

"It would be my pleasure."

Danielle dialed the number and handed it to Amanda. She ordered a personal-sized cheese and pepperoni pizza and a large Diet Coke.

After Amanda hung up, she moseyed to her room. The hotel had soft music piped through the halls. She passed the swimming pool with a Jacuzzi and wished she had a bathing suit.

Taking the elevators to the second floor, she stopped at the fifth room down the hall. Opening the door, an old woody smell tickled her nose. "Phew, it's stuffy in here."

Amanda dropped her duffel bag on the bed and pushed down on the mushy mattress. It felt like a deflating balloon under the pressure of her fingers. She sauntered over to the window and opened the drapes. Her room overlooked a half-empty parking lot. She could see the pizzeria that Danielle had recommended.

Removing her sneakers, she went into the bathroom to wash up. Pulling the shower curtains aside, the worn white ceramic tub was inviting enough to soak. *A bath would be great.*

Amanda sat on the bed and turned on the TV, clicking through the channels. Stopping to watch a reality show, she opened the whiskey bottle and took a swig, cringing at the boldness of the amber liquid.

Twenty minutes later a knock on the door jolted her off of the bed and she grabbed her wallet. A short, graying older gentleman with round glasses and a faded beige cowboy hat greeted her.

"Good evening, here is your delivery." He handed her a small square box and a large soda.

"Thanks."

"That will be ten dollars and fifty cents."

Amanda gave him fifteen dollars and he dug in his jeans pocket to retrieve her change. As he did, a necklace dangled out of his windbreaker. It was an emerald pendant with a silver cross etched inside.

Joshua had the same pendant! He told her it represented a symbol of unity among the marines while stationed in Afghanistan and Iraq. And these men, some two hundred of them, received this keepsake and made a pact to wear this pendant always. In ten years, they were supposed to meet up again for a reunion. Coincidentally, Gregg, the almost divorced one-night stand man in Chicago, mentioned he had a similar pendant.

The man asked. "Are you alright?"

Amanda pointed to his chest. "Um, where did you get that pendant from?"

"This was my son's. He died in Afghanistan. This is all I have left of him."

She nodded, knowing the feeling of loss. "I'm terribly sorry. My brother had one, too. He is gone; leukemia—" Amanda had almost said yesterday, but that would have sounded superficial. She was in a motel by herself and her brother was dead.

With watery eyes, the man gathered the change. "Here you go, Miss. I'm sorry for your loss as well."

She pushed it back. "No … No. That's for you, keep it. Thanks for the pizza."

Amanda closed the door, flopped on the bed and took a sip of her Coke. The pizza smelled good, but she'd lost her appetite. She grabbed a plastic baggy from her duffel bag. Inside was the same exact pendant. She opened it and wept, letting her hands run over the cold metal jewelry.

Five weeks earlier, Joshua was admitted to the hospital for the final time. Two bouts of intensive chemo over a period of nine months hadn't resolved anything. The leukemia had spread all over his body. The doctors said it was only a matter of time. They caught the cancer too late and now they would wait. Wait until death defeated her brother's failing organs.

Easter came at the end of March, Joshua's last holiday. She watched as he played with his food. Josh had been pensive the last few days, neither one of them was speaking much.

That particular morning she and her brother attended mass in the hospital's little chapel. Raised Roman Catholic, they never practiced their faith, so Amanda found it odd they would even go to church.

She pushed her big brother in a wheelchair and watched as he prayed for the longest time after receiving Holy Communion. *Is he scared to die?*

Back in the room, Amanda fumbled with the TV remote and put on an old sitcom rerun.

Joshua frowned at her. "Turn that off, will you. I'm tired and I don't want to see that garbage."

"What's the matter?"

"Turn it off, damn it!" Josh slammed his fork on his plate and threw the food to the floor. Bits and pieces of turkey and gravy splattered the wall. A biscuit rolled to the far corner.

"Hey!" Amanda clicked the remote and jumped from her chair to clean up the mess.

"I'm sorry. Leave it. I'll buzz the nurse later. Sit with me."

Amanda lumbered back to her chair and stared at her brother. She couldn't recognize his gray eyes anymore. They were like little specks in his bloated, pale face. His unruly dark hair was practically gone; he wore a black knit hat in place of it. His arms were thin and frail with tons of needle marks from being poked with IV's.

She touched his cold fingers. "What's wrong?"

"I have something for you." He fumbled through his gown and pulled out his pendant necklace.

"Josh, what are you doing? That's your battalion pendant."

Her brother unclasped it and presented it to her. "I'm giving it to you. I can't take it with me. Take it, go on."

Amanda's lips quivered. He was so proud to be part of this incredible battalion; he had made a commitment to reunite with them and now he was giving his precious necklace to her. *What should I do with it?* She felt guilty for being healthy and was overcome with grief.

Joshua shook his head. "Don't cry, please. We both know tears have gotten us nowhere. We've had it tough, little sis. But we made it work. So will you."

Amanda wiped her eyes. "How do you know that?"

"Because I'll never leave you. Keep this pendant and when you think of me, I'll be there."

Amanda grabbed the necklace from her brother and held it in a tight fist. Through gritted teeth she said, "I hate you."

Joshua smiled, "I know. The feeling is mutual."

Chapter 7

Lying on a bumpy bed Amanda opened her eyes and blinked, the pendant still in hand. The TV was on and so were the other lights in the room. The morning sun shone through the shades and the nightstand clock read 7:44. *Oh my God! I must have fallen asleep.*

Rolling over, hunger pains raged inside her as the smell of food overwhelmed her senses. The box of uneaten pizza and full plastic cup of Diet Coke lay next to her on the nightstand, untouched. Sitting up, Amanda devoured a few pieces of cold pizza. When her tummy was full, she considered her next move. *I need to go back to the station and get out of here.*

It was Friday and close to ten when Amanda checked out and started her two mile-trek to the train station. Her mind was consumed with memories of her brother and the pendant he had given her. Amanda didn't dare put it on her neck; she kept in a plastic pouch, and hoped it would be a good luck charm wherever she landed.

A few cars drove by as Amanda roamed through the streets of this sleepy town. She passed a diner, glancing at people eating their breakfast. Oldies music wafted through the air from a mechanic's shop across the street. She approached the train station; a simple-looking, white-brick building with a couple tracks behind it.

By the time Amanda entered the modest lobby, it was almost quarter to eleven. She eyed a vending machine near the restrooms, wishing for a strong cup of coffee after drinking flat, watery soda mixed with the whiskey she bought from the convenience store the night before.

There was a black couple standing by the doorway leading out to the tracks. Directly across from them was the ticket window; she approached it cautiously.

"Morning," hooted an elderly, thin man with a pointy nose.

Caught off guard by his shrill voice, Amanda replied. "Hi."

"Where to?" he quizzed. On his striped shirt she noticed a blue patch with the name *Howard* emblazoned on it.

"Not sure." Feeling foolish, she read through the list of fifteen destinations on the wall. "Are these all the cities the train goes to?"

Howard folded his arms and leaned into the window, "More than we can take on. From here, that is."

"Great. Let me think about it for a moment." Amanda fidgeted as she scrutinized the listing. The east coast didn't appeal to her; she was sick of cold weather after being in Chicago. As her eyes drifted from city to city, one caught her attention. She'd never been to San Francisco. *Yes! California it is.*

With her decision made, Amanda said, "Um, California."

"Where in California?"

"Right, I'd like a one-way ticket to San Francisco."

"Okey, dokey. I'll tell you when the train leaves. It doesn't go out there every day."

Crap. If it didn't leave today, Amanda would have to return to the motel.

As Howard checked the computer, Amanda's portable phone buzzed.

"Hello?"

"Miss Lenger?" It was a female voice.

"Yes, this is Amanda Lenger."

"Ms. Lenger, I'm Brenda Rivers, I'm one of the social workers at the Veterans Administration Hospital. This concerns Joshua Lenger."

My brother? She stepped away from the window, motioning to Howard to wait.

"How can I help you?"

"We've been trying to reach you for the last two days. Your landlord had given us this number. We cannot release your brother's body without your signed consent."

Amanda let out a deep breath. "What? You're kidding. I completed all the paperwork requested of me, including the consent form."

"I'm sorry, ma'am, but the form wasn't signed."

"Oh," she replied, annoyed at the situation. She remembered the envelope with the key Josh had given to her. Amanda took it out along with the Post office's address. *I can kill two birds with one stone. Maybe I can have the document faxed to me at the post office Joshua asked me to go to and check out this box at the same time.* "Can you fax the form to me?"

"No, ma'am, I'm sorry to tell you this, but your signature has to be on the original document."

Shit! Amanda scratched her forehead. She wanted to get out of Chicago and now she'd have to go back and sign paperwork—one stupid form to get her brother's body buried somewhere. Her dream of escaping to San Francisco was disappearing.

"This is ridiculous, I'm out of town."

"I apologize for the inconvenience. When do you expect to return?"

"I don't know." *Never.* "I'm at an Amtrak station in Iowa. I'd have to check. Can you hold?"

"Of course."

Amanda cupped her cell and approached the window. "Does a train leave for Chicago today?"

The clerk perused his computer. "You're in luck. It leaves in a half-hour."

"When will it get into Chicago?"

"By four."

"I'll take it."

Amanda moved her hand from the mouthpiece. "What time do you close?"

"I'm here until six."

"Can you please give me directions to your office? I'll be there later this afternoon."

She jotted down the address on an old receipt and ended the call.

After hanging up, she paid Howard forty-one dollars. *The envelope!* Reading the address, she asked the elderly man. "By the way, where is this post office: 13245 E. Wilkins?"

"On the other side of town, a few miles east."

Damn! I won't have enough time to go there and come back here. Amanda threw the envelope in her bag and slid down the wall onto the floor. *You're an idiot, Amanda! I've dug myself into a big hole.*

Emptiness and sorrow set in. She looked out the window in hopes of distracting herself; she saw two boys get out from their car and embrace family members. *I wonder where they're headed. Better than me.*

Amanda pushed herself up and strode across the small lobby of the station and outside again. *What have I done? I shouldn't have left Chicago so fast, hours after my brother passed. What was I thinking?* She wished Joshua was with her. He always took charge wherever they went.

Sitting on the curb for a few minutes and wishing for clarity, Amanda took out the whiskey bottle and snuck sips. From her wallet, she pulled out a picture of her brother and stared at it. "Help me to make the right decisions in life, please, I need you."

The sun and the whiskey warmed her body. Hugging her knees, Amanda bent her head and closed her eyes. She'd have to be more decisive with her life choices.

Soon it was time to leave, a tipsy Amanda found her way to the boarding platform. Putting a wobbly foot on the first step of the car, she grabbed the handrail, but paused. Looking up into the blue sky for any sign of wisdom, she nodded as if reality and her future circumstances finally dawned on her. *I need to go to Chicago and give my brother a proper burial.*

A flock of geese crossed her sightline. When the birds passed, the sun-light blinded her vision.

Steadying her balance, her purse fell to the ground, spilling its contents. Embarrassed, Amanda scrambled and shoved everything into the purse. She then marched up the stairs into the train returning to Chicago.

Part II: THIS IS NOW — LIFELINE

"Embrace all who you might meet. For much learning can come forth."

Musical Inspiration for this Section

"Lifeline" by Mandisa

Chapter 8

May, 2012. Chicago, IL.

Sitting at the intersection of Bradley Avenue and Harbor Boulevard in her idling car, teardrops slipped down Amanda Reynolds's face as she watched a parade of floats pass by. One particular float decorated in red, white and blue, carrying local soldiers who had returned from Iraq stirred up emotions inside her like an erupting volcano.

A long banner shouting, *Welcome Home, Troops* waved in the balmy Memorial Day wind.

"You asshole," Amanda choked on her words. "I've missed you terribly since you've been gone."

Seeing the grateful young men and women in uniform triggered a distant memory of the time when Amanda turned twenty-one. Joshua had come home for the weekend to celebrate her special birthday. It was a crazy night that took her days to recover from, but a wonderful reunion none-the-less.

Dressed in his Marine attire, Josh took Amanda to Mother's, a popular Chicago tavern on Rush and Division. They sat in the lower-level bar listening to a loud heavy metal band playing in the corner. He ordered four tequila shots, putting two in front of her. In the seven years since leaving Des Moines, Amanda hid her secret obsession with alcohol from her brother, an addiction which started the night she saw her mom indulging when she was only thirteen.

Amanda eyed the yellow liquid in the tiny shot glasses. "What's this?" *I tried this stuff once and I hate it. It smells like shit. What am I going to do?*

"It's Tequila. I know you've never had this, but it sure is good."

Amanda forced a smile. *Oh, if you only knew.*

"Watch me." Joshua licked the webbed skin between his thumb and index finger, took the saltshaker and shook it on his dampened skin. Licking the salt off, he grabbed the glass of tequila and masterfully downed it. From the small plate between them, he grabbed a lime wedge and stuck it in his mouth to counter the sharp-tasting liquor.

Amanda took a sniff. "Whoa, this doesn't smell that good." She preferred whiskey. *Josh would kill me if he knew I drank regularly.*

"What are you waiting for? I don't have all weekend." Joshua repeated his perfected process with his second shot glass of the golden liquid.

Nauseated, Amanda's stomach did a flip-flop. The room was cloudy with smoke. She hated the smell of cigarettes; it reminded her of their mom.

"This is my little sister," Joshua commented to the bartender, Dean. "She's twenty-one today. I'm teaching her to do shots."

"Ha. Well, happy birthday to you."

Dean was an older gentleman with soft blue eyes and a dimpled chin. He and her brother ogled her, waiting.

Crap, I gotta to do this and get it over with. Following the steps with the salt, she swallowed both shots, one right after another and then sucked on the lime wedge.

Joshua cried. "Hold on! One shot at a time, dummy."

Dean snickered. "Impressive. She threw those back like a pro."

The taste of tequila was numbing, it had a bitter aftertaste and Amanda wanted to gag. Instead, she squeezed more lime juice in her mouth. She and Joshua continued to do three more rounds. Once the liquor took hold of her, the metal music and smoke-filled room didn't bother her anymore and the rest of the night was heavily blurred.

Joshua might have turned twice over in his grave if he had known alcohol had been a secretly-steady friend to Amanda. There was no denying that stress had gotten to her in the last decade, their mom had changed into a different person, she and her brother left Iowa, living in a big city with no other family, and lastly, experiencing Josh's death.

After her brother's passing the dependency became more obvious as evidenced by her and Ryan's lifestyle. Amanda had relied on alcohol like their mother; it was a vice she had struggled with for some time. Sober for four years now, she suddenly craved a drink.

"Here's to you, Joshua. I remember the good ol' days." Amanda pretended to raise a glass toasting her dead brother and the soldiers' safe return home. **"No more tequila for me."**

Honk, honk.

Amanda looked into the rearview mirror. "Geez, hold your horses buster."

The last of the floats finally passed on Harbor Boulevard as she waited for the line of cars to move again on Bradley Avenue. A few minutes later she turned into Glenn's Grocery parking lot. The store was crowded with customers shopping for their Memorial weekend dinners.

Shaken by the bittersweet memories the parade had brought to mind, Amanda rushed inside to buy her own party necessities. *Just a few things and I'll be out of here.* She weaved through customers trying to recall her list without glancing at it. It had also been four years since she and her husband, Ryan, had hosted a Memorial barbecue at their house, four long years of sobriety and many, many Alcoholics Anonymous meetings.

Once Amanda gathered her food items she wandered into the liquor department. Ryan said he'd go, but today it had been a tough battle with the girls. Her daughters, Emily and Rose, had been exceptionally bratty.

Rose, being only four-years-old, accidentally broke her older sister's favorite doll. Emily, seven and innately bossy, was furious and screamed at her younger sibling, which naturally provoked uncontrollable crying and whining from Rose. Amanda tried to calm both girls, but they wouldn't stop. Finally, Ryan coaxed them into going outside to play on the swings. By then, a frazzled Amanda pleaded with her husband to let her go to the store by herself.

Hesitantly, he handed over the car keys, telling her, "I was going to get some booze, anyway. You know Michael, he likes rum. Let me take care of it, okay?"

"Ryan, honey, I need to get my bearings. Not to mention some *me* time. I'll get the liquor. Don't worry, it will be fine." *It's not like the liquor bottles are opened.*

"Sure, but please be—?"

"Careful in the liquor department. Yes, trust me. I'm not going to do anything stupid." A relieved Amanda waved as she trotted out of the house.

Amanda examined the neatly organized bottles on the shelves like they were fancy shoes. The various colors and sizes made her mouth water. *I can do this.* Perusing one of the aisles, she located her former liquid of choice, vodka. Putting two bottles in her cart, she circled around the aisle, picked up a bottle of rum, *for Michael,* grabbed two cases of beer and then checked out.

Outside, after putting the groceries in her trunk, she gingerly removed a bottle from one of the bags and carried her *old friend* to the front seat. *I've missed you. Damn, what the heck am I doing?*

Amanda opened the bottle, dipped her finger into the clear cocktail and put it into her mouth, sucking the liquor from her skin, like a starved man marooned on a desert island. Her body shuddered as she remembered the physical sensation she always experienced with this elixir. Amanda carefully poured some into her half-drunken fruit-enhanced water bottle. She capped it and shook the bottle. Slowly, she twisted the lid, brought it to her salivating mouth and took a long, savoring drink of the mixture. *Oh, my God! This is better than sex.*

Without another thought, she took another drink, and another, until the plastic container was drained and the vodka bottle was half-emptied. She chilled in the parking lot, feeling the effects of vodka.

From the visor, Amanda observed herself in the mirror. Even at thirty-six, her bone-white complexion had retained its youthfulness. Her straight dish-blonde hair continued to look shiny. There were dark circles under her light-green eyes from lack of sleep the night before, but other than that, no one could tell what kind of past she had lived.

A wave of guilt washed over her body. *What the hell did I just do? I have controlled myself for so long. Why or why did I give in?* She had managed to stay sober after many years of drinking, burying tainted childhood memories that even her own husband wasn't aware of. As her body convulsed from alcohol spasms, a veil of sorrow covered her.

Amanda pounded the dashboard. **"Damn you, Joshua! Damn that stupid parade!"**

Her cell vibrated.

Not now! "Hello."

"Hi, Mommy, are you on your way home?" Emily's high-pitched voice came through the receiver.

With perspiration forming on her brow, Amanda wiped herself and snatched the vodka bottle again. "Soon baby."

"I love you Mommy."

She poured more into the plastic bottle and haphazardly spilled some the precious clear drink on her jeans. "Love you too, sweetheart, see you soon."

Clicking off, Amanda took a few more sips, emptied the remaining liquid outside and capped the bottle. *I've got to get rid of this.*

Slipping two pieces of spearmint gum in her mouth, she spotted a trash can near one of the store entrances. Starting the car, she reversed and drove toward it to dispose of the evidence.

"It's all good. Here comes, Mommy."

Chapter 9

Two Weeks Later.

Ryan pressed his intercom button. "Yes, Eilene?"
"Your daughter, Emily, is on the line." Ryan glanced at his watch. *Why is she calling me now?* He had two full hours of preparation before his big marketing presentation for one of his top clients. He pushed aside his notes. "Put her through."

"Hello, Sweetheart."

"Hi Daddy."

"What's up, baby doll?"

"Mommy's asleep and she won't get up to play with me and Rose."

"Asleep?" Ryan straightened in his chair. "What do you mean? Go get her."

"I can't. She won't move on the bed, not even when I shake her."

In the background, Ryan could hear Rose weeping.

"Emily, what did Mommy do?"

"I don't know."

He scratched his head, "Did Mom have coffee today?"

"I think so."

Ryan knew from past experience that Amanda drank liquor in her coffee cup. She'd been sober for four years. The last couple of weeks though, he'd seen a change in his wife's behavior. She was jumpy, goofy and extremely happy.

"I'm coming home. Hang up, go sit in the living room with Rose and wait for me. Do you understand?"

Emily started to cry. "Yes but is Mommy dead?"

"No, no she's not. It will be okay, kiddo. Don't worry. I'm on my way." *What the hell is happening?*

Hoping his daughter listened to him, Ryan hung up and called his secretary into his office.

Eilene's four-inch heels clicked on the hardwood floor. She poked her head through the door, "You rang?"

I can't stand that clacking noise! Ryan didn't answer but rather cleared off his desk while putting on his blue suit jacket.

"Um, where are you going?"

He swiped through his calendar on his Smartphone. "I have an urgent matter at home. Call Bill Fisher and cancel our meeting for today. Reschedule it any other day or time this week. And please, apologize for me. Apologize a lot for me. I have to go, pronto."

Eilene's brow creased. "Is everything alright?"

Ryan rushed passed her. "Not now, Eilene."

"Your lunch?"

"Cancel it all, damn it!"

Ryan took the elevator to the underground garage and ran to his black, two-door BMW. He opened the door, fell into his seat and took several deep breaths to calm himself.

He was convinced Amanda had drunk herself into an alcoholic stupor. It was what put her over the edge before; that is how she ended up in AA. *At least this time, she didn't get in the car and drive with the girls in it.* The last time she totaled the car but had been alone. Amanda was lucky to have walked away with just a few bruises. If she was passed out as he suspected, the damage to his girls would be far worse because Emily and Rose were there.

I should have said something earlier when I noticed an empty bottle of vodka in the trash the other week. He'd had a few drinks with Amanda occasionally joining him, promising him she had it under control, but it wasn't a worthy excuse.

Damn it! Their sex life had improved dramatically in the last few weeks as well. *I should have questioned her? Stopped her!* She'd been clean for a long time, but with her casually drinking, he blamed himself. *This is my fault. Why did I believe she could control it? Why did I let her drink even once? It should not have happened.*

Ryan sped through the ramps to the entrance, dialing 9-1-1.

Chapter 10

Wearing a purple skirt with a white blouse, Cecilia Stanger, the Reynolds' spunky white-haired seventy-plus neighbor, was already on the front steps of the house when Ryan pulled into his driveway.

He jumped out of the car and greeted her. "Thanks Cecilia for taking my call and doing this. I'm so sorry to inconvenience you with this urgent matter. You're the only one I can depend on since my parents live so far away."

With a concerned expression on her face, she answered, "Go on. It's no problem. I'll take care of the girls."

"I appreciate it. The ambulance will be here any minute."

He passed her, opened the front door and ran through the house calling for his daughters. "Emily? Rose? Where are you?"

With one sobbing and the other hiccupping, Emily and Rose met their father in the corridor. They both wore colorful outfits and mismatched socks. He crouched down, holding them closely to his chest. *Thank God! They're okay.*

Pulling away, he peered into his eldest daughter's eyes. The shape and color were the mirroring image of his wife's. "Emily, you did right by calling me, thank you." Rivulets smeared her face. "Don't cry anymore." He looked behind him. "Miss Cecilia is here and she's going to take care of you for a short time. She has a new book she wants to read to you. Mommy is okay, I promise. Please, go with Miss Cecilia. I'll see you in a little while."

Ryan stood. *I hope they leave before the ambulance arrives.*

Rose cried, clinging to her father, "Daddy, Daddy. Mommy, hurt. Help her."

He gently ushered them to the front door. "It will be okay, sweetie. Go on with Miss Cecilia. Daddy will take care of everything."

The older woman had already collected some of the girl's toys, extra shoes, and clothes. She waved to him as they went out the door.

He watched them through the living room window until they were inside Mrs. Stanger's house. Ryan then raced up the stairs two at a time until he reached the landing. His heart beat so fast, he wasn't sure what he'd find. *I hear the ambulance, what a relief!*

Making a right turn and sprinting into their bedroom, he saw his wife lying on the bed in a fetal position wearing her cream-colored nightgown.

Throwing his blazer to the floor, Ryan grabbed her. "Amanda, Amanda, wake up."

She didn't stir. He bent to hear her breathing. *Phew!* She reeked of alcohol.

The doorbell chimed. "Upstairs!"

Two burly paramedics were beside him in a matter of seconds.

"What's the problem?" queried the bigger of the two.

"I think she's passed out. She's been drinking again. I don't know how much liquor she's had," Ryan faltered. "She's a recovering alcoholic."

The smaller paramedic checked her vital signs. "Yep, out cold and her breathing is slow, too slow."

The bigger paramedic, Russell, interrupted, "Okay, let's gets moving right away. Mike, get the stretcher and we'll take her in."

Within minutes, Russell and Mike had Amanda settled in the ambulance. Ryan gazed in despair as the ambulance backed out of the drive with flashing lights advertising a crisis.

Ryan hopped into his car, put on his sunglasses to avoid eye contact with already curious neighbors, and followed behind the ambulance to St. Philips Hospital.

Droplets of perspiration fell from his brow; his brown curls were disheveled. *This needs to stop. I can't believe I've neglected a matter as serious as this? What made her do this again?* They had all the comforts of life, a modest home, two wonderful kids, two cars and, he assumed, a great marriage. *We went through this before but she had gotten better. What could be wrong now?*

He pounded the steering wheel. "Damn you, Amanda!" He telephoned Cecilia to check on his kids. She informed him they were doing fine and could spend the night if need be. As Ryan drove, his mind was distracted. At least his kids were okay. *I need to make sure my wife is safe.* When she was feeling better, they were going to have a serious discussion to get to the bottom of her setback.

Ryan cussed again thinking about the presentation he was supposed to have done that afternoon. *All my preparation for this meeting reduced to shit. My boss must be so angry at me. Oh, my head feels like it's going to explode!*

Chapter 11

Something gripped Amanda, she struggled to get loose.

"It's okay. It's me."

She blinked; trying to adjust to the bright light above her. "My God, where am I?"

"In the hospital."

The sight of Ryan's face, pale with a five-o'clock shadow, came into focus. He was wearing a suit. "What happened? Why aren't you at work?"

Ryan shifted on the bed. *You mean where I should be instead of here?* "Because you've had alcohol poisoning."

Amanda tried to get up but a wave of nausea jerked her down like a heavy weight. "The girls? Where are the girls?"

"With Cecilia."

She sank further in the bed. Her right arm stung from the IV. Groaning, she remembered her coffee cup. *I got drunk in front of the girls.*

Her husband fiddled with the covers.

Amanda shrank away. "I'm sorry. I'm so ashamed of myself for messing up again."

"We've been through this already. You stopped drinking." He stood up and strode to the window. "And now, again. Why?"

She twitched. "I made a mistake, *again.*"

Ryan blurted. "Right, we know that already. I need an explanation."

What triggered this relapse? Amanda recalled the float. And then she knew. She thought of Joshua and her stomach churned. The memories of her deceased brother had come flooding back to her upon seeing the float full of uniformed soldiers. *I can't believe a damn float made me so weak that I relapsed again.*

Ryan had been patient with her during her previous treatments, attending AA meetings, even taking care of their daughters—her precious children. *What will they think of their drunken mother? The last time they hadn't seen her crash and burn.*

"I need time alone to figure things out."

Ryan's face reddened. "*You* need time alone? Great, I cancelled a huge meeting. This will cost me my promotion, my bonus but you need time alone. How am I supposed to support us when you're drinking again? I saw the bottle in the trash. I ignored the signs and feel like a total idiot."

Amanda moved slowly, twisting at the frayed ends of her ugly-green hospital gown. She wanted to hug him but nausea and a dull pain zapped all her energy. He was right; she'd been selfish by risking her life and her family's safety. *I'm a mom for God's sake.*

"I'm waiting." Ryan scowled.

She had to tell him about her past, all of it. Her marriage was teetering on the edge of destruction. *I could lose my husband and kids this time for sure? I have to fix this.* Amanda took a deep breath. "I don't know what to say. I need help."

"There are other ways of dealing with these urges, you know. You could have called your AA sponsor or talked with me."

"I know."

"You think you can dismiss your family obligations and leave?"

"No, it's just hard to explain."

Her husband paced back and forth. "You're an alcoholic, Amanda. You can't drink anymore, not even socially. *Not ever.* That's your problem. And I'm a sucker for believing you were completely rehabilitated after the first time. I'm just as much to blame as you."

"It's not your fault. Don't blame yourself."

"Who will take care of the kids?" he asked, incredulous. "I can't take time off."

"I don't know. We could ask your parents."

"Terrific. They'll enjoy hearing you'll be going on a trip and leaving them to raise our children. What's wrong with you?"

"Please!" she begged.

"What's the matter, Amanda? Tell me."

There were so many skeletons in her closet. *Where do I begin?* She needed to confess but was finding it difficult to find the courage to do it right there. Sighing, she said. "It's complicated."

Ryan stopped and folded his arms. "I can see that."

Chapter 12

Two weeks later, Amanda was experiencing severe alcohol withdrawal, including debilitating migraines and increased heart rate because she had binged on so much liquor in a short period of time.

Things were no better at the Reynolds' household as relations with Ryan were strained. Her husband was working longer hours and the kids were being extra cautious around her.

Emily was especially distant and moody toward her mother, always wanting her daddy or Miss Cecilia, who stopped by regularly to see the girls. Amanda pretended their home-life was normal, but she knew her children were traumatized.

Am I turning into my mom? She'd have to take steps to end her addiction or become the older Louise, the one in Mount Pleasant, Iowa.

To escape the confines of the house and keep herself occupied, Amanda took the girls to the local library. While her daughters participated in the children's programs, she researched alcohol holistic rehab centers. She needed another form of treatment besides AA. *I need to get out of Chicago and get rehabilitated for good this time.*

In addition, she needed to let go of the sudden thoughts of Joshua, a past Amanda succeeded in keeping hidden from her spouse. Not wanting to burden anyone anymore, she'd promised to get clean.

Searching through a number of rehab centers, Amanda found a renowned addiction facility in Taos, New Mexico. The Taos Healing Institute—a holistic treatment center for high-risk alcoholics. There was an application process and if accepted Amanda was expected to fulfill a thirty-day intensive detox treatment program. She'd have to identify her root-addiction issues and learn how to manage temptations.

The owner, Gretchen Miner, was an eighty-nine-year-old retired painter, and in the healing business for over thirty years. A recovered alcoholic, Gretchen had mentored many patients with her fail-proof instructions by slowly moving them away from their dependencies and refocusing those cravings toward something else. Based on its solidarity and the peaceful setting that Taos offered, the institute was the perfect place for her. Feeling confident after reviewing patient testimonials, Amanda approached Ryan the next evening, ready to explain *some* truths to him.

Ryan sat in a recliner in the den clicking through TV channels when Amanda meandered in. Sitting across from him on their dark brown loveseat she cleared her throat.

"I never told you this, but my mom abandoned me and … and I had an older brother. He was four years older than me. His name was Joshua. I'm not originally from Chicago as I told you. I'm from Des Moines, Iowa."

Ryan pressed the power button on the remote. "Okay."

Amanda continued, "My father died in a car accident when I was seven. He was a truck driver and was hit head-on while driving through Fargo, North Dakota during a severe winter storm. Before the accident, my mom was a loving woman, playful and full of joy. My parents' relationship was incredible. My dad loved and cherished my mother. But then, in an instant, she became a widow and a working, single-parent, having to raise two children alone."

Her husband's mouth dropped as if to say something, but he didn't.

She stood, tightening her hands into fists. *I have his attention now, I can't quit.* "Not more than eight or nine months after my Dad was gone, different men started coming through our front door. Mom began drinking, something I had never seen her do. Our family unit dissolved and she basically forgot about us. When I was thirteen, I started experimenting and got myself addicted to alcohol." Amanda rubbed a hand down her face. "When Josh was eighteen and I was fourteen, he made a big decision, to take me with him and run away from our mother. With the money he earned from working a part-time job we left and fled to Chicago. That's the truth, honey."

Ryan bolted from the chair and rushed to his wife. "Why haven't you told me any of this? You've been lying about your parents being dead and that you were an only child. Why? Why did you lie to *me*?"

Amanda shifted on her feet. "What would have been the point to tell you? How do you think I feel, all this truth-telling, these hurtful memories that I really have no desire revisiting."

Her husband drew away. "But obviously your painful recollections continue to revisit you. Look what you've done in front of our kids this time."

She nodded, "I know. You're right. I have no more excuses."

Ryan came closer, "What happened after that?"

Amanda took a deep breath. "Things were good for a long while. I transferred to Kelvyn High and got a part-time job when I was sixteen. Joshua joined the Marines and went overseas, but I continued to depend on him to take care of me." She paused. "After ten years on our own, Josh got really sick. He was stationed in Germany and was sent home for tests. He was diagnosed with leukemia. We went through a couple rounds of chemo, but the cancer was too far along. In a year, his body deteriorated and he died, leaving me all alone."

"Wow, I'm sorry. That had to be so hard on you."

"It was."

"Is your mom still alive?"

The image of her mom at the trailer park burned in her mind like one of those birthday candles that never gets extinguished no matter how many times you try to blow them out, Amanda had to shake it off. "I don't know. I visited her once, saw her just after Joshua passed. He made me go and find her in Iowa," she coughed. "I didn't have the courage to speak to her when I saw her from a cab window."

"What if we looked for her? Talk to her, I'll help you."

Amanda raised her voice, "You're joking, right? I don't want anything to do with that woman! Can't you understand?"

Her husband stepped forward. "No, I don't because you're not alone anymore; you have me and the girls."

"I'm terribly sorry for getting riled up at you, but I'm *not* looking for her again." She wanted to take all her memories of an abusive mom and the upsetting image of her dying brother and stuff them in a bag, to burn them into ashes and throw them into the wind.

Ryan grabbed her by the arm. "Let's do AA again. It's a great program. Call your old sponsor, or better yet, let's find another sponsor. I don't care. Let's get you some help."

"No, AA sponsors don't work for me."

"You didn't try hard enough."

Amanda shook her head. "I hated those meetings. I'm sorry but I honestly did. The formality crap of Hello, my name is so and so, and I'm an alcoholic. We shared stupid sob stories about how we got drunk."

Ryan smirked, "Cut that out will you. Those sob stories are about real people. They have their reasons, just like you. Those people stick to it because they want to be healed permanently."

"Well, this time I want to do it my way. I have to go away. I need to get treatment specific to my needs, not some canned set of steps. *Plus*, I know I have to stop drinking for good, or else I'll keep thinking about the same things over and over again."

"Amanda," Ryan appealed.

"I've divulged my shameful past to you. Isn't that enough?" She tugged at her hair, thinking. *Burn the past. Remove it from my recollection completely. Liquor is a reminder of my past.*

"Don't call it shameful. Your circumstances are unfortunate. But this alcohol addiction can be defeated. We can do it together!"

Amanda pictured the military float in her mind again. It had opened a flood gate of emotions so wide, she was unable to contain them any longer. "Ryan, it's not about *we*; it's what I have to do by myself."

Her husband picked at his brow. "I don't know if leaving will solve anything. I think you'd be running away from your problems, alone."

She pointed at him, "No, you're wrong."

Ryan stuffed his hands in his pockets. "Fine, let it out. I'm assuming you know where you want to go."

Amanda nodded. "Taos."

"Taos, New Mexico! Are you nuts?"

"Please, help me help myself."

Ryan fell back in the recliner not sure what to do. *Is it because of me and my drinking? This is all my fault.* "You're not leaving me for another man, are you?"

She sat on his lap. "Gosh, no, there is no one else. I have to heal *me* and be a sober wife to you and still be the mother to our children."

Ryan put his head down. "How long is this going to take?"

"If accepted, which I believe I will be, the program is a thirty-day rehabilitation regimen, similar to a boot-camp."

Scratching his head, he said, "How are we supposed to pay for this regimen?"

Amanda leaned into him, "Like we usually do, a little at a time."

Ryan sank deeper into the recliner. "It's not like we don't have any other bills you know. We haven't even taken a vacation in a few years. It's always been about your alcohol problems. Frankly, I'm sick of it."

She nuzzled into his neck. "I'm sorry, you're a terrific husband and I love you with all my heart but I have to do this."

Ryan was scared of what was to come, but he loved his wife so he was willing to do whatever it took to heal her.

"Okay, I'll help you help yourself. But this is the last time."

Amanda embraced him. "Yes. I promise, the last time."

Chapter 13

It was near the end of June, a warm day brightened the Saturday morning. A few more weeks had passed since Amanda announced her decision to attend The Taos Healing Institute in New Mexico. She'd been accepted to the program, and Ryan stood by as she made her flight and rehab reservations. They had since learned that the elderly woman had a ninety-eight percent success rate.

Amanda's flight was at two. It was past eleven and she was in the bedroom getting ready. The girls were downstairs watching morning cartoons. Ryan was on his way up the stairs to see his wife, feeling rather groggy thanks to night-before jitters. Sapped from her previous alcoholic breakdown, it felt like deja vu`. *This time she'll be gone for a whole month.*

Ryan observed her from the doorway. His wife looked pretty. She always did. It was no wonder he'd fallen in love with her. Amanda wore a white polo top over denim Capri's, and beige strapped sandals.

"You need help closing that?"

"No thanks." With a last yank, she zipped the suitcase shut. "There, got it."

"The limo will be here shortly. I can carry it down for you." *I'm giving it my best shot, can't you see? Helping you help yourself.*

"Where are the girls?"

"Ah, downstairs." *They'll miss you and I'm the one who'll get to deal with the ramifications.*

"Thanks, are you okay?"

Ryan nodded, grabbed the suitcase and moved out of the way, knowing his wife would want some time alone with their daughters.

"I'll take this outside and wait for the car." *I need to get air, anyway. I'm already feeling a strangling sense of loss.*

Amanda gave him a peck on the cheek. "I appreciate it."

He went down the stairs past the living room, calling to his children. "Girls, your mom's coming. Be sure to give her big hugs and kisses."

Emily was curled up on the couch. "Does she *have* to go?"

Ryan set the luggage on the floor. *I wish she wouldn't.* "Yes, she does." Then, he picked it up again and left, not wanting to see his child's reaction.

Chapter 14

Standing on the landing, Amanda held onto the banister a little longer, hesitant to descend the fifteen steps. Confident with the feel of the oak under her fingertips, she slid her hand down the railing.

When Amanda reached the bottom, her heart palpitated. *What do I say to my children? How am I going to explain that I'm an alcoholic with bigger issues plaguing every fiber of my mind and body?*

Rose tumbled off the couch, rushing to her.

"Mommy, mommy, we're watching *SpongeBob Square Pants*."

Amanda knelt and hugged her energetic four-year-old. "How fun, sweetie."

The child jerked away. "Mommy, why do you have lipstick on?"

Yes, I do have lipstick on. *I don't normally wear it during the day.* "I'm."

"—Away, Rose. Mommy is going away," Emily interjected as she approached.

"Where to? I want to go with you," Rose stammered.

Nervous because her little girl was about to burst into a crying fit, Amanda grabbed her hands holding them in hers. "Hold up. I'll be home soon enough."

"That's not what Daddy says."

Amanda cocked her head. Oh, my dear Emily. *I'm so sorry for hurting you. Please don't hate me.* "Your father does exaggerate the facts sometimes. Let me explain." *Not true. Ryan told them the truth. And why wouldn't he? It is part of his child-rearing rule book.*

Emily took a step back as if surveying her mother.

Rose impatiently tugged at her pants. "Why are you going away?"

Amanda cleared her throat. "I have this project I'm working on for a few weeks. It's in New Mexico and I'll be on a ranch with this kind lady who needs help." *It's me that needs the help.*

"Where's New Mayco?"

Emily elbowed Rose. "Don't believe her."

"Emily!"

"Mommy has a coffee problem and she's leaving us with Cecilia and Grandma Maria while Dad is at work."

Rose stomped her feet on the hardwood floor. "Stop drinking coffee and don't go."

Amanda stroked her youngest daughter's face. "It will be okay, sw … sweetie."

"It's true, right Mommy?"

"Girls, girls. Please stop."

Amanda sighed at her firstborn. Even at seven she and Ryan knew Emily was special—intuitive and stubborn. Ahead of her first-grade friends and classmates, her vocabulary and understanding of life situations were equal to that of a third or fourth grader. She was an adult living in a pint-sized body, constantly wanting to be part of her parent's conversations. It was no wonder the girl had become distrusting of her mother these last few weeks, especially after having seen her passed out on the bed in a drunken stupor.

Amanda went to caress Emily's flaxen hair, but the child dodged her hand. Tears stung her eyes. "Yes, I have a little problem and I'm getting help. It is far, but, if I don't go, I can't be a good mom to you both."

Rose jumped into her mother's arms giving big wet kisses. "You are the best Mommy already. I love you."

Amanda cuddled with her younger child. "Can I have a hug and kiss from my big girl too?"

Emily pulled at the lace on her tank top. "Will you miss us?"

"Gosh, yes." *I need your approval, kiddo. Be strong for me.*

"Will you call?"

Amanda squeezed Rose against her chest and then put her down gently. Squatting, she looked deeply into chestnut-colored eyes. "Whenever I can, honey, I promise."

"Can we call you?"

"Yay, Mommy, can we call you?" Rose twirled around.

Amanda shook her head. She knew the requirements of the center. No incoming calls unless it was an extreme emergency. "I'm afraid they don't allow it."

A car horn sounded; startling them and breaking up their moment.

"Hugs?" She begged Emily again. *Please forgive me.*

Her daughter fell into her embrace, burying her tearful face in her mother's neck. "I don't want you to go. I want you to stay here."

Amanda gripped her lovingly. "I'll be home before you know it."

With one final squeeze, mother and daughter separated. "Go and watch TV. Daddy will be in shortly."

The girls ran back to the couch. Amanda turned away and wiped the streaks off her face. Taking a deep breath, she paused at the front door. Outside, Ryan leaned against the brick wall, hands in his cargo shorts. He looked over his shoulder just as she pushed the door open.

"Limo's here."

"I heard."

"He's ready to take you to O'Hare."

"Thanks," she mouthed, unable to utter another syllable. Heavy emotions churned her insides.

Ryan drew her close to him. "Get better."

Amanda could feel the tremble in his grip. She blinked several times, unable to stop the cascade of tears coming from her eyes. "I'll give it my best shot."

"Call us when you land."

"You bet." Amanda kissed her husband.

Not wanting to linger any longer, she sprinted down their narrow drive. Sitting in the backseat, she bit her lower lip, feeling a heaviness on her shoulders, waving goodbye as the car drove away from the curb.

Watching their manicured lawn and brown bungalow home retreating from sight, Amanda whispered, "God, if you're listening, please help me."

Chapter 15

The taxi glided east on I-90 headed to the airport. Next to her was a beige and red-checkered Louis Vuitton knockoff, and in the trunk, a small dark blue luggage with only a few pieces of clothing inside; the proprietor told her not to pack many things, but to bring layers, summer nights got a little cool in Taos.

Traffic was stop-and-go. Amanda lifted her wallet from the purse, taking out a photograph of her daughters; Emily and Rose were dressed in identical outfits that day, pink fluffy skirts and white blouses. The picture was taken a few months earlier at a J.C. Penney. She'd had a coupon for a free Easter sitting and brought the girls in. Holding the photo, a tear ran down her cheek. *I need to get better.*

The driver, a young bald-headed man with black square frames asked, "What time is your flight?"

"Two-o'clock. We're on time."

Putting the picture away, Amanda closed her eyes, replaying the day she had drunk herself into an alcoholic stupor, or what she could remember.

It was an awful day right from the start. She awoke with a migraine. It felt more like a hangover headache, her head throbbed. It was no accident because the night before she drank several vodka and cranberries with Ryan after the girls had gone to sleep. They were on their deck discussing his upcoming client presentation, and then she went to bed right after.

Emily and Rose were scampering around all morning playing with their Barbie dolls and they kept getting on her nerves even while they played together. She screamed several times for them to stop making noise, but they didn't listen. Amanda drank three mugs of black coffee and still the headache hadn't subsided. Finally, she went to her medicine cabinet and swallowed four aspirins.

A half-hour later, the pain continued to pulsate. *What is wrong with me?* Opening one of the cupboards in the kitchen, she extended her arm until she grasped a bottle of vodka hidden behind a couple cans of tomato sauce.

While the girls watched TV, Amanda took another mug, poured two shots of vodka and knocked it back. Minutes later, a fiery sensation consumed her. The temptation was too great and she filled the mug up again, to the brim. She couldn't remember how many cups she'd drank.

Ryan told her at the hospital that she had finished the bottle and started another, also hidden all the way in the back of the cabinet. *I hate myself for what I've become.*

Peering through the rearview mirror, the driver commented, "You alright?" Amanda just nodded. "What airline?"

"United."

The driver approached United departures, and then popped the trunk while Amanda rummaged through her purse for money. Once outside, a warm breeze caressed her face. She loved summer in Chicago, the warm wind, the smell of dandelions and car fumes. This is what she remembered when she was with her brother. But for now, she'd have to be away for several weeks, in Northern New Mexico's semi-arid climate and higher altitude.

She checked in, the attendant weighed her luggage and put it on the belt to be processed and loaded on the plane. O'Hare was busy with weekend travelers. Amanda waited in a long TSA line before walking toward Gate 21. On the way, her stomach growled. She strolled past several restaurants before deciding on a Starbucks coffee and an apple fritter. Zigzagging between passengers while walking toward the gate, she expertly balanced the drink, a bagged treat and her purse.

A few families scooted passed her, lugging their belongings while keeping a close watch on their children. Seeing these parents caring for their youngsters reminded Amanda of the final moments she'd spent with Ryan, Emily and Rose. *I should have done this rehab in my hometown like Ryan wanted.*

At the gate, Albuquerque crew for Flight 297 boarded the plane and the clerk announced boarding by groups.

Amanda found her seat, 27A, a window seat next to a long-legged man. He got up, almost knocking his cowboy hat against the overhead. Taking it off, a long yellow ponytail, neatly tied, hung over the back of his neck, the color matching his twisty blonde moustache.

"Excuse me."

"No problem, ma'am."

When seatbelt and safety checks were completed, the plane taxied to the runway. There were three other planes ahead of them. Looking out the window Amanda sighed, *I hope this is worth it.*

"Name's Jed, I'm from New Mexico."

Amanda turned and considered the gentleman. He reminded her of an older version of Trace Adkins.

"Amanda. From here."

"Why's a city girl like you traveling to Albuquerque?"

She crossed her arms. *Wow! The man gets right to the point.* "Personal business. What's a country boy like you doing in a big city like Chicago?"

He chuckled, "Shucks, ma'am, you're spot-on. I'm no city slicker. I stand out here like a purple pickle in a pumpkin patch."

"For sure. You're no shorty."

"Blame my father. Six feet-five at fifteen, and he was six-eleven before his twenty-fifth birthday. I'm just shy of six-seven myself. I'm not as tall as he was. God bless his soul. The man died two years ago at eighty-seven."

"Wow, long life."

"Eh, you're young. No sense worrying about dying."

Amanda agreed, feeling the man's eyes upon her. "I surely won't be young forever. By the way, you never answered my question, why were *you* in Chicago?"

Jed twisted the ends of his moustache. "Hmm, you're right. Young, pretty and smart. You don't miss a beat, do you?"

Amanda laughed. She liked Jed. He was friendly. "Thank you for the compliment. What's your story?"

"My brother-in-law, Roger, runs a law firm, Zigler and Sons in the city. Have you heard of them?"

"No, doesn't sound familiar. There are lots of law firms in Chicago, so I'm not surprised I haven't heard of that one."

"My baby sister and Roger are getting a divorce; they're in a heated custody battle over their two boys. My nephews are eleven and fourteen. Things aren't going so good for my little sis, so I came up here to give my boy, Mr. Roger, a little counseling of my own."

Befuddled, Amanda didn't know what to say. "Uh, did it go okay?"

"Humph … I reckon it did."

The plane lurched forward, interrupting their conversation. The captain alerted the crew to prepare for takeoff. Amanda, grateful for the distraction, squeezed her eyes shut. She hated the takeoff and landing part of flying.

The engines revved to full power, Amanda held her breath, waiting. The pilot released the brakes as the wheels sped down the runway. As the engines accelerated to the required speed, the plane lifted off the concrete and began to climb higher into the sky.

Amanda exhaled and settled in her seat, removing her wallet from her bag and taking out another photograph of them together. *The girls have changed a lot since this picture was taken at a barbeque two years ago.* Emily's hair was longer; she loved wearing it in pigtails. Rose was younger with her sweet, chubby baby face, her hair not quite as long, was ear-length and wavy. Ryan was ageless. Smiling, he had a light-hearted disposition about him. His bright eyes matched his youthfulness. Gazing at her own image, she appeared less tired even though sadness surrounded her eyes.

Have I ever been happy? Ryan was such a wonderful husband, helpful and loving in more ways than she could ever hope to have in a man. He was great with the girls, valued at his job, and admired by his colleagues and superiors. It was his calmness that had attracted her to him. *Who knows where I'd be if it wasn't for Ryan.*

Ever since Joshua passed away, a part of her had died with him too. Her family was dismantled, no connections, and no warm lingering memories. Amanda had been living a lie with her own family until now. She prayed for a resolution and for her mental perspective to change. *Two hours and forty minutes in this tin can, hope I can make it.*

Jed peeked over her shoulder, "Good-looking family."

"Thank you."

"I have two kids of my own. One son is twenty-four; the other is twenty-six. My younger is in the Marines, the other in the Navy."

"Two boys in the military? Wow! Where are they stationed?"

"Younger, Jake, in Afghanistan. Older, Luke, in Iraq."

"How nerve-racking it must be to have both children in the military. Thank you for allowing your sons to serve our country."

Jed puffed his chest. "My wife and I pray that they don't get their heads blown off, or any other body parts. I need those boys to come home in one piece. I have a lot of land to farm and could use their help."

Amanda nodded, "I'm sure."

Jed rested his head; she took it as a cue to end the conversation. Still holding the photo, she focused on Ryan's face to keep her mind occupied.

In Chicago, it had taken three days for the paperwork concerning the release of her brother's body to clear military protocol. They had provided a coffin and a burial plot at the Virginia Veterans Cemetery in Amelia. The military held a memorial service attended by Josh's general and co-captain. A plaque with his name on it would be placed at the Veteran's Memorial Office on Michigan Avenue and Ohio Street, honoring men and women who served in the Middle East, died in the line of duty or otherwise.

During those tough few days, money was almost non-existent, she thought about calling Gregg, her almost one-night-stand, about the burial process. She remembered his number, but didn't have the courage to go through with it. *I'm sure he's forgotten me.*

Amanda's hope of starting fresh had also faded. She'd lost her nerve. More importantly, she needed the security of a place where she knew the area. Her fear of the unknown was putting a burden on her shoulders. For the time being, she opted to stay in Chicago until a better opportunity came up.

Amanda had rented a cheap motel room, the hostel she and Joshua had lived at for a time was full, and so she had no other choice. She searched for work, even trying to get her old job back. Her boss didn't want to take her back, claiming she hadn't been diligent enough in her responsibilities. And that was like a dagger to her heart, cramping her self-esteem even more.

After a few more days of feeling sorry for herself, Amanda found a waitressing job at the Living Kitchen in Logan Square, an organic eatery serving locally grown foods. It was popular with the neighborhood, the tips/pay was good. The chef was also the owner of two other locations, one in Los Angeles and the other in Miami.

Two months later, the owner allowed her to work two shifts, mornings and afternoons. The tips increased and Amanda was able to get an open contract for an apartment in Logan Square not far from the restaurant. It was a small one-room/bedroom, on the third floor of a brick building. Her tiny balcony overlooked a children's park. It beat living next to a train track like she and her brother had done years before. This neighborhood was quiet and roughly four blocks from the diner. Having abandoned her old car before her trip to Mount Pleasant, Iowa, she walked to work every day.

Time flew by. Before Amanda knew it, ten months had passed since Joshua's death. One-night hookups and short-lived boyfriends spurred on by a lot of alcohol came and went. The relationships were dull and often left her feeling dirty, but it helped her cope with lonely nights. She was also having dreams of her deceased brother, even as she continued with her disgusting lifestyle.

One busy Tuesday morning, Amanda was covering five tables at once when three men in dark suits came in, one was Ryan. He wore glasses then, black, thin-framed rectangular. Another waitress was taking care of two big groups and asked Amanda if she wouldn't mind serving them.

She agreed to take the table and headed over to greet the new patrons. As she weaved toward their table, she and Ryan checked each other out. The men were polite and cordial, ordering black coffee and omelets. By the time they were done eating, Amanda had learned each of their names; they worked for Heartland Fidelity Investment Company. When they left, a generous tip greeted her as she cleaned off the table, remembering Ryan's bright smile.

The next day, Ryan showed up, alone. He made small talk about the weather and the Cubs. Then, he came again, and the next day, until the third day, he asked her out.

Of all the guys she had hooked up with or dated, none made her feel so protected and happy. He lifted her whole being up after losing her brother. He made her laugh and smile again.

Ryan and Amanda dated for six and a half months before getting married. It was initially a strong attraction for them both, but they were soon fast friends and their relationship flourished. It felt right, they were ready to start a life together. Amanda found it hard to believe she was blessed to finding a man who was gentle, loving, spirited and willing to marry a woman like her.

Ryan was financially stable and already bidding on a three-bedroom house in Naperville; a southwest suburb of Chicago. During that time, her husband still worked in the city and she often met with his inner-city friends to socialize.

Ryan and Amanda dined at expensive restaurants and danced at luxurious clubs. Married life was blissful. They partied a lot. It was an exhilarating time for Amanda because of her humble upbringing. The one thing she did in excess of was drink, and she and Ryan did *a lot* of drinking.

Three years later Emily was born and the drinking continued. When Rose came along, Ryan became the responsible one, he learned how to handle his liquor. By this time Amanda had spiraled into a full-blown alcoholic, sneaking liquor whenever and wherever she could. After her morning coffee, while the kids were distracted by TV, or when she was doing chores, she concealed it in a coffee mug. Her new drink of choice was vodka. There wasn't an overbearing odor and it was clear, so it looked like water.

Ryan changed jobs, taking one in the suburbs. It was a great opportunity for him and them. Amanda was happy for her husband, but she also missed their city friends. She carried on with her drinking until the situation became worse, no longer caring for herself or the house. The reality of her drinking was revealed when she left three-year-old Emily and Rose, not even a year old, home alone while she drove erratically to the liquor store to pick up more booze to keep the buzz on. She ended up crashing the car and entering AA. Eventually, Amanda sobered up.

As the plane flew westward, Amanda reflected on how things had changed since the parade. Seeing the floats carrying the uniformed men and women had stirred up old memories of Josh, and she'd cracked. Amanda had scared her children with her irresponsible actions. This trip was her last effort to heal herself.

The captain came on the intercom and announced they'd be landing in thirty minutes. Amanda blinked to shake off her cat-nap. Jed shifted in his seat.

The man took a sip of his drink. "Hello again." Amanda stared at his plastic cup. "Oh, they passed out beverages, but you were sound asleep. I didn't want to disturb you."

Amanda breathed a sigh of relief. "No worries." *Thank God! How would I have fended off this temptation? He reeks, I think he's had a few.*

Jed stretched, "I'm ready to get out of this plane, aka sardine can."

Looking out the window, she observed the dark-red mountains, not commenting.

The man leaned over; his breath smelled like a scotch bottle. "There's my state, ain't it a beauty. You'll love it."

Amanda leaned back to let Jed peer through the window, inhaling the alcohol vapors from the man's breath. "Looks great." *Relax, girl. You can't drink, remember?*

The plane landed at the Albuquerque International Sunport Airport. And in no time, they taxied into a terminal and disembarked.

At the baggage carousel, Amanda plucked her suitcase off the belt and said goodbye to the older gentleman. "It was a pleasure. Good luck to you and to your farming. I hope and pray your boys get home safely."

Jed tipped his hat. "I hope you wrap up your personal business soon and get right back home to your family."

Amanda gave him a thumbs-up. Then, purchasing a snack from a vendor stand nearby, she marched through the doors marked *Shuttle Services.*

Chapter 16

Outside, dry warm air hugged Amanda's face. It was five Chicago time, four o'clock in New Mexico. Cars and buses passed her as she stood at the curb looking for a bus, *Sundance Shuttle Services.*

Pacing up and down the sidewalk, she spotted a blue twelve passenger shuttle half a block away and proceeded in that direction. As she approached, the bus's side door was already open. Inside the driver seat was a plump, middle-aged woman wearing a red sun hat and dark sunglasses reading a newspaper.

"Excuse me, hi," she waved. "My name is Amanda Reynolds and I believe you're my bus ride to Taos."

The woman straightened up and quickly folded the paper. "Oh, my goodness, my apologies. Got caught up with the fashion section and lost track of time." She grabbed a clipboard. "You said your name was Amanda Reynolds?"

"Yes."

"You're on my roster. Pleasure to meet you, I'm Leona Davis." The driver noted the time on the clipboard. "Right on schedule too. Here, let me help you with your baggage."

"It's okay, I can do it," hoisting it up herself.

Amanda climbed into the bus, there were five seats on each side of the van and two along the back window. Above the seats was a stowaway rack to hold personal belongings. She made herself comfortable on the first seat kitty-corner from the driver. Leona got back in the driver seat and started up the engine.

"Are we waiting for any others?"

"No ma'am, you're my only customer today."

"Oh," was all Amanda said as she glanced around the interior. The outside of the bus was a little weathered, but inside the black leather seats were nice and shiny. It smelled like someone had sprayed potpourri. Lucky for her, it was her ride for the next two and a half hours to Taos.

Leona turned, "Ready to hit the road?"

"Sure."

Ms. Davis weaved through cars, taxis and shuttles before getting onto North I-25. A few miles in, she spoke, "Have you been to Taos before?"

Honky-tonk music played in the background as Amanda took in the scenery. "No, my first time."

"Taos is close to the Pueblo, the longest sustaining community of people dating back to 3,000 B.C. We've been incorporated since 1934. Here's a good one, Taos means *place of the red willows*."

Amanda blinked, "What exactly are red willows?"

"I didn't know what they were either. They are a small tree native to this area and some parts of California. They have reddish-brown bark and light green leaves."

"Sound pretty."

"I'll point them out to you."

"Thanks. I'd like that."

"Oh, by the way, we have the best microbrews."

Amanda laughed, "I had no idea."

"Yes, they are huge here in Taos. If you like beer, you'll have to try Green Chile Beer."

She waved her arms. "No thanks, anything with Chili in it, especially beer, I'll stay far away from."

"It's not so bad. If you like beer, I'd recommend a few of our microbrews. The pilsners are tasty this time of year."

It was tempting to Amanda, but she wasn't here to sightsee or drink. She needed to get sober for good by managing her temptations. Only then could she work on controlling past memories that have creeped up in her life.

"I appreciate it but I need to tell you something. I'm an alcoholic."

"Oh, golly me," Leona smacked her thigh, "I didn't know. I'm sorry."

She slid over and took a seat right behind the driver. "No need to apologize, I'm going to The Taos Healing Institute."

The woman coughed. "My goodness, I apologize again. I didn't put two-and-two together when I checked the destination. My age must be showing. Ms. Miner is a wonderful lady. We are a small town and I have known her for nine years."

Intrigued, Amanda leaned closer, "If you don't mind me prying, how do you know Gretchen Miner?"

Leona looked in the rearview mirror, removing her sunglasses to reveal light blue eyes covered in green eye shadow. "My sister's kid, Antonio, received some help from Gretchen a few years ago for drugs. He was seventeen-years-old, in and out of rehab. My sister and brother-in-law tried multiple interventions, but he was a user, very addicted. Antonio lost his battle with the damn demon two years ago. He never even made it to his twenty-first birthday."

Amanda was shaken by the news. "I'm so sorry to hear about your nephew."

Leona shrugged. "Eventually, it would have caught up to him. Damn kid never did listen very well. My sister went to shit when he died. After a time, she found a way to live again. She has two other kids to raise; you know, there's never enough time to grieve when one is being pulled in so many directions."

They were quiet for a bit. The sound of the shuttle's engine hummed in the background. Amanda reflected on her own addiction. She was determined to get sober for her girls. She took out the picture of her daughters again.

"I have to get better," she murmured.

Leona spoke. "Since I put us both in a somber mood, let me tell you more about Taos other than the breweries."

"Sure. Love to hear it."

The woman tapped her fingers against the steering wheel. "Good, this highway is named the Low Road. There are two main ways to get to Taos. One is this way, like I said. It will take us two hours. This highway rides along the Rio Grande. We'll stop after Santa Fe, where we can look at the gorge. The other highway is High Road, which is an extra hour or so of driving."

Amanda looked out the window, observing a long stretch of highway with desert-like landscape on both sides. "Besides the driving time, what else is different between Low Road and High Road?"

"This road is not as pretty as High Road. There are more towns, galleries, shops and pueblo homes on High Road. Here, you'll still see some of that, but the villages are more spread out. Low Road has gorgeous valleys, and the Rio Grande, of course."

"Are you originally from here, Leona?"

"No, I'm a transplant from Arizona, actually. My husband and I moved here fifteen years ago after we did a tour of northern New Mexico. We fell in love with the scenery and moved down to Albuquerque with our two sons. We're empty-nesters now, both of my boys are married, and we have two wonderful lively young granddaughters. My hubby, Travis, is the principal at our elementary school. This is his last year before retirement. Me, I was a kindergarten teacher for over twenty years, I retired four years ago. Last summer, I got bored and started driving tour buses to Taos."

"Wow! Congratulations on your granddaughters, and with this job. Do you like it?"

"I know what you're thinking. An old geezer like me driving a tour bus? You don't see many women." She coughed. "Pardon me, got a tickle in my throat. Honestly, I like driving. This is part-time. My other love is spending time with my baby girls."

"Good for you."

"Oh, my grand babies are as girly as can be. Raising boys are sure different than girls. You married? Have kids?"

"Yes, I have two daughters myself. My oldest is seven, and my younger is four."

Leona fanned herself. "God bless you. Girls can be drama queens; dancing and dressing up. My grand babies are quite the entertainers."

Amanda chuckled. She could relate. Emily was her diva, incessantly asking for new clothes and jewelry, while Rose was more athletic, preferring jeans and gym shoes to tutus.

The older woman glanced over her shoulder. "We got off track. I'm supposed to be telling *you* about Taos. You'll like it. It's a tiny, isolated town. There's also the 800-year-old Taos Pueblo as I mentioned before. People still live in them. Get their water from the river. No TV, either. I have no idea how they do it."

"Actually, it sounds cozy."

The woman continued, passing a semi-truck and then switching lanes. "These darn trucks. They make me nervous. Okay, where was I? Oh yes, Taos is legendary. Celebrities like Julia Roberts and the late Dennis Hopper called it home. Speaking of Mr. Hopper, I bet you didn't know he wrote the script for *Easy Rider* here. A rebel he was. He's buried in Taos."

"Incredible."

"You can say that again. A lot of writers and painters have made their trek to Taos over the years." Leona snapped her fingers. "There's the famous Mabel Dodge Luhan, she started a writer's colony, she convinced D.H. Lawrence to come to Taos and he did. Oh, and we have the paintings of Georgia O'Keeffe; she was a recluse who painted local landscapes. You got to see them. They are so beautiful. I could go on and on."

"Thank you for the information," Amanda replied, "I'll be honest, I didn't do sightseeing research when I was looking for a healing center."

Leona grinned through the rearview mirror. "I tell you, my sons loved coming here for vacation. It's why we moved. How about you? Where have you vacationed, lately? Any place fun?"

Amanda considered the question. "Our vacations never took us this far southwest. We've only done driving vacations with the kids because airfare is so expensive."

"Don't I know it?"

"We've gone to Wisconsin Dells, St. Louis to see a Cardinals game and we've gone up to Michigan during the fall to see the leaves change. Emily, my oldest, wants to go to Disney World in Orlando. We're saving up for that. Hopefully, we'll go next year."

Leona slowed behind a vehicle. "When I was a kid, my parents took me and my older brother on camping trips. I learned all about fly fishing and white-water rafting. I'm so happy to have had the opportunity to pass those experiences on to my kids. Are you camping people?"

Amanda held her breath. Her mom and dad definitely weren't vacationers or campers. They never had enough money to go anywhere. Her father worked Monday through Saturday. On Sunday they went to church. When the weather cooperated, the family would go to the park and get ice cream afterwards. Their family life was simple, and her parents loved each other. After her daddy died, their visits to the park were infrequent. As she grew older, she resented other children whose parents took vacations regularly.

"We're not really camping people. When I was a child, we took day-vacations like I do with my daughters, nothing too exciting." *I wish.*

Well, there was one … She couldn't forget the one big trip that changed her life, the one with Joshua when they drove to Chicago after leaving their alcohol-sotted mother.

Upon exiting the apartment building after their confrontation, Amanda collapsed in front of Joshua's car. "I can't do it, Josh. I can't. I don't want to leave Momma. I'm scared."

He helped his fourteen-year-old sister to her feet. "Get up and stop crying. We have no other choice, do you hear me? Don't you want to finish high school and get your diploma?"

She stared at the concrete.

"Listen and look at me, it's not happening here. Mom is a mess. She can't take care of herself or you, especially not me."

Amanda brushed a few strands of hair away from her eyes, blubbering. "And you think you can take care of both of us?"

"You're my little sister. I won't let anything happen to you or let anyone hurt you."

Josh was mature for eighteen. He was the *big brother*. When their father passed, he stepped up and tried to be her father-figure and he was only eleven. She had made it through her first unknown—losing a dad. Her next quandary was having the courage to leave their mother.

Fleeing Des Moines and relocating without their mom took guts. Guts she didn't have, *but does my brother?* They heard a clatter from their third-floor apartment. A window opened and Louise's gruff boyfriend stuck his head out the window. "Get out of here you pieces of shit. Go on, scram."

Joshua flipped him off, opened his passenger door and guided Amanda inside the Pinto running on its last leg.

They drove in silence for over an hour on unfamiliar roads until Amanda couldn't stand it anymore. Frightened, her mind was in a tizzy and her heart was pounding. "Where are we going? Turn back please."

Her brother kept driving. "Nope."

She crossed her arms. "Then, where? You haven't told me."

"Chicago."

Her arms fell to her lap. "That's so far away."

Her big brother smirked. "Don't worry, think of it as an adventure."

Joshua made sure it was an adventure. They traveled six hours in his 1980s junk heap. He'd found the cherry-red Ford Pinto at an estate sale, cheap.

They had a picnic lunch at one of the rest stops that had a children's playground. Even though they were too big to play, they swung on the swings and climbed the monkey bars. Giggling and racing around, it was a great release to romp in the summer air.

Joshua even let her drive a few miles on the highway. The hours flew by and they stopped for snacks at gas stations. When they entered the city on a windy Thursday afternoon and saw the many skyscrapers and buildings off I-290 onto Congress Parkway, it took their breaths away.

It was the greatest vacation ride she'd ever had. But in the back of her mind, Amanda knew the ramifications of their sudden departure. She was a minor traveling with no legal guardian or parent. If they were discovered by the authorities, she'd have to go back home to her mom, or, even into foster care. The unknown was frightening, but she trusted her brother.

Joshua saved her from a broken home and tried showing her how to take control of her life. She had fallen many times since, but managed to pick herself up each time. Something created a new void in her recently, causing her to spiral. Amanda hoped she could make things right again, this time for good for herself and her family.

Somewhere between talking about vacations, site-seeing in Taos and recalling her trip to Chicago, Amanda tuned out her surroundings, only to be brought back by Leona's excitable voice. "Mrs. Reynolds, we're stopping here. This is the magnificent Rio Grande."

Amanda focused on the rest stop they were turning into. There were half a dozen cars parked. The sun was bright on the horizon. She got up and followed Leona out of the van to a grassy area overlooking the river. Below, in the canyon, she witnessed the awesome rushing river. From this distance, the water resembled a curly straw of blue-green liquid. It was windy, and their hair whipped around in the wind as they hiked onto a bridge.

"Breath-taking," Amanda remarked.

They were standing on a cantilever truss bridge over 600 feet above the crimson cliffs and mocha canyon that made up the Rio Grande Gorge. The gorge was 800 feet at its deepest point. She could make out tiny specks of white and gray in the foaming white water, rafters moving downriver.

Leona agreed, "I knew you'd like this view. I've been here hundreds of times and never get tired of looking at this amazing creation."

"It's unbelievable." Amanda couldn't think of anything else to say.

"I'm forever in awe of God's wonderful handiwork when I take in that which He has done."

What would my children think if they saw this? Even Ryan could appreciate this. One day.

They stayed for a few minutes with Leona pointing out the red willows by the river before returning to the highway. The road was crowded as they entered Taos. Amanda was excited. She enjoyed her tour, but was looking forward to checking in at the institute.

A few miles from Goat Springs Road, the van screeched to a halt on Spider Road. Amanda saw a sign pointing to The Taos Healing Institute. It was a narrow gravel road lined with blowing grass and tumbleweed. It reminded her of an old western. The van hiccupped, bumped along the way and stopped in front of a house. It didn't look like an institution, just a ranch with a wrap-around porch. The air was dusty as she climbed down from the van.

The screen door popped open and a wiry spry elderly woman with shoulder-length white hair walked out to meet her. She was wearing tan jeans and a plaid, burgundy blouse with the cut-off sleeves.

As the woman drew near, Amanda noted her face, lined with wrinkles, but her light brown eyes held a youthfulness.

Extending her hand, the woman had a soft voice with a southern drawl, "Howdy, you must be Mrs. Amanda Reynolds? I'm Gretchen Miner. It's nice to meet you face-to-face. Welcome."

"Likewise, thank you. Please call me Amanda," she replied, her body feeling wobbly. *Why am I so nervous all of a sudden?*

"Come along, let's get your belongings. You packed light, right?"

"Yes."

Leona stepped off the van and handed the suitcase over. "Here you go, Mrs. Reynolds."

Amanda smiled, "Thank you, Leona, for everything."

"My pleasure. Good luck to you, ma'am."

Ms. Miner stepped in. "Hello there Miss Leona."

"Hiya Gretchen."

"How are the grandchildren?"

"Beautifully-exhausting."

"Ha, keeps you young. Give my best to the family."

"Will do." Ms. Davis waved goodbye, got into the van and doubled back.

Amanda sighed, watching the van kick up red and brown gravel under its tires. *Time to change my future.*

Chapter 17

Gretchen held Amanda's luggage as both women walked to the clay-shingled house. Up five steps onto a rustic front porch, the floorboards were weathered but sturdy. There were bird feeders and wind chimes hanging everywhere, and the railings were dotted with cactus plants.

"You must be tired from your trip, eh?"

"No, a little hungry, though. I nibbled on a sandwich I bought from the airport before getting on the bus."

"Lucky for you I have something special."

"Oh, okay."

"Come in," Gretchen held the door open, "I'll show you around."

Upon entering the foyer, the smell of spicy chili peppers and a strong odor like something was fermenting came at Amanda's face like a fan turned on full-blast.

She sneezed, "Excuse me. What's that strong peppery smell?"

"God bless ya." She rubbed her hands together. "Oh, that's our dinner. Gretchen Miner's famous Chili, you'll love it."

Amanda smiled politely. *Wow, I hope I don't sneeze when it's going down my throat.*

There were colorful, handmade throw rugs covering the hardwood floors. Gretchen caught Amanda staring. "They are American-Indian made, in case you're wondering."

"Nice."

"I'm from Arizona, as southwestern as you can get in Taos. I have four half-sisters who are American-Indian. They take after my step-father. My sister, who lives in Santa Fe, made these for me."

Amanda nodded in admiration.

Let's begin here." Gretchen waited for her to follow. "To our left is a sitting room. I have a ton of books and you're free to browse. I may have to start using the fireplace soon, the nights do get chilly around here." Two mushroom-colored couches occupied the room facing a magnificent, white-stoned fireplace in the middle of two walls lined with bookshelves. "To our right," Gretchen stepped aside, "is the dining area." A rectangular-shaped oak table surrounded by eight empty chairs took up the center space. Along the wall, there was a glass cabinet filled with handcrafted dishes. Gretchen pointed, "Through this hallway is the kitchen."

This was a spacious area with modern appliances and a center island cooktop stove. There was a round, white table with four chairs in a corner near a large bay window overlooking a concrete patio with a small table and a couple of lounge chairs. Through the kitchen down another hall, Gretchen took Amanda to the bedrooms. The woman pointed to the door to her master bedroom, which she didn't open, and then the two other rooms, both next to a lavatory.

The one bedroom contained two bunkbeds, a dresser, and a small desk. The other, Amanda's room, was furnished with a twin-sized bed, a plain wooden desk and a dresser. The furniture was outdated, cream-colored, but appeared to be clean and functional. Gretchen pointed around, "From your bedroom you can go to the sitting area. It's one big loop. You can't get lost."

"Thank you for showing me around." *Funny, I didn't see a single TV. Oh well, I'm not here to enjoy myself.*

"My pleasure, go ahead and get settled, feel free to use the toilet and I'll get supper ready."

"I need to call my husband and let him know I got here safely."

The elderly woman crinkled her brow. "Sure, don't make it long though. My rules are strict. I'm here to heal you. I don't want you telephoning him again, please. This is your time to get better, ya know that, right?"

Amanda nodded, ambling into her room. *Gosh, Gretchen is a pain in the ass with personal calls.* She dug in her purse for her cell.

The phone line emitted a crackly static sound through her earpiece. While waiting for Ryan to pick up, she got comfortable on the bed and studied the colorful collage of red, orange and yellow geometric shapes of the comforter.

"Hello?"

"Hi, it's me."

"Amanda, I can't hear you. The line sounds like it's breaking up."

"I know, I can't hear you so well either. I'm here. Flight and drive were good. How are the girls?"

Her husband exhaled, "What do you think? They miss their mother."

Amanda fidgeted, "And, I don't miss them, or you, I suppose? Can I say hi to Emily and Rose?"

"Sure."

The girls got on the phone both trying to talk at the same time.

"Mommy, Mommy, we miss you."

There was laughter and screeching. "Hi babies. I love you."

"Love you too, Momma!"

Ryan grabbed the phone. "Hey, get better."

"Wi … Will do."

"Call us again soon."

She straightened up, wiping her eyes. "About that. I can't call you that much while I'm here."

"Why not?"

"The woman is strict, her rules. She doesn't want distractions, I'm sorry, hon."

"Call as soon as you're able, or text, if you can. Good luck."

"Thanks, I, uh, love you, Ryan."

"Love you, too."

Amanda moved her purse and stretched out on the bed. An oak fan hanging from a white-painted ceiling offered her a refreshing breath of cool air. Closing her eyes, she massaged her temples. *I don't know if I can go through with this?*

"Yes, you can!"

Amanda sat up. "Huh. Who's there?"

"It's me, silly."

Joshua was sitting on a rocking chair in front of her bed, dressed in white shorts, a blue shirt and gym shoes.

Frightened, Amanda jumped off the bed, "Oh, my God!"

"It's okay! It's okay! Don't be scared." Joshua went over and embraced his little sister. "I'm so glad you can see me, I was a little worried."

"I don't understand," she stuttered, backing into the closet door. "You're supposed to be—"

"Dead? Yes, I know." He inched closer. "I don't have much time. I am here to support you on your journey."

Amanda hugged herself, unsure, what else could she do. She was trembling and blinking at the same time. *Is this a figment of my imagination? Is he a ghost? He looks so healthy.* Joshua was still there every time she stopped blinking. Her heart was beating a mile a minute. "Okay."

"Good, be sure to give Gretchen whatever she needs to help you." Joshua kissed his sister on the cheek, opened the door and walked out.

"Uh, yeah, whatever."

After he left, Amanda smacked herself across the face. *I must be tired.* She hadn't seen her brother since he died twelve years before, and now here he was talking to her IN THIS VERY ROOM. *This is preposterous. I think I'm going crazy!* Stunned and a bit dazed, she threw her suitcase on the bed, frantically searching through the clothing she'd brought. *Joshua, here in the flesh and looking cancer-free?*

Amanda absent-mindedly plucked out a pair of flip-flops and exchanged them for the sandals she had on her feet. *There, better. Get a grip of yourself, must be alcohol withdrawal.*

She slipped out of the room and went into the bathroom. Splashing cold water on her face, she stared at herself in the mirror. *I'm dreaming. There wasn't anyone there.*

Entering the kitchen the smell of chili filled her senses. Gretchen looked up from stirring the contents of the stockpot. "Are you okay? You look like you've seen a ghost."

Amanda shivered, "Fine, fine," she responded dismissively, sneezing again. "Am I your only visitor?"

"Yes, why do you ask? I had a last minute cancellation. Is there a problem?"

"No, I ... never mind." Amanda dragged her feet. *I think the lack of alcohol in my body is making me feel strange.*

"You have me all to yourself. Come here and sit down instead of standing around. I'll serve the chili."

There were two place settings on the table. Amanda sat opposite the window. It was already eight and the sun was setting.

Gretchen filled two bowls and brought a basket of hot rolls over to the table. "What would you like to drink?"

"Water."

"As you wish."

Gretchen carried a pitcher of water and a bottle of Jack Daniels to the table. Seeing the bottle of booze, Amanda's eyes widened. "What's this all about?"

Sitting down, the older woman replied, "Want some?" The woman poured herself a shot and took a sip. "It goes great with chili."

"No, thanks, I thought I was here to resolve my alcohol issues?" *Come on, just one drink. No, I can't!* Amanda reached for a glass, filled it with water and drained it in two gulps.

Gretchen raised her cup in a toast. "We'll get to work on that soon, don't you worry. Dig in."

After clinking her refilled glass of water against Gretchen's shot of whiskey, she scooped up a spoonful of chili. The ground meat was so tender and the beans and tomato chunks were bursting with flavor.

"This is fantastic, best I've ever had."

"My pleasure, it's a family recipe, over fifty-years-old. My grandmother's concoction."

They ate in silence, enjoying the flavors. Amanda sneaked glances at the bottle of whiskey. Even though she'd become a vodka drinker because it was harder to smell and easier to mask, this dark amber liquid was her first indulgence. The urge to drink made her stomach squeeze and tighten up. *Thanks Mom, this is all your fault.*

Gretchen rose, grabbed another glass, and poured some of the liquid into it. "Here, go ahead. I know you want to."

Amanda was mortified. *This lady must be a mind reader. First my brother shows up and now this woman is pouring me alcohol, the same liquor Mom drank, and depended on for so many years.*

She couldn't deny her urges any longer, and grabbed the glass, taking a swig. It burned her throat almost choking her. "Sorry, it's been awhile since I've had whiskey."

Gretchen leaned forward. "You get used to it right away."

Angrily, Amanda ogled the older woman. "I thought you were a recovering alcoholic?"

"I am."

"And you're drinking again!"

Gretchen cleared the table without answering, disappearing for a few minutes. When the woman returned, she placed a sheet of paper and a pencil in front of her.

"Before I tell you what you have to do with that," she pointed to the paper, "I want to discuss a few other things regarding your stay."

Amanda sagged back in her chair.

"We get up at six. You will join me on the porch for yoga. I've put workout attire in your closet. We will have breakfast and afterwards do chores like sweeping, dusting and washing. We'll take a walk in the field in the backyard and return by lunchtime. After lunch, we do more chores and stretches. Later, we'll cook dinner together, eat and then retire. Other days, like tomorrow, I have to shop for a few things."

Amanda put her hands out on the table. "Wait, chores? I paid you $3,000 to help you with chores? Where's my therapy?"

"Incorporated in all the chores we do. Are we clear?"

Screw that!

"Good. Now, back to this," Gretchen pointed to the paper again, "I want you to write down everything you can think of about your addictions and why you need help. After you're done, leave the paper on the table. I suggest you go to bed when finished. We have a busy day tomorrow."

A fuming Amanda gawked at the blank sheet. *Chores and stretches? This is ridiculous. I don't deserve to be treated like this.*

She heard her brother's voice in her head: "Be sure to give Gretchen whatever she needs to help you." *Argh.* With pen in hand, Amanda scribbled on the paper, pressing down a bit too hard.

Chapter 18

$\mathbf{A}$manda awoke to the sound of wind chimes. She had a pounding headache. Finding the alarm clock on the dresser, she noted the time. It was a little before six and it looked like it was getting light outside. Next to the clock was an empty glass, the same glass she drank the whiskey from, or *was it a different one?*

Sitting up, Amanda stretched her arms and yawned. *When did I fall asleep?* Slipping into flip-flops, she teetered to the door, nausea erupting within her stomach. The aroma of roasted coffee permeated the hall. Inhaling, another wave of nausea hit her, she grimaced. *Take control. This is not good.*

And then it began to happen, a heaving feeling started in her belly and was making its way up through her chest. Amanda took several short breaths, thinking it would stop, then like a volcano it arose. Covering her mouth, she quickly tip-toed to the bathroom and puked in the toilet. *Oh, thank God! At least I made it.*

After cleaning up, Amanda dressed in the workout clothes that were on the rocking chair across from the bed. Entering the kitchen, she stopped abruptly. *Ugh. No!* On the counter were bottles of liquor, stacks of gum, a canister of coffee, bottles of soda, and several bags of chips.

Turning away from the stove, Gretchen announced, "Morning."

Amanda steadied herself, "What's this?"

Gretchen snorted, pointing to the display. "I know it's a lot of stuff. I feel like we're on a reality rehab show and I am sharing your temptations. These—" she waved with her hand—"are your addictions, my dear."

"Oh."

Gretchen sighed. "Honey, my instincts are telling me you have a deeper reservoir of pain you aren't sharing. But don't worry. We'll uncover it together soon enough."

The night before Amanda had recorded what she identified as her plaguing addictions. *You happy, Josh? Why this analysis?* The evidence was there in front of her eyes.

Gretchen had already prepared fried eggs and pancakes in small warming pans.

Who does she plan on feeding? There's enough food for an army of ten, not just the two of us.

"I see you put on the elastic pants and loose top I left for you."

Amanda glanced at her outfit. "Yes, thank you. They're comfortable."

"Before we eat, we are going to do yoga to get the blood flowing."

Amanda squeezed her eyes in disapproval; she was feeling a dull wave rippling through her abdomen. Her mouth was dry and her tongue scaly. She wished she could chew gum but knew that wouldn't be happening. *I hope my stomach can take it.*

They went out on the porch into the crisp air. Lying on the wooden deck were two yoga mats. Gretchen instructed Amanda to sit on the orange one, while she sat on the blue one. Ms. Miner laid back and began lifting her legs high and doing circular motions like riding a bike; the woman tilted her head expecting Amanda to follow suit.

For the next half-hour, they squatted, lunged and balanced themselves on one leg. Amanda was feeling sicker and sicker, but she was too frightened to admit it.

When finished, they each rolled up their mats and Gretchen took them inside. Amanda hung out on the porch, inhaling deeply to calm her nausea and settle her spinning head. A moment later, she lurched forward and vomited over the railing. *Yuck, shit!*

Gretchen came out and calmly offered her a glass of seltzer. "This will help." She glanced over the railing. "I'll get that later."

The woman left, leaving Amanda alone. She barely remembered writing her addictions, she was so angry doing that chore. *How much did I drink?* She swallowed the soda, burped a few times and went in to find Gretchen clearing her plate from the table.

Amanda sat down, humiliated, "I'm sorry for the mess."

The older woman glared at her and said. "Listen, I don't care about the mess outside. Don't drink all my liquor."

What! "I drank all your liquor?"

"Yes, ma'am, you did." Gretchen walked over to the sink and lifted the bottle for her to see. It was empty.

Appetite gone, Amanda's head pounded harder. *I need sleep.* "I'm so sorry."

The woman hissed, "Don't drink all my liquor again!"

Furious, she pushed her chair out and stood up, rage boiling through her like an angry mob. "What kind of healing are you providing if there is alcohol around?"

Gretchen strutted toward her. "First, don't disrespect me in my own home. Secondly, I suggest you keep your emotions under control. Eat your breakfast. We have work to do."

Amanda sat down and massaged her brow. "I can't eat. My head is killing me. Can I rest for a bit?"

The mentor hovered over the table. "Like hell you will! This ain't a vacation. We have work to do I said." she turned toward the food on the counter. "Do whatever you need to do to get focused so we can get you sober."

Amanda gaped at all the addictions and the pans filled with the breakfast foods. Trembling, she rose from the table and helped herself to a pancake, some scrambled eggs and a banana.

Returning to her seat, she chewed the food slowly. Every few minutes, she felt like she needed to heave, but thankfully she didn't. Amanda's nausea ceased after gulping four cups of black coffee and chomping on three pieces of gum, while nursing a diet coke in between.

Gretchen observed her while drinking a steaming cup of Joe. "Enjoying yourself?"

Between chews, Amanda nodded. "You have no idea how I've wanted to have coffee *and* cola *and* gum. It's so delicious." As soon as the words came out, she stopped chewing.

Gretchen stood, opened a cabinet, and uncapped another bottle of Jack. She poured herself a half-glass and downed it. Then she placed the bottle in front of her. "This is what you really want, am I right?"

Amanda pouted, pushing her glass of cola and the bottle of liquor away. "Why are you teasing me? It's not fair! This isn't the way to help me; you're trying to fuel my addictions, not alleviate them."

"You're right, life isn't fair. But I don't want to be fair. I want to be firm and you need to learn control. From the looks of it, you already have two strikes against you." She held up her fingers. "One, you have no control, and two, you're not in the best shape for a woman in her mid-thirties."

Ouch, that hurts. Amanda looked at her body. She wasn't heavy, but she was a little fleshy here and there because she didn't exercise. Feeling foolish and deflated emotionally, she whispered, "Gee, thanks. So what do I need to do?"

Gretchen removed the cups and the bottle. "First, help me put all these items I bought, your addictions, into the garage. Say goodbye to them because from now on you're going to eat only what I feed you." She patted her on the back. "Today, we're taking a ride to an organic store in town."

After removing Amanda's addictive foods from the counter and stacking them in a corner of the garage, the two women got into a shiny, ice-blue vintage vehicle. "What kind of car is this?"

Gretchen patted the steering wheel. "This beauty is a 1967 Chevy Impala."

"Wow! It's in great condition."

"97,000 miles on this baby. And it is just a baby."

The elderly woman put the key in the ignition and the engine thundered to life. She backed out onto Spider Road.

"My late husband bought me this car for my sixty-ninth birthday." Gretchen winked at Amanda. "That was twenty years ago, if you're doing the math. He loved old cars as much as I do. He found it at an auction in Texas and drove it here. Hardly any miles on it still. We drove it to Vegas, Colorado, Tennessee and Texas. She's a good car and a great ride."

"I can't believe you're eighty-nine-years-old?"

Gretchen grinned, "Shocked? Me too, I thought I would've been dead long ago. I was married to Roy for thirty-nine years."

"When did Roy pass?"

"Been eighteen years, stubborn old fool. He smoked a pipe for almost half his life, never wanted to give it up either, even after he found out he had lung cancer. He suffered a lot, his own damn fault though." Gretchen sighed heavily, "He was good man, a hard worker. God, I miss him."

Amanda nodded, feeling sad for the woman's loss and missing her own family.

The windows were down, the sun was blazing and the air was a little cool. The wind blew through their hair. On Paseo Del Pueblo Norte, Amanda saw a sign for Kit Carson Memorial State Park. "I read up on Kit Carson on the net. So this is where the park is?"

"You got it; Kit Carson was quite the outdoorsman. An explorer, a trapper and a rancher in the 1800s, he used Taos as his base camp for fur-trapping expeditions. His grave is in the park and the park even offers RV and camping amenities."

Gretchen kept on driving. Amanda watched people strolling along the sidewalk in front of restaurants and shops. They drove another few minutes, squeezing into a space in front of Cid's Food Market. She exited the car and followed the elderly woman into the store.

With list in hand Gretchen asked, "What do you usually cook at home?"

Amanda shrugged, "Honestly, I'm not good in the kitchen. In fact, I don't cook. We buy a lot of packaged dinners and frozen foods. They're quick and the girls like them." The store was well-lit and smelled of fresh bread and coffee. Gretchen grabbed a cart and started for the produce aisles. "You see," she said as they approached displays of raw vegetables, "this is what you *should* be eating, raw healthy foods, better for your mind and body. Not junk. The chili I made last night was with a combination of organic tomatoes, fresh beans and ground beef from grass-fed cows."

Amanda listened to her mentor. They weren't a "green" family. She grew up with a drunken mother and when she lived with Josh they ate a lot of canned foods and macaroni and cheese. However, she learned a little about organic foods when she waitressed at The Living Kitchen, but never paid attention to the food preparation, she just served it.

"I know you're right." Nervous, Amanda added, "Can you teach me?"

"Come along, I have a long list of things to buy."

They spent the next hour perusing the aisles as Gretchen explained the types of foods she should be purchasing, such as oats, organic teas, free-range eggs, grass-fed meats, goat's milk, avocados, red and yellow peppers, celery, and salads. It was an eye-opening experience for Amanda. And it wasn't like she didn't have the time to cook; she was a stay-at-home mom, she didn't care for it and Ryan never complained, so she hadn't thought about changing her routine.

As they meandered through the store, Gretchen commented. "Your body is a temple, and what you put into it becomes the fuel your body needs for energy. What you don't need, you won't miss, believe me."

The store personnel were great and knew Gretchen Miner well. They asked about her garden, her paintings and her sisters. Amanda felt at home in the company of this exceptionally spry nearly ninety-year-old woman.

They checked out and filled the trunk with food. During the short drive back, Amanda broached a different subject with Gretchen regarding her own addiction. "You're a recovered alcoholic? How did you become a non-alcoholic?"

The woman laughed. "Yes, to the first question. I'm now a 'non-alcoholic'. It took time, but I can't teach others to cleanse without being clean myself, eh?"

Amanda shook her head. "I've seen you drink, and yet you say you're cleansed?"

Gretchen grinned. "I am. As for you, I studied what you wrote on your sheet of paper. I have been observing your behavior from the moment you got here, and I took a huge risk against my own well-being with the whiskey because ... I was once like you."

"Oh."

The wise healer made a turn and continued driving. "You see, part of getting sober is the need to control your temptations and change your habits. I had poor habits: drinking, smoking, not getting enough sleep or exercising. Roy could tolerate his unhealthy habits, but I wasn't going to do that. My body was deteriorating on the inside and I ignored it for a long time."

Amanda moved closer. "Would you mind telling me what happened?"

Gretchen shrugged and looked toward her. "Without going into detail because we are here for you and not me, it's like this; I would have drowned because I got so drunk once at a pool party. That was my wake-up call. I changed, refocusing my cravings and channeling them into what I call emotional landscapes."

Amanda studied the woman. "Wow. I'm glad you're okay. What do you mean by 'emotional landscapes'?"

"It's pretty simple. Whatever I'm feeling in the moment, I paint it. I don't use any paint brushes or anything. I dip my bare hands in the paint and basically splat it on a canvas."

"Can I take a look at your work some time?"

"Sure, after we sweep the porch. I think you'll like them. Sold a few paintings too."

"Right. Your chores," she grumbled.

Back at the ranch with the groceries having been put away, Amanda helped Gretchen fold laundry and sweep the porch. The floorboards were constantly dusty because the wind blew the pea gravel from the driveway onto the steps. Before they knew it, it was noon, Amanda was feeling queasy again. *Am I hungry or am I experiencing withdrawal symptoms?* The sun was hot so she drank a couple glasses of water infused with lemon and cucumbers, hoping that would help ease the weirdness in the pit of her stomach.

Gretchen gathered her ingredients; romaine lettuce, a tomato and a cucumber. In no time she had a large bowl of salad ready for them. She added chopped walnuts, dried cranberries, slices of avocado, even whipping up her own balsamic vinaigrette. Then, they both dived into their salads.

The mentor stared at her. "What's your story, Amanda?"

"What do you mean?" she asked between bites.

Gretchen chewed. "There are varying stages of alcoholism which I'm sure you learned about in AA. I don't need to bore you with the details. From what I've witnessed thus far, you use alcohol as a crutch. It's your MO, your way of maintaining and coping, your escape mechanism. You could be working out and eating right instead. What gives?"

Amanda remembered what Joshua had told her, to be upfront about her circumstances.

The woman extended her arm. "Before you tell me, I want you to know that you look like a nice lady, I don't want to take money from someone and not be able to help him or her. I may not be your answer. Do you know what I mean?"

Amanda nodded, putting her fork down. She took several deep breaths and talked about Joshua's death, the roller coaster-like emotions of losing a sibling, visiting her mom at the trailer park in Iowa and leaving abruptly at the sight of what her only parent had become. She confessed having gone to AA and relapsing again at the Memorial Day parade and the confusion that accompanied it. She was close to telling her about Joshua appearing in the bedroom the day before but Amanda decided against it. It boggled her mind. *It never happened.*

Spontaneous tears slipped down her cheeks. "I don't know what's going on. My kids are suffering. Drinking has been my *escape* like you said. It feels so good and I feel empowered. I thought I could manage it, but the addiction is overpowering."

Shaking her head, Amanda continued, "I love my family, yet I feel there is a void or something that needs closure. I'm not sure how to do it."

Gretchen squeezed her hand. "Oh, I'm sorry for this rotten experience. I hate to ask, but this will help me to understand you better. Have you talked to your mother recently?"

What? Again! First it's Ryan asking about my mom and now this woman! She shuddered, "Are you kidding me? No. I'm never returning to Mount Pleasant. I can't."

"Why not?"

Amanda placed her plate in the sink. *To see the reality of the woman my mother chose to become? No way.* "I'm not here to see my mom; I want to get clean."

Ms. Miner rose and faced her. "This place is not a pill that you can take and suddenly all your problems go away. I can help you with your addictions. I can teach you to eat healthier. I can teach you to exercise. What I cannot do is heal the raw emotions that are consuming you."

Amanda petitioned desperately, "Are you getting rid of me already? *No, please.* I feel like I haven't accomplished anything. I'm not clean. In fact, I've been feeling nauseous. I know my body is raging and rebelling without alcohol. I need help, Gretchen, please! Besides, I've only done yoga, chores, swept, cleaned, and learned a little about organic foods. I need to learn more from you to fully kick my bad habits. You look like you have your life together. I want the same thing."

The older woman hugged Amanda. "Thank you, but you make it sound like you're on vacation. You can't run away from the underlying triggers of your addictions. And I'm no psychologist, but I have an inkling, it's your mother."

Amanda sighed. *My mother. My brother.*

Releasing her embrace, Gretchen asked, "Do you have any hobbies?"

"Hobbies? Like sewing?"

"Yes, anything to deter you from wanting a drink."

Amanda thought for a while and came up with a list of things she didn't like. She hated reading, didn't like writing, or keeping a journal. Exercise wasn't exactly exciting, just needed. She finally recalled her fondness to music. "I like listening to different kinds of music, especially classical and jazz."

Gretchen clapped, "Great, how does it make you feel?"

"It relaxes me, reminds me of my father. He used to play jazz and classical music in the garage."

"I personally like painting, it's my thing. You should consider taking up something else besides listening to music. Focus on others besides yourself like volunteering at a homeless shelter, dog shelter, whatever, and carve out some exercise time too. I'll show you my paintings, but better yet, let's do this. Would you be willing to join me in a painting session?"

Amanda bit a nail, "Sure."

"Good, I have to run an errand. I'll be back in an hour or so. Put on older clothes and be ready. You're going to paint this afternoon. Let's see if this will reveal any issues causing your unhappiness."

"Where is your paint room?"

"In my shed."

Five minutes later, Amanda sported a faded peach-colored T-shirt, coffee-colored cargo pants and brand new tennis shoes. They weren't fancy, but they weren't ugly/get dirty clothes either. Alone, she walked out on the porch. The wind had picked up and dust was twirling around. *Oh, this dust. Gretchen would surely be grunting about having to sweep the porch.* She picked up a broom and swept, again.

She accumulated a pile of dirt and gravel, searching for dustpan to pick it up. Looking around, Amanda noticed the garage door was open and wandered over. *Why would Gretchen leave it open with the wind blowing outside?*

The back wall was lined with shelves filled with storage boxes. In front of the shelving there was an old lawn mower, a weed whacker and a workbench with numerous tools on top. *Probably her husband's.* On the opposite side lay the boxes full of her addictions. She eyed them; her mouth watered as she spied a vodka bottle.

"No, I'm not going to do it." Amanda said to the boxes.

Something shiny caught her interest; she walked away from the temptations. On the middle shelf of a high three-shelf stand, sticking out behind a yellowed shoe box was a round musical jewelry box. Its exterior was painted silver with cream-colored stripes; it was decorated with the seven dwarfs. A pink apple rested on top of the box.

When Amanda opened it, the interior revealed an enchanting scene, the dwarfs' cottage. Standing in the middle was a tiny figurine, Snow White. She flipped it over to reveal a key. Winding the key, Snow White twirled to the tune of Johannes Brahms' bedtime lullaby.

Amanda shivered, not having heard that tune in years. Memories of her mother rushed into her mind.

Amanda was six-years-old. Joshua had fallen off his bike while zigzagging around a baby turtle sitting in the middle of the sidewalk. He had some cuts and bruises around his face and forehead, but otherwise he was okay. She and Mom had gone to the pharmacy because they had run out of ointment and band aids, while their father finished attending to Josh's wounds.

Passing one of the aisles, Amanda noticed a round Snow White jewelry box. When she opened it, a lullaby played. She was so smitten with the figurine twirling to the music that she couldn't put it down. Her mother refused to purchase the music box, it was a little pricy.

The workers at the trucking company where her father, John, worked were threatening to strike and her mom wanted to save up as much money as she could. Amanda continued to plead her case in the aisles, and again at the cash registers while waiting in line, until her mother gave in. That year, and only that year, her mom played the tune every night at bedtime for Amanda until the day her father died.

Amanda sank to the floor as pools of tears formed in her eyes. The jewelry box was different than the one she had owned as a child, but it certainly reminded her of the loss of her father, and the rage she had felt for Louise when she stopped being the mother she had been to her and her brother.

When Amanda and Joshua fled to Chicago, she had unintentionally left her jewelry box on the dresser. *Whatever happened to it?* Wiping her eyes, she placed the box back on the shelf.

Exiting the garage, she caught sight of her *addiction* boxes. The damn vodka was poking out of one of the boxes like a trophy. Emotionally shaken, Amanda pulled the bottle out and carried it to her room.

Amanda awoke on her bed. A ginormous headache echoed in her head. She was face down, when she lifted herself and turned, Gretchen was sitting in the rocking chair across from her.

Holding up an empty bottle of vodka, the woman interrogated her. "What did I tell you about drinking my liquor?"

Amanda sat up, noticing she was still wearing the same work-out clothes. "I'm sorry, I couldn't help myself."

"Give me a break! You are wasting my time and yours. How are you supposed to get healthy for your kids and your husband when you're drinking this stuff all the time, huh, explain that?"

Right again, damn. Wearily, Amanda fell back on the bed. It was so easy to relapse. Getting rid of her demons was going to take a lot more self-control. And she had to make the choice to stop turning to them.

"What time is it?"

"Time for stretching exercises and breakfast." Gretchen headed to the door. "Get up, nap time is over."

Amanda glared at the clock, 4:30. *Darn it.* She rose and pulled up the shades. It was dark out. *Did I actually sleep through the rest of the afternoon and night?* Her mouth was dry and her stomach ached, a stinging feeling and nausea at the same time. She stumbled out the door.

Gretchen was standing on the porch looking toward the horizon, just where the sun would be rising. The air was cold, Amanda hugged her body for warmth.

Silently, they opened their mats and began stretching. Amanda followed as best as she could, considering the burning feeling in the pit of her stomach. It was a long while until they finished.

As the sun was beginning to make its first appearance of the day, the chilled air turned warmer. Gretchen hardly spoke during the time they were on the porch with the exception of instructed exercises.

She finished rolling up the yoga mat. "I'm really sorry. I know I'm not cooperating, please forgive me. I was looking for a dustpan to scoop the dirt from the porch and ended up snooping instead. I shouldn't have."

"Apology accepted."

"Can I ask you question, though?"

Gretchen nodded, "Go ahead."

Amanda hesitated, not wanting to cry. Swallowing the emotion, she asked, "Where did you get the Snow White jewelry box on the shelf in the garage?"

Gretchen fluttered her eyelids. "It's my niece's. My sister gave it to me for safe-keeping when her daughter died."

"Oh, I'm sorry."

"Cancer, twenty-six years ago. I had the jewelry box in the house, but I couldn't keep it there anymore. It reminded me of my beautiful niece too much. She was a special little girl. Born with chronic health issues, she lived cancer-free for eleven years. But the good Lord took her home; she doesn't have to suffer any longer. I put the box in the garage with the intention of finding a new place for it somewhere in the house. I'd forgotten about it. I'm ashamed to admit it's been sitting on the shelf for ten years."

Amanda cracked her knuckles. "I used to have one like it. My mom bought it for me when I was six." She paused, feeling her eyes tear. "Seeing it and hearing the lullaby brought me to a different place. I miss my father. I was reminded how it was with my mother before he died. I caved in."

Gretchen hugged her. "That's why you are here, to heal. I wish I hadn't left you alone to deal with that dreadful memory."

Amanda closed her eyes, "Thank you."

"Daylight's coming. Let's get some nourishment. We have more chores to do. Afterwards, we'll talk about foods you can eat that will give you energy." Food sounded like a great plan. Famished, Amanda followed her mentor inside.

Chapter 19

Ryan stretched his arm across the bed sheet yearning for the familiarity of her skin and her soft body. Instead, the pillow was still fluffed up and her usual space empty. He gazed up at the ceiling, missing his partner. It had only been a few days since his wife had left, but it seemed much longer.

Cecilia, their neighbor, had been a Godsend. She was cooking meals for him, Emily and Rose. His parents were flying in the following week for a couple days to help out while he worked. *There is so much to juggle.* Schedules and babysitting was normally Amanda's job. Ryan pulled the pillow over his face recalling the dinner incident the previous evening with Emily. He had yelled at her for accidentally knocking a plate of pasta on the floor. The stress was getting to him. His baby girl didn't deserve his fury. *Can I make it these next few weeks with Amanda gone?*

Ryan threw the pillow on the floor and got out of bed. It was not quite 3:30. In a few hours he'd have to leave and tend work obligations all over again. In the master bath, he splashed cold water on his face. *I have to get rid of all the alcohol if I am to be a supportive with my wife's new life. Geez, my scotch, bourbons and whiskeys will have to be tossed, and soon.* Ryan shook his head as he stared at his pale face in the mirror. *I'm tired.*

Stepping back into the bedroom, he bumped into something. "Emily, you scared me! What are you doing up?"

His eldest squirmed, "I can't sleep, Daddy."

Ryan squeezed her shoulders. "Makes two of us. We need to rest, though. I'll walk you back to your room." With that said, father and daughter tip-toed into the hallway.

Chapter 20

July

They spent the next three weeks exercising, cleaning, and learning to cook homemade meals. Amanda had lost six pounds thanks to her healthier diet of vegetables, lean meats, and drinking more than eight cups of water a day.

The days passed, Amanda's afternoon mood swings and evening headaches lingered. Gretchen assured her it was withdrawal from alcohol and other addictive foods she had previously consumed. Her body was healing and changing for the better at the same time.

One afternoon, Gretchen went to run an errand and left Amanda by herself in the house. It was hot outside with the temperatures soaring to 90 degrees. Feeling restless and a little homesick, she took her phone and headed outside to sit on the porch steps. Amanda gazed at the dirt path leading out of Gretchen's property. It was eerily quiet despite the whistling of wind chimes on the porch. The garage was closed. Grinning, she remembered the last incident. Thankfully, her addictive food and drink items were in the boxes where they belonged behind a locked door.

She got up and walked to the back of the house. Situated on the south side of the property was a structure no bigger than a small bedroom made of weathered wood and metal beams and covered by thick plastic sheeting. Walking toward it, she noticed a wooden door with a clear plastic window. Upon careful inspection, Amanda saw two shelves on each side of the room containing rows of potted plants. *Wow, an indoor garden!* There was vegetation hanging everywhere with special lights in the corners and two oscillating fans on opposite sides.

The garden intrigued Amanda. Hoping to explore the inside she pulled on the door, but it was padlocked. *I need to talk to Gretchen to find out more on what is she growing? I could do this at home to help my family eat healthier.*

Amanda looked around seeing a rustic brown and yellow barn. She meandered toward it. Shaking the large door, it was padlocked as well. A black, wrought-iron chair stood against the outer wall of the barn, Amanda sat on it. She missed Ryan and her daughters, but Gretchen was adamant about not connecting with family while she was in treatment. Regardless, Amanda was concerned about her husband since he was doing double-duty with the girls. Fumbling with her cell, she couldn't wait any longer. *I'm calling him now.* The line rang three times before someone answered.

"Reynolds' residence."

Amanda recognized the voice of Cecilia Stanger, their neighbor next door. "Hi Cecilia, it's Amanda."

"How are you?" she squealed.

"Doing well and the girls, how are they doing?" She heard giggling in the background. Jealousy ran through her bones at the thought of Emily and Rose playing without her there.

"Playing princess. Hold on; let me give you to Mr. Reynolds. He just walked into the kitchen. Godspeed to you."

Amanda gulped listening to the phone being passed.

"Hi." Ryan spoke.

"Hi."

"How are you?"

Amanda squinted up at the sun. She was beginning to sweat. "My best to get healthy."

"We miss you."

"I miss you guys too. Are the girls okay?"

"Driving me nuts."

Amanda cracked a smiled. She could relate. Taking care of a seven-year-old and a four-year-old was no easy feat. They required constant attention, especially her younger child, Rose, who was into everything. "Sorry."

"Are you getting better?" Ryan's normal burly voice sounded flat and tired.

"So far, it's been a bit of a bumpy ride." Amanda paused hearing tires rolling on gravel. "I … I gotta go. I'll call you later." She closed her phone and slipped it into her back pocket.

Ryan stared at the receiver for a split second before putting it on its cradle. Turning around, four large brown eyes examined him.

"Who was that, Daddy?" Emily asked, flushed from playing.

"Mommy."

Rose squealed, "Mommy, Mommy. I want Mommy."

"Is she coming home yet?" Emily queried her eyes moist with emotion.

Ryan's heart throbbed. "Soon she'll be home. She says she misses you."

Rose clapped, hugged her father and skipped into the family room.

Emily crossed her arms, unconvinced, "If she missed us so much, she wouldn't have left in the first place. It's taking too long, Daddy."

I know. He tried embracing her, but Emily shrank away, running to the stairs. Ryan jerked up. Cecilia came up behind him. "Give her a few minutes. Let her calm down. Dinner will be ready soon."

"Sure. Thank you," he replied lumbering out of the kitchen. *For God's sake Amanda, I hope you're getting better.*

Amanda covered her eyes. She was feeling heartbroken more than anything. She missed them and was anxious to return home. Gretchen kept her occupied and on a short leash. At home, who'd hold her accountable? She couldn't have access to alcohol or the addictive foods she used to eat. She'd have to start fresh, to clean out her whole house. Ryan worked hard and Amanda didn't want to burden him. It was going to be tough getting organized, re-stitching her relationship with her children.

Gretchen trekked to her from the house. She was dressed in black from head to toe. Her hair was pulled back in a tight bun on top of her head and she sported a black paint-spattered sleeveless hoody, Capri pants and black plastic boots. "I thought I'd find you here."

Amanda straightened, regaining her composure. *I can't let on about the phone call.* "Ah … I decided to take a stroll. Saw your indoor garden over there."

"I love gardens. I like seeing things transform, just like my patients," she heehawed. "Oh, I'm also growing basil, cilantro, parsley and a few tomato plants, nothing fancy."

"I don't even know how to plant. Ryan is the gardener. He grows roses and some other flowers I can't even pronounce." As soon as Amanda said her husband's name, she felt her heart breaking.

Gretchen put an arm around her. "Soon you'll be home. I promise."

Amanda surveyed her mentor's attire, "What's with the black? It's hot out here."

"It's my painting gear. I know we talked about it, and we haven't gotten a chance to do it yet. Do you want to join me?"

"Of course, I've been waiting for this."

Gretchen unlocked the padlock, "If I were you, I'd change clothes."

Amanda examined her attire, jean capris and a red short-sleeve top. "I don't have anything I'd mind getting paint on."

"In that case, let me give you something to wear."

Ten minutes later, Amanda was wearing a tie-dye short-sleeve shirt, black jeans and dark green garden boots. Gretchen lent her a hair tie. "I'd put your hair up, it gets messy in there."

"Okay." She grabbed the rubber band and drew her disheveled golden-brown hair up into a ponytail. Together, they opened the creaking, large wooden door and entered. Once inside Gretchen yanked on the cords dangling from the ceiling, illuminating the shed's interior.

Looking around the structure, Amanda commented, "You call this a shed? This is a barn."

The older woman chuckled, "I have other things in here besides my paintings, shovels and planting gear. I never thought of it as a barn, but by the looks of it you're right."

Amanda sniffed, "It sure smells like paint."

She observed murals of magnificent artwork. In one corner lay a picture of a naked woman crying on a yellow chase; on the opposite wall a large bowl of smashed fruit and a blistered hand reaching for an apple; across was a picture of clouds and rain; but one prominent picture that caught her attention was a large face—the face of Jesus. Amanda inched toward it. It was a painted on a black canvas, the face was colored grayish-white.

"When did you do this?"

Gretchen appeared next to her. "A month and a half ago, as a matter of fact. I was feeling spiritually inclined, the picture came to me in a dream, so I painted it."

"I love it." *Gosh, I don't even have any religion in my life.* "We're Catholic, but we don't attend church like we should. I need to work on my spiritual development too when I get back."

"Thank you, Amanda. When I need a lift or I'm feeling inclined to express myself, I come here. This is my escape, my way of channeling those temptations that consume my mind, those I had talked to you about."

Her mentor turned and went to another corner of the barn, hauling on two large blank canvases. She placed them back-to-back on separate easels over a plastic sheet in the center of the room illuminated by two dangling bright lights overhead. She pushed two rolling tables topped with paint and brushes next to the canvases.

There were five large jars filled with white, yellow, blue, brown and black paint, large enough for a medium-sized hand to fit inside. Gretchen put away the brushes and unscrewed the tops of the paint jars.

"Do you need help?"

"Nope."

Amanda watched as Gretchen took out white rags from a drawer and placed them neatly at the feet of the rolling tables. "To clean yourself when you're finished."

"Right." Amanda felt uncomfortable around the artist. She was organized and her drawings weren't amateur in the least. Plus, she didn't know how to paint, let alone plant, cook or even be a good mother and wife. She plopped herself on the concrete floor and hugged her knees.

"What's the matter?"

"Doing some self-loathing."

The older woman kneeled beside her. "Use that self-loathing in the art you're going to create."

Amanda blew out a heavy sigh, "I'm sorry, I'm not artsy, Gretchen. In fact, I'm hopeless."

"Quit that, let it go. Are you willing to make an effort?"

"I guess."

"Well, that's half the battle, isn't it? Here," she took out a shower cap from her pocket, "you're going to need this for your hair. One more thing, we aren't using the paint brushes for this exercise, your bare hands and arms will do."

"Oh." Puzzled, Amanda put on the cap. Gretchen did the same. They walked over to their canvases and the elderly woman showed Amanda the colors to use and how to be free in her artwork.

"I'll be on the other side, if you need me." She strolled to her canvas, already splashing paint on the sheet.

Amanda ogled her blank canvas for a few minutes. Memories of her childhood flashed into her mind.

The first time Louise had put lipstick on her daughter, Amanda was around four-years-old. Her mom carefully outlined her pouty lips with a lip pencil liner and expertly filled in the center with bright red lipstick. She giggled, drawing little lipstick hearts on Amanda's cheeks, telling her the hearts represented how much she loved her. Amanda smiled at that memory.

She remembered a darker incident. She had been awakened by the sound of something falling. Upon investigating, she and Joshua discovered their mom had fallen through the glass coffee table. Joshua telephoned 9-1-1, they spent several hurried minutes cleaning up the shards scattered all over the worn carpet before the ambulance came. When the paramedics questioned their mother later, she told them she accidentally tripped and fell. In reality, Louise had been drunk, thinking the coffee table was a bed. That night, Louise got four stitches above her left eyebrow.

Amanda examined the jars. Taking her right hand, she dipped it in the black jar. The liquid was cold and heavy. Raising it, she slammed it against the sheet and watched as a hand-print larger than her own, from the impact, revealed itself. The black paint began dripping down the canvas creating an eerie picture. With her other hand, she dipped into the red jar and smeared her left hand across the black print. She did this with the other colors, crisscrossing the previous designs. New blended colors were emerging to the average eye, the canvas was a collage of streaks and hand-prints. But for Amanda, the creation was a release of sorrow and the fury she felt about her mom, which she had subconsciously harbored during the last twenty-two years. Continuing to work out feelings of sorrow she endured for her brother's passing, she slapped the canvas and grunted as each spray of color flooded the white background.

Images of Louise drinking and stumbling came to her mind. She remembered the searing pain each time her mom slapped her across the face. In retaliation, Amanda struck the canvas harder, plunging her hand into the black paint again and again, until her forearms were coated and dripping with the dark color, doing what she could to erase the uncomfortable vision of the last time she saw her mom standing in her doorway at the trailer park.

Suddenly the image of Josh's face came to mind along with his last words at the hospital, "Make it right; make it matter." Amanda splashed paint on the canvas until it was covered in dark shades. Exhausted, she dropped to the floor.

Wiping her arms and hands with the towels Gretchen had provided, she stumbled to her feet, unable to look at the mess she'd made on her canvas.

Gretchen came over, taking in her painting.

Amanda cleared her throat. "I told you, I can't paint worth a lick."

"That's quite a *lick* you created. It's fantastic!"

Her heart raced, "No. No, it's not. In fact—" she threw the towels on the floor, "it's not right, nor does it even matter." She lunged, ripping the canvas from the easel until it fell to the floor.

Amanda rushed out of the barn into the dusty air. She ran and ran until her lungs burned. She collapsed on the ground in front of the porch steps willing her mind to delete every unhappy memory of her mother.

The older woman caught up to her, out of breath. "It's okay, really."

"Gretchen, Gretchen, did you see my brother?"

"Shush, I got you."

The healer hoisted a bawling Amanda and half-carried her into the house.

Chapter 21

A loud buzzing filled the air. Turning over, Amanda noticed the clock radio light pulsing, 6:15 a.m. There were no paint residue on her skin and she was wearing yellow and orange polka-dot pajamas. Her eyes took in a dark blue suitcase up against the wall beside the door to the room.

Throwing the covers on the floor, Amanda jumped off the bed, put on her sandals and torpedoed out of the bedroom. Entering the kitchen, her stomach growled at the smell of freshly cooked eggs.

Gretchen greeted her, "Well, good morning to you."

"Why is my bag packed?"

"Eat first, we'll talk after you've had some food in your belly."

"I'm not hungry."

"Like hell you aren't, you look pale. Take a seat and eat."

She ran to the table and sat down as Gretchen ambled over with a plate full of scrambled eggs and fruit. Taking up a fork, she dove into her breakfast, leaving just the crumbs a few minutes later.

Across from her, Gretchen picked at sliced cantaloupe and strawberries, "You were hungry, apparently."

Taking a long drink of freshly squeezed orange juice, she didn't answer immediately, "Can you tell me why my bag is packed?"

Gretchen set her fork down, "I can't help you anymore. I've given you some basic tools and resources to better your insides. Your cravings and addictions are dormant for the moment until the demons resurface. I promise you they will." The woman leaned over the table. "My goal was to cleanse you and teach you how to eat and drink healthy. Someone else will need to help with those darn demons, to expose them and help you remove them from your mind forever."

Amanda held her head for a minute. Looking up, she said, "I'm afraid to go home."

"I know, but you aren't going home. I have a friend in Nashville who has agreed to try and help you. He's expecting you."

"What? When?"

"Today, I've already booked your flight. I have a taxi coming at 8:30. Flight's at noon."

"You have it all covered, don't you?"

"Those demons are like heavy clouds hanging over your emotions. The alcohol and addictions are both a temporary band-aide."

Amanda bit her lower lip, "This is scary."

The older woman patted her hand. "You need an emotional cleanse. I love your company, but you need something more than what I can provide." She rose and placed her dishes in the sink.

Turning, Amanda asked, "What happened yesterday?"

"I believe you blacked out from emotional overload. Basically, you had a breakdown which in my opinion was long overdue." The woman shook her head, "You even asked me if I saw your brother."

My brother. I told her I saw Josh? "Oh no! I'm so sorry for making a mess in your barn, for drinking your liquor and being such an unacceptable house guest."

"It's supposed to be like this." Gretchen fussed with the dishes in the sink.

Amanda joined her. The woman put her arm out. "No, it's okay, go and get ready. I'll take care of things here."

"Let me help."

"No. Get."

At exactly 8:30, a white and orange checkered cab coasted up the gravel drive. Gretchen and Amanda were already on the porch awaiting its arrival. The sky was blue and the air calm.

The two women briefly hugged, even while Amanda tried holding on for a few more seconds. Gretchen stepped back, "Remember, good eating habits are contagious. Your girls will be proud of you. Continue to exercise and stretch every day."

"Thank you, Gretchen, for your hospitality and everything else you've done for me." She no longer needed gum or coffee or anything with caffeine. Most of the time she had energy, of course there were the occasional waves of nausea due to cravings, but she was doing her best to take hold of them.

"Listen, those demons aren't going to go away by themselves. You need to face them to deal with them."

"I will." But even as Amanda said those words she feared the difficulty ahead. *Am I prepared to face the past to conquer my future?*

Gretchen passed her an envelope, "I've detailed what you'll need for your trip to Tennessee. Mr. Huckfinn is a good man, he will help you. This," she gave her another envelope, "is the rest of your money for the remaining days you were supposed to be here."

Amanda took the first envelope, but refused the second one. "I can't do that to you."

Gretchen shoved it back. "Take it, it's yours."

Reluctantly, she took the other one and stuffed both in her purse. Grabbing her things, she ambled down the steps to the driver standing on the gravel drive. Amanda glanced back, but the woman was already inside.

Sighing, she slid into the taxi. *Round two.*

Chapter 22

The taxi driver, Danny, informed her that the fastest route to the airport was via the Low Road. Amanda thanked him, recalling the sound of the gushing water of the Rio Grande and the beautiful landscape of the two-lane road. *When I'm fully recovered, I want to return with the family and explore the scenic High Road.*

"Where are you flying to?" Danny peered in the rearview mirror. Dark sunglasses covered his eyes.

"Nashville."

The driver tipped his sunglasses. "Nashville, eh? What a great city. Your home?"

"No."

"Vacationing?"

Shaking her head, Amanda answered, "I wouldn't call it that." *Enough with the questions, I'm not in the mood for chitchat.*

The driver seemed to have gotten the hint and focused on driving and she looked out the window. A part of her felt she let Gretchen down by succumbing to her vices during her stay, another part of her gave her confidence to carry on. It had been a yo-yo of an experience.

Amanda learned better eating habits and different ways to prepare simple cuisines, skills that she could pass along to Emily and Rose. But the true test was controlling the temptations when old memories seeped into her mind.

Amanda let the warm air from the open window blow in her face. She took out her cellular phone and wrestled with calling Ryan. *He'll freak out if he knows I'm flying to Nashville.* Her family was expecting her home in a few days.

Turning it on, she saw a text from the night before. It read: … Emily is taking your absence pretty hard. … Love you and miss you. We are counting the days until you come home.

Amanda deleted the text. *I should go home. What am I doing?* Gretchen's words whispered in her ears. "Take care of those demons. Do it for your girls."

Amanda thought of her brother. *Was his appearance a few weeks earlier a figment of my imagination?* She couldn't figure it out. *Should I have told Gretchen?*

Two hours later, Amanda was back at the Albuquerque Airport. She had an hour to spare, including check-in before she was scheduled to fly into Houston for a connecting flight to Nashville. It was going to be a half-day trip this time; United Airlines offered no direct flights to Nashville from Albuquerque.

There were a few people in line at the counter. The representative was a young Native American female and friendly. Her dark ponytailed hair exposed her perfect chin and flawless olive-colored skin. The woman graciously took Amanda's baggage and directed her to the correct gate.

Amanda strolled through the airport, eyeing the restaurants. There was a deli, a coffee shop and several concession stands. Amanda marched past them. Her stomach instantly craved coffee and gum, but she promised herself there wouldn't be any more *dependent* purchases. *Control it, Amanda! Control it!* Straightening her shoulders, she increased her pace.

A man and woman with two girls sauntered in her direction. She thought of Emily and Rose. *I miss them.* Emily was her little co-mommy, so protective of Rose. Even though the two girls constantly fought, they loved one another deeply and were inseparable.

Amanda stopped and watched them as the family passed. The man's demeanor and his attire of Khaki pants and black short-sleeve shirt reminded her of Ryan. An aching formed in her stomach. She longed to see him. What kind of husband would willingly agree to let her be gone on this journey for a month?

Amanda followed a sign to her gate. Settling in a chair and checking her cell phone for the third time, she pressed the speed-dial number to her husband's work, when someone bumped her leg.

"Excuse me," said a male voice.

Amanda moved without looking up and ended the call. "Sorry." *Let me try again.* She raised her head and Joshua slinked next to her. "Oh, my God! Josh!"

"Didn't think you'd see me again, did you?" Amanda gawked at her deceased brother. Joshua was wearing blue jeans and a short-sleeved Chicago Bears T-shirt. "Don't worry, nobody can see me, nor will they think you're crazy for talking to yourself."

Amanda pinched his arm. "Are you even real?"

He looked amused, "Hey, that hurt."

She crossed her arms. "This is absurd. I can't believe this is happening." *At Gretchen's house, and now the airport?*

Joshua patted his sister's shoulder. "I'm sorry your stay with Gretchen ended so abruptly. I want to tell you I'm proud of you for not indulging yourself in the things she taught you to avoid, especially here at the airport. And I wouldn't call Ryan right now; he's in the middle of a six-million dollar meeting."

"What are you trying to tell me?" Amanda felt her eyes bug out. "You're supposed to be dead, six feet under in Amelia, Virginia, but instead you're sitting next to me giving me a pep talk?"

Josh snickered, "Gotta run! See you soon, sis." And with that, he disappeared with a crowd of passengers coming off the plane Amanda and others were waiting for.

This can't be happening. I must be dreaming. Shaking her head, Amanda rose and walked to the window to watch the cleaning crew board the plane. Hands shaking, she stuffed them in her windbreaker, taking slow deep breaths. Amanda felt dizzy so she sat down in another seat in front of the window, holding her purse tight. *Did I just see and hear my brother speak to me?* She fiddled with her cell phone again, ready to call Ryan, but remembered Joshua had told her not to. *He's probably working around the clock to get this six-million dollar deal done.* Stuffing it in her purse, she decided to call him in Houston instead.

Twenty minutes later, the flight crew boarded United 5156. The plane took off at noon as scheduled. The captain came on and announced a flight travel time just shy of two hours.

Amanda sat in a window seat, reclining to relax after witnessing her brother's appearance again, and all that had transpired at the ranch. To calm her nerves, she flipped through a couple magazines when she remembered the envelope from Gretchen. Taking it out of her purse, she opened it to reveal information about her next mentor.

Harvey Huckfinn was a retired rodeo rider. He'd spent twenty years riding, roping and bulldogging bulls and untamed horses. But reoccurring back problems had caused him to retire. He spent the next twenty years teaching young cowboys how to rodeo. Harvey spent his time tending to his organic egg farm and reading historical fiction. At the end, a P.S. alerted her that he had a southern charm which could sometimes be mistaken for flirtation, but it was meant mostly to be protective, that she should not take it as offensive

The rest of the note contained his address, email and phone number. Amanda folded the paper. *What credentials about demons does this man have?* As she pondered this her eyes grew heavy and she dozed.

Later when Amanda awoke, she heard they were landing in Houston. Putting away the contents from her tray, she fastened her seatbelt and watched from her window as the plane taxied into Houston's George Bush Intercontinental Airport.

Once she got inside, Amanda purchased a large orange juice, an apple and a ripened banana and headed to Terminal 6A. In less than forty-five minutes, she would board Flight 4139 heading to Nashville.

Rushing from one terminal to the next, a pit stop to the ladies room and buying her fruit snack, she forgot to call Ryan until she sat next to a brown-eyed girl wearing bright-pink designer glasses, studying a book on various plants.

"I can't believe I forgot," Amanda muttered. She got out her phone and texted. Hi. … Can't talk at the moment. … Will call you later this afternoon. Love you.

The plane took off without a hitch. Travel time was less than an hour and a half. As Amanda munched on her snacks, she chatted with a young woman named Julie. A sophomore from Tennessee State, Julie was in the Agriculture and Consumer Science program. Her passion, finding alternate solutions in order to create fuel from plants, proved to be enlightening. Their conversation was cordial and humorous as Julie recounted stories about her sorority sisters and what they did to her when she joined. The girl did most of the talking. She was obviously exploring life, living it and loved sharing ideas on living green with strangers.

Before they knew it, the plane landed at Nashville International and Amanda's anxiety increased. This was her first time in Tennessee. The letter from Gretchen only contained Harvey Huckfinn's brief bio and address, and she wasn't sure where that was or what kind of treatment was next. It also stated Harvey was picking her up. She unfastened her seatbelt as the plane taxied on the runway, listening to Julie's never-ending chatter about her schooling and upcoming events.

Armed with a piece of paper for guidance, she followed the rest of the passengers to the Level Two Baggage claim area with Julie accompanying her until phone calls slowed the college student down, and the two women wished each other well. Amanda never felt so out of the loop about things as she was feeling now. Then again, things had been worse, being to the point of no control, and passing out in front of her girls.

Amanda needed to call Ryan. *Forget what Josh said.* It was Wednesday afternoon, she hoped he'd be at his desk. Taking out her cell, she heard Ryan's phone ring two times, until his secretary, Eilene answered.

"Ryan Reynolds' office."

"Hi, Eilene, it's Amanda."

"Hello Amanda. How are you doing?"

"Well, thanks."

"Good, um, I'm glad."

Amanda detected a sudden awkwardness in the woman's voice. *What did Ryan tell her?* Six years with the company, Eilene was loyal to Ryan and executed her job responsibilities perfectly.

"Is Ryan in?"

"No, sorry, he's in a meeting."

"When will he be available?"

"Not sure, I can leave a message and have him call you as soon as he's done."

From past experience, it was unlike Eilene to be so vague; she was his co-pilot. Amanda was feeling even more anxious and contemplated her next response. If she asked Ryan to call back, there was a chance they'd miss one another and then they'd be playing phone tag. Better to try him again, later.

"It's okay, can you tell him I'll call later?"

"I will."

"Thanks, Eilene. Bye."

Hanging up, Amanda continued on. She was a little miffed, Ryan's secretary wasn't very forthcoming with her. *I wonder if he told Eilene I was a drunk and in rehab?* Her husband wasn't in the habit of telling others their family business, but it might be possible this time. *It is my second relapse.*

Amanda shuffled her feet in the direction of the taxi stand. Her cell phone buzzed. *Ryan must be back already.* As she checked the screen, the display showed an unfamiliar number.

"Hello?"

A southern male voice sang through the line. "Harvey Huckfinn, here. Is this Mrs. Amanda Reynolds?"

"Yes. I'm sorry, did you say Huckfinn?"

"Yes'm, Mr. Huckfinn. I'm outside, taxi 7635." Amanda clicked off. She assumed he'd have his own car.

Going outside, a warm humid gas-smelling heat slapped her in the face as a long line of idling taxis stood before her; she searched for 7635. At the end of the line, she saw the taxi and headed for it.

Sitting on the hood, smoking a cigarette, a short, barrel-chested man was dressed in a blue plaid button shirt sporting a large black cowboy hat covering thick dark unruly hair. He also wore the tightest dark blue denim jeans Amanda had ever seen on a man. His ensemble came complete with a pair of alligator-skinned boots. *Hmm, he's a cross between Lyle Lovett and Johnny Cash.*

In a single motion, he dropped his cigarette out of his mouth and smoldered the butt onto the pavement with the point of his left boot. "Howdy, Mrs. Reynolds, I'm Harvey Huckfinn. It's a real pleasure."

"Mine, too, Mr. Huckfinn."

"Please, call me Harvey. Everyone around here does."

"You can call me Amanda."

The man tipped his hat. "Yes, Ma'am, I mean Amanda."

Harvey took her luggage and tossed it in the trunk. Amanda glanced his way; he was graceful, but not cocky. His grey eyes were attractive, she briefly wondered about his personal affairs before shaking the thought from her mind. *This is my journey.* Gretchen wouldn't have recommended him if she weren't sure he was what she needed.

Making her way to the backseat on the passenger side, Harvey growled at Amanda. "What are you doing? Sit up front."

"But I thought—?"

"Horse radish," he snorted. "I'm no cabby."

"Um, why are you driving one?"

Harvey crossed his arms. "My Ford's in the shop. My mechanic is a part-time cabby. I'm borrowing his car. We'll stop at his shop to pick my car up. It's on the way. Hope you don't mind."

Amanda got in on the passenger side. "Not at all."

"Good, let's go."

The older gentleman slithered in beside her. He was energetic and agile for someone who was chunky around the mid-section. He took the I-40 W ramp toward I-65/I-24 Nashville. The car was clean but Amanda detected Old Spice and cigarettes in the air.

They merged onto I-40 W. Harvey made small talk about Nashville. A Tennessean, he was right at home providing Amanda details about his city and state.

"Your first time in Tennessee?"

Amanda nodded, "Yes, are we near the downtown area?" She always had a fascination for Tennessee, especially Nashville. She loved the new country music that was popular these days and southern barbeque, especially ribs. It was on her list of cities to visit with her family. Excited to be here, there was still lots of work to do to get well before going home.

Harvey smiled, a dimple formed on his right cheek. "… About forty minutes, depending on traffic. I've made it in thirty minutes now and then." He pointed to her window. "By the way, we are passing downtown Nashville now."

It was late afternoon and the skyline was beautiful with the last of the sun's rays glinting off the many towering structures. After a few minutes, they got onto the I-24 East exit toward Memphis I-440.

It was quiet for a while, like two strangers sharing a ride, both knowing this wasn't a casual visit. Next they merged onto I-65 South. Harvey hoping to engage Amanda asked, "Want to know some Nashville history?"

"Sure." Her full attention was on Harvey while he drove.

"Betcha didn't know Nashville is referred to as 'Middle Tennessee'?"

"No, why is that?"

Mr. Huckfinn laughed, his belly shook. "Jeez, beats me. But it sounded good, eh?" Amanda rolled her eyes in amusement.

"Anyway, Nashville is in the middle of the state. But this city is more than just country singers and record companies. I can't complain, our economy is thriving and we have some gorgeous neighborhoods thanks to many artists besides singers/songwriters who want to live here. We're pretty artsy-fartsy."

"I bet."

He resumed, "Let's see, we have the Ryman Auditorium. It is a National Historic Landmark now. The Grand Ole Opry Convention Center, Country Music Hall of Fame and Museum and Vanderbilt University is also here. The Hermitage, the ancestral plantation home of President Andrew Jackson, I can't forget that. Here's a good one. Tennessee is home to Jack Daniels Whiskey, but oops," he smacked himself on his head, "I shouldn't have said that."

Amanda sighed. "Great, thanks a lot."

"I'm sorry, Gretchen already told me about your 'friends'."

She grinned, "No worries, I'm working on keeping those tempting friends far away."

Harvey patted her leg. "Good to hear." He then removed a cigarette from a brushed-gold container. "Smoke?"

They passed exits for Brentwood. Amanda shook her head. "No, thank you."

"You mind if I do? It's a very bad habit. I picked it up during my rodeo years and I can't stop."

Amanda hated cigarettes. It was a constant reminder of her mother and the times she frequented bars in the early afternoons, drinking while other patrons blew smoke in the air. She needed to be honest with him. "I hate to say this, but it brings back many unpleasant memories. Please, if you don't mind?"

Harvey glanced at the road and down at his hanging cigarette. He put the cigarette back in its container. He eyed her mischievously, "What if I chewed?"

"Sure, but I don't like it much, either."

"Understood."

Adjusting the air conditioning, Harvey removed a Skol container from his pocket. He grabbed a bit of chew and stuck it in his mouth, all the while keeping one leg on the steering wheel and a foot on the gas. Capping the container, he placed it on the dash and drove normally. "Did you like Gretchen?" They passed exits for Franklin.

"She's a lovely lady. She taught me how to get rid of my toxins and new ways to eating right."

Harvey acknowledged, "Don't I know? She's what a hundred and her ticker is still tocking away."

They both giggled. "Not a hundred, eighty-nine."

"No shit, women outlive men all the time. Did you like the eggs she served you?"

"What eggs?"

"The ones Gretchen cooked up for breakfast."

"They seemed pretty good."

Harvey huffed, "Only 'pretty good'? Well, they're from my farm, Hucky's Organic Eggs."

"I didn't know she bought her eggs from you. She never told me." Smiling, she asked, "And, what's with the name, 'Hucky's'?" They merged onto I-840 W.

He opened his mouth; a piece of chew was stuck to a couple bottom teeth. "Huck Finn was already taken, so I went with Hucky's instead."

"What made you get into the egg business?"

"My family has been in the poultry industry for over fifty years. You see, down here in Tennessee, poultry, soybeans and cattle are the primary farming business. As for myself, I've been around chickens all my life. I never liked the chicken slaughtering business so I started harvesting eggs, good, fresh, and no hormone-induced egg production. Betcha didn't know I knew Gretchen, either? Yep, known her for a long time."

Finally, exits for Spring Hill came into view. Harvey took the second ramp and turned onto a two-lane road. Manufacturing plants gave way to acres and acres of farms on both sides of the road.

Amanda was curious to know more about her new mentor's relationship with Gretchen. "How did you two meet?"

Harvey found a Coke can in a side door pocket and spit. Relaxing and lowering his hat, he began to tell his story. Twenty years earlier, Harvey was in the rodeo. Not a lot, but still involved enough in the mix. The job had taken a toll on his back, one night at the Nashville Rodeo Festival he was sitting in the crowd watching a young man he was grooming attempt bareback bronco riding when Gretchen and her late husband, Roy, sat next to him. They carried popcorn, orange juice, a baggy of fruit and two bottles of water. He watched them as they scooted on the bench beside him with their snacks in a heavy plastic bag.

Harvey was annoyed. Rodeos weren't movie theaters where you munched on snacks watching the entertainment. This was serious business. He figured they were rich folk. It was obvious they were outsiders because they should have known better than to sit so close to the wooden fence with all that food.

So, Harvey moved over to give himself room, but Roy, taking that as a cue to move, inched closer accidentally spilling popcorn on Harvey's jeans.

After five minutes of apologies, the three of them watched the rodeo. His protégé, Marcus, rode his stallion like a pro. He lasted over eleven seconds, a long time riding without a saddle and only holding onto a 'leather rigging'. Harvey told them it was more like a suitcase handle. The bursts of movement from the horse yanked on all of Marcus' muscles but the kid still held on.

"I was so proud of Marcus. He did fantastic. He was going to qualify for the finals with that time." He sighed, "Then, the worst happened."

Amanda blinked, "What?"

He spit into the cola can. "Marcus fell off the horse. The 'pick-up men' didn't have a chance to scoop the kid up in time. The damn animal kicked him in the head." Amanda gasped.

"Roy and I leaped, but Roy was faster, he jumped the fence. He ran in his expensive loafers across the dirt field and started checking Marcus for vitals. He asked someone to call paramedics. By the time they came, Marcus had lost conscious and gone into a coma. His parents took him off life support fifteen years ago. He lived in a vegetative state for ten years. And that's how I met Roy, a smoking drinking surgeon and his lovely wife, Gretchen, a clean-bodied 'no toxin' woman. But, she can handle her Jack Daniels with no problem."

"I know. I've seen her guzzle it."

"Poor old bastard, Roy, lived like he was dying, all that smoking and drinking. Gretchen didn't like it. Man left this Earth filled, though, loved life. Back then, Gretchen was starting out with the healthy stuff. I told her I was in the egg business. Farming chickens, free-range and she asked if she could buy some. I had them shipped to her. She liked them, the rest is history. Oh," he spit again, "they used to have a cabin here, but sold it. She and Roy are true to their land, in Taos. Myself, though, I've never been there."

Amanda closed her eyes recalling her experience. "It's breathtaking, all the red in the rocks and mountains. The air is great, with the exception of the wind, but Taos is a quaint town. Everybody is friendly. You should visit."

"I know, Gretchen says so all the time. Spoke with her this morning about you," he winked.

"Really?"

"Got the scoop, the whole story."

She folded her arms. "Is that so? What's your story, Harvey?"

He spit. "What I told you is not enough?"

"I read the bio and thanks for sharing. Tell me about your 'demon-ridding abilities' because you've come highly recommended."

"Have I, eh? Well, don't you worry? You'll see." Harvey drove into a gas station, the weathered yellow sign read, *Lou's Auto Mechanic*. "Let's get my Ford outta here first."

Ryan lumbered out of one of the conference rooms on the thirty-second floor. It had been a tough sell but he had acquired a new six-million-dollar client. He should have been happy, but he was mentally wiped. Making a stop in the small kitchenette, he refilled his coffee before heading to his office. He had a big proposal to work on for another client and had to stay late. He needed to ask Cecilia if she could remain with the girls through dinner.

His secretary, Eilene, stopped him as he passed her desk. "Ryan, I have messages for you."

He took a sip of coffee. It tasted burnt. "Sure, who called?"

The woman looked tense as she read one of the messages, "Emily's day care, she punched one of the children."

Ryan gawked at his administrative assistant. *Jesus!* Pulling at his starched collar, he responded, "What do they want me to do?"

"Pick her up, I think." He ripped the message from the woman's hand and started for his office. *Damn it!* "Wait! Here." Eilene gave him the other two messages. "The other is from Cecilia. She didn't say specifically what she needed, but she sounded agitated. This one," she put the paper up to his face, "is from your wife. Don't call her, she said she'd call you back."

Ryan was frustrated. *I've got so much work, the kids missing their mom, and this thing with Emily.* He forced a smile. "Thanks, Eilene. I'll take care of things from here." He walked into his office and slammed the door. Raising his fists, he growled, "You couldn't have picked a better time to get well, Amanda!"

Then, stepping around his desk, Ryan slouched in the chair, picked up the phone and dialed Cecilia's number.

Chapter 23

Amanda and Harvey climbed out of the taxi and entered Lou's Auto Mechanic shop. There were rows and rows of cars to the left of the parking lot for repairs or pickup. It was a small building with three lifts and an attached reception/cashier station.

Inside, the smell of oil, sweat and metal tickled her nose. Three worn chairs with black tattered fabric and an old TV with rabbit ears occupied the waiting area. On the opposite side there was a ceramic countertop filled with magazines and a bowlful of bubble gum and hard candy. Behind the counter a man in overalls dozed, his head leaning on folded arms.

Even with the chatter from the television and the banging from the workers in the garage, the man, who appeared to be in his early sixties, snoozed.

"Lou? Lou? Get your ass up!" Harvey hollered.

Three Hispanic workers spied them from the garage window and resumed work on the cars.

The man grumbled, "What the Hell?"

"Hell what, you say!" Harvey roared.

"You're going to give me a heart attack, you clown." The man sat up staring bullets. Lou wore dirty overalls with a blue denim shirt underneath. A trucker's cap covered his bald head. Despite a trimmed, white-and-gray speckled goatee and grooved wrinkles, Amanda thought he was attractive.

"Car's ready, Harvey."

"What was wrong with it?"

"You had an oil leak, your muffler was not on right, a few loose clamps, and you needed new spark plugs. Juan there," Lou cocked his head, "is giving it a final once over, should be ready soon." He narrowed his eyes, as if noticing Amanda for the first time. "Who's this pretty lady?"

"A friend of Gretchen's."

Lou's hazel eyes bore into Amanda; she felt the weight of his stare. "I'm Lou."

"Nice to meet you. I'm Amanda."

Shaking hands, his calloused grip was strong against her delicate palm. The workers looked at her too. Feeling self-conscious, Amanda backed away from the counter.

Harvey pulled out his billfold, "What do I owe you?"

Lou punched numbers on a calculator. "A hundred bucks should cover it."

Harvey whipped out the bill and slapped it on the counter. "All good?"

The man took the money and shoved it in his front pocket. "Perfecto."

Juan drove the truck out of the garage and parked it, leaving it running. Harvey walked over by the door. "Thanks for the fix." He threw the keys and Lou caught them perfectly, like a football receiver. "See you, bro."

Amanda followed Harvey outside. He took her baggage and threw it in the flatbed. They got into the silver Ford F150 pickup. "Your journey with me begins now."

"I'm ready."

They drove in silence for a few minutes. Amanda admired the scenery as they passed several farms, a few plantations and a couple of churches on the two-lane road. Harvey took a quick right, driving on gravel for another few more minutes until they came to a black gate. In the center were two letters, HH. Harvey punched a few buttons on a gadget he had in his pocket and the gates opened.

Tall trees lined the gravel driveway on both sides. Their car eased into a circular drive, a fountain stood in the center. There was a statue of a peasant girl standing in a pool; she was holding a flowerpot with holes, water spouted out of them.

"Interesting," Amanda remarked.

"You like it? I don't care for it. I liked it when I purchased it but not anymore. It's kind of creepy. It does attract a lot of exotic birds."

She squinted, "Creepy? What do you mean? It looks innocent to me."

"I'll drive closer and you'll see the girl's eyes, they look watery. I used to think she was human wandering the grounds when I was asleep."

Amanda scrutinized the statue as Harvey slowed the vehicle. "There," he pointed at the stone figure, "See what I mean."

She strained, but noticed nothing out of the ordinary. "They look normal to me."

He patted his fingers on the steering wheel. "Figures, you're on her side because she's a girl."

Harvey circled the fountain, and his home came into view, a modest-looking cabin of dark wood, cherry-like in color with a long wraparound porch covering most of it. Amanda spied a large, enclosed chicken-wire fence directly behind the home.

"Your farm is awfully close to the house?"

Harvey shut off the engine and got out. "It better be. How else could I keep an eye on my sixty chickens?"

Amanda closed the truck door, admiring the property. "True. Do you run this operation all by yourself?"

"No, ma'am, I have a few hired workers who gather the eggs and then we send them to a packaging house a few miles away for shipment, mostly local, several grocery stores in Nashville and Gretchen of course."

Amanda started to reach for her suitcase when Harvey stopped her. "Wait. We'll get that later. Come meet my family." He led her around his house, their shoes scraping on the gravel drive. Nearing the fence, clucking and something that sounded like *wra-wra-roo* filled her ears. It was loud, she observed chickens fluttering around in the enclosed yard; it was comical to watch as they chased each other, feathers fluttered to the ground.

Hanging close to the fence, Amanda asked, "You let them run around like that?"

"I pride myself on raising cage-free chickens. They are free to run, preen and socialize happily."

"What do you feed them?"

Harvey bent down hoping to catch the attention of a rooster. "Come here, buddy. Come to Papa. Oh, there's Max. He helps keep predators away, coyote, fox, dogs, squirrels, you name it. To answer your question, I feed them a vegetarian regimen. I don't give them any hormones or antibiotics. Their yokes are dark orange. I'm proud of my chickens. My eggs are delicious."

Amanda squatted next to the man. "I have no experience raising chickens. Are they a lot of work?"

Max crowed, making the cock-a-doodle-doo sound. She sniggered, getting to her feet. "I've seen 'cock-a-doodle-doo' written out but never heard it live. It sounds exactly the same."

Harvey grinned, "You sure don't know chickens, do you?"

"No. I'm a city girl."

There were some white chickens and brown-colored ones. "Why do you have different colored chickens?"

Harvey winced, rising, holding onto his back. "Darn it! When I bend down for a long time it gets a kink in it." He stretched from side-to-side and straightened up. "There, much better." He stretched once more. "Okay, let's see, I have two types of hens. Hens of course are the ones who produce the eggs. The browns are my Rhode Island Reds. You see," he gestured to several clucking near a coop, "they are best for laying a rich medium brown egg. The white ones there, farther on, are my Leghorns, ultimate egg machines. They give me pearly white eggs."

Amanda stood up. "I see, how many eggs are you getting a day?"

"Each hen produces an egg a day, at least three or four a week, give or take. I have fifty-eight hens and two roosters. Max is one of them, and then there is Simon, I can't see him just now."

"Your coops look neatly arranged, Harvey. At least I knew what *they* were called," Amanda muttered.

Without warning, three Leghorns started chasing one Rhode Island Red in circles, clucking and poking at it as it tried to run away from the others.

"Goodness, what are they doing to that poor thing? Shouldn't you do something?"

Harvey remained calm, "Nope, they're just playing. They'll be done in no time."

And just like that, the chickens stopped and went their separate ways. Amanda was confused, "Wait, what just happened?"

He stroked his chin. "There's something incredible about the social dynamics of animals. I can't claim to know about every animal, just my chickens because I'm with them every day. Would you like my take?"

I'm curious. "Please, tell me."

"Chickens can piss each other off, chase each other around, get it out of their system and forget about it. It's called forgiveness. "Humans," he paused, "err too many times. We're wretched sinners. Not perfect and we make mistakes. Yet those that are hurt never learn to let go and forgive, creating a cess-pool of anger within their gut."

Amanda stumbled backward digesting this revelation. She felt like a spear had slashed her in the stomach. Not having a mom around most years, she had sealed herself off from past memories, becoming hardened and resentful. Then Joshua left her, the only person she ever trusted, no wonder things crumbled because she dived head-first into alcohol and other addictives to forget her past, but not truly forgive.

She gazed at the chickens. They were farther down in the pasture, oblivious to what happened, going on with their business.

Harvey came closer, "Are you alright?"

"I hope so. Thanks for the explanation. I think I have to work on forgiveness."

"You came to the right place. I'm glad Gretchen referred you. Let's get your stuff and go inside."

They headed for the house while Amanda observed her surroundings. "You have a great business here, I hope it's always successful."

"I appreciate that. It's only my part-time gig. I'm a pastor at a church as well."

Amanda gaped, "You, a pastor?"

Harvey turned, "Mostly counseling young social outcasts. Come on in. Want a glass of orange juice?"

She chortled. "Sure, sounds healthy."

Inside, Amanda noticed little furniture in the home. There was no dining room, only a family room with a couch, coffee table and a large screen TV. On one side of the wall was a large bookcase. *There must be a few hundred books on the shelves.* There were classics like Moby Dick and Huckleberry Finn, several books on Aristotle and a few editions of the Bible.

Harvey came back from the kitchen and gave her a glass of orange juice. He held up his own.

"Freshly squeezed?"

"Of course," he clinked his glass against hers.

Amanda took a large gulp. "I love the bookshelf. You have a great collection."

"Thank you. I'm a voracious reader."

"You don't have a lot of furniture."

"I'm only one person so what do I need? I do need a dependable car. Glad Lou fixed it. Come here, finish your juice," he urged her to relax on a brown and green cloth-covered couch.

Amanda furrowed her brow. "Shoot, I forgot to call my husband. He thinks I'm still in Taos."

"I'll leave you alone, I need to get supper started anyway." Harvey left through a corridor Amanda presumed led to the kitchen.

She checked her cell for messages. There were none. It was after five, *Ryan should still be at the office.* She'd try there first, and then his portable if he didn't answer.

The phone rang once. "Oh, hi Amanda, I'll get him right away."

The line clicked through.

"Hi there."

"Hi," Ryan replied, "I'm so glad you phoned back. I saw your text but then got worried when Eilene told me I couldn't call you. We need to talk. We have a problem."

"Oh, honey," a lump formed in her throat. Amanda was chipping away at a heavy boulder she carried on her shoulders, but was troubled about his issues too. Taking a deep breath, she said, "Tell me. But I don't know what I can do to help. I'm in Nashville now."

"**Nashville!** What happened to Taos?"

Setting the empty glass on the coffee table, she tried to stay calm. "The Taos Healing Institute wasn't what I needed. No, let me rephrase that. I learned a ton about healthy eating and what you need to put into your body, my body, *our* bodies. I'm going to be healthier when I come home, I promise," she hesitated. "I have other issues, Ryan, that need addressing, emotional ones like forgiveness."

There was a long pause and Amanda shifted in her seat.

"… Emily hit a girl at daycare," he said, his voice soft.

"What?" *Oh, no!*

"She's not playing nice, or listening to her care giver. I had to pick her up today. I'm in over my head. Emily and Rose need you."

I was afraid this would happen, leaving him home with the girls. "I have a few days left but I'm not sure how long I'll be here. I'll keep you posted."

"You don't understand! You have to come home right away!"

Having caused stress in the family already, she knew she owed it to them to get well. "Ryan, I can't. I know you are carrying the family burden for the moment, and you have your job. I'm so grateful for your support. What if I relapse? What good will this detox session have done? Our daughters need me fully healed."

"Emily is being a bully. I'm swamped with a million dollar deal and Rose hasn't been sleeping well. You're in Nashville and I'm here with our children?"

"Ryan," guilt was consuming her. *I should, I shouldn't. I have to go. I MUST stay here.* She needed to do this and finish it; finish her journey. "I need to finish this. This is my last hope."

"Where are you calling me from?"

"I'm at this man's house. His name is Harvey Huckfinn. He's a friend of Gretchen's, the woman who treated me in Taos. He specializes in what I believe I need."

Ryan coughed through the line. "Are you coming back on Saturday, at least?"

Amanda got up from the couch and moseyed to the bookshelves. Letting her hand graze one of the Bibles, she said, "I just got here today and I don't know what I'm supposed to do, I'll call you on Friday."

"Sounds like a spa retreat."

"You want to talk to this man?"

"No, I believe you. I can't be mommy and daddy forever. I have a lot on my plate and I miss you."

"I miss you too but I don't want to be the person I was. I want to change. I am changing. That's why I need to do this. Please understand." She heard a loud clatter coming from the hallway. "I need to go. I'll call you soon. Love you."

"Can I call you?"

"I don't know. I won't have my phone on me. Leave a message. I'll call you in a couple days, promise."

"Sure."

Amanda sniffled. *They will have to hang on.*

Ryan hung up the phone and pinched the bridge of his nose. *What a mess. I wish this setback never happened.* A knock on the door interrupted his thoughts. "Yes, come in."

Eilene entered with a steaming cup and two cookies on a plate. Setting them down in front of him on his desk, she said, "My mother used to tell me there is nothing so terrible that some hot tea and sugar cookies couldn't fix."

Ryan cracked a smile, "Thanks. I appreciate it."

The woman hovered over his desk. He sensed her concern for him. No doubt she'd heard his conversation with Amanda through the thin walls.

"It's okay, Eilene, really."

"If you need anything?"

Ryan was grateful to have an administrative assistant like her. He sat back in the chair. "Listen, I'm going to stay late. Cecilia is with the girls. You can go if you want."

The woman nodded, "Sure, boss. Eat those cookies."

He watched her leave as she shut the door behind her. He took a bite of the first cookie. *My dinner.*

Amanda followed the sound to a bright olive-green kitchen with white everything—cabinets, countertops and appliances. There was a cracked cantaloupe lying on the hardwood floor. Harvey was trying to clean it up.

"Son of a gun," he snapped.

Amanda sprang to his side, "Here, let me help, and please watch your back."

He rose slowly passing her a roll of paper towels. "I'm sorry, that *was* our fruit."

"Don't worry we'll salvage what we can." The smell of onions and tomatoes filled her nostrils. "It's yummy in here. What are you making?"

"I hope you like bean soup. Saw this great recipe on the Food Network. Do you watch it?"

"No, but I will now." She threw the wet paper towels in the garbage and placed the salvaged half on the cutting board. Harvey handed her a knife and plate as she sliced long wedges, placing them in a circular arrangement on the dish.

The bean soup was excellent; Amanda helped herself to another bowlful. She hadn't eaten much since leaving Taos and was starved. After a few bites, she noticed Harvey's eyes upon her. She put her spoon down. "You have a lot of questions, I can tell. Go ahead ask me."

He folded his hands. "Okay, how did it go with your husband?"

"Not so good. He's overwhelmed. I'm here and they're there. I don't blame him; his job is demanding. Our two little girls are also very demanding." She rolled her eyes. "We're having challenges with the older one. It's hard on him watching me go downhill again. I'm supposed to keep the family together, I've screwed that up. I haven't been upfront with him regarding my past, either. He's been kind of in the dark throughout our entire marriage, until recently."

"I see. What do you want to accomplish here for yourself, Amanda?"

She took a drink of water. "I've learned my addictions are a reaction to an underlying emotional deficiency. I know why I chewed gum, drank soda and alcohol, and allowed unhealthy things into my body. It was my way of coping. I've felt a sense of—"

"Resentment."

How did he know that? "Yes! My mom became an alcoholic and neglected her *motherly duties*. My brother and I had no choice but to leave. I was only a minor."

Standing abruptly and feeling emotionally burdened, Amanda grabbed the ends of the table, holding tight, her knuckles turning white, facing Harvey. "What kind of parent does that to their own flesh and blood?"

Looking deep into her eyes, the older gentleman calmly responded, "A broken one."

Amanda shifted on her feet. "Right."

"If I recall from what Gretchen told me, you're broken as well. What parent gets completely wasted in front of their children, and passes out while her firstborn has to call her father and tell him her mommy won't wake up."

She pounded the table, "Dammit, that's not fair."

Harvey scooted off his seat and stood up. "You've scarred your children. They saw you." Amanda fell into her chair and sobbed.

The man walked around to her, "I'm sorry, but I have to be honest with you. You heal yourself by learning to forgive other's transgressions. Remember the chickens?"

She wiped her face. "Yes, but it's not that easy."

"It never is, but I'll show you how to, I promise. You have to have faith."

"I know but my family needs me."

Harvey touched her arm. "They do, I know that. You understand you are doing this for yourself, though, because if you're not healed your family will suffer forever."

"I know."

He grabbed some tissues from the countertop and gave them to her. "Let me show you to your room. I'm sure you want to unpack. The rest of the evening is yours to do as you please. I'm leaving to take care of a few things for my chickens. Tomorrow morning I'll take you to prison."

Amanda stopped wiping her eyes. "Prison, I don't understand."

Harvey beamed, "Gotcha!" She laughed. "Nice to see your pearly whites." He squinted at her. "You city folks sure have nice teeth. By the way, what do you all eat up in Chicago?"

"It sure isn't great bean soup and organic eggs. Heredity might play a role."

"Good genes must have come from your parents. Anyhow, as I was saying earlier, I'm a pastor at the church up the road, *The Chosen Saints*. But during the week I visit our local detention center, a prison for teens, I counsel the boys and girls, mostly boys. I need to warn you, you're gonna see some hurt kids. My goal is to help them with forgiveness. This should be good for you too."

Amanda stared at Harvey in shock. *Chickens? A part-time Pastor? Prison? Why on earth would Gretchen send me here? Oh, my Lord! What in the world have I gotten myself into by coming here?*

Chapter 24

Amanda tossed and turned all night. She heard voices, things slamming, and noises outside. Rubbing her eyes, she sat up in bed, "What is this ruckus?"

"It's Harvey and his employees; they are loading the truck with—"

"Joshua!" Amanda let out a screech while scrambling under the covers.

"Eggs." Her brother sat on the bed with his arms crossed.

"What's your problem, scaring the crap out of me?"

"Sorry, now get up. It's after six."

Amanda yawned and stretched, "What is it with these people; ready to go at the crack of dawn?" Joshua bellied over. She shot him a glance, "It's not funny."

"Right, in case you've forgotten, this isn't a vacation." He held out his hand. "You don't want Huckfinn thinking you're a slouch." Amanda grabbed his palm, and scooted off the twin-size bed. "You slept alright?"

"Just peachy."

Josh made himself comfortable on a recliner across from the bed, "Ready for the new day?"

"I don't have any expectations."

"Good."

Amanda saluted him. *What does he know?* "Whatever, or should I have expectations? What is it you want?"

Joshua drummed on the armrest, "Nothing, just checking on you."

"Really, it's been a long time coming, brother." Amanda bent down to pick up a fallen sock. When she got up, he was gone. *This is ridiculous!* She sprawled on the bed and raised her arms up high. *I'm talking to myself. I'm really talking to myself because there is no one in this room but me.* Amanda changed out of her pajamas and into jeans and a short-sleeve black top. Sliding her feet into a pair of clogs, she made her bed and slipped into the bathroom.

Washing her face, she heard commotion from the kitchen. When Amanda entered the room, a round woman was making a colorful concoction in a blender. "Morning, Signora Reynolds."

She waved, "Morning, is Harvey around?"

The woman's accent was thick. "He outside. I make eggs, toast. Juice, here," she pointed to the blender. In no time, the woman had breakfast and a vegetable smoothie on the table.

"I am Martha."

"Amanda. Thank you."

Giving her a napkin, she said, "You eat. Mr. Harvey coming."

Amanda devoured her meal, topping it off with a bowl of fresh fruit.

Harvey waltzed in. "There you are. I see you met Martha, my estate assistant. She makes the best tamale this side of Tennessee. Isn't that right, Martha?"

The woman beamed at her boss. "Mr. Harvey, you too kind."

Harvey wore dark brown slacks and a white long-sleeve shirt. He approached the woman. "I have lunch covered. Can you make us dinner though; around five-thirty?"

"Yes. No problem, I be here later will cook for you and Mrs. Reynolds."

Amanda watched their interaction. There was a trusting comfortable way in which they communicated. She could sense they had a good relationship similar to Ryan and his secretary, Eilene. *That woman can finish Ryan's sentences and she knows what he needs.*

Amanda handed Martha her empty plate. Harvey drank orange juice while inspecting papers on the counter.

Turning his attention to her, he asked, "Everything to your liking?"

"Wonderful, the food was better than I could ever make. Thank you."

"My pleasure. If you're ready, we can go." Amanda rose from her chair.

Outside, the sun peeked through the giant trees surrounding the property. It was cooler than she expected, but she presumed it would get warmer as the day progressed. Harvey motioned for Amanda to go ahead and get in his truck while he talked with his workers. The flatbed was filled with a few large boxes of egg cartons. *Wow! Who are all these eggs for?*

"There are ninety dozen eggs in there," Harvey said as he came closer, a few days' worth of breakfast for the twenty kids and twenty employees at the detention center."

"That's a lot of eggs."

"Great eggs," he corrected her.

"Selling eggs to the center, awesome."

Harvey guffawed as he opened his door, "It would be if I charged for them. But, I don't."

Amanda did a double-take. *Free eggs?* She followed Harvey's lead by getting in.

The road to the detention center was scenic, towering trees lined both sides. Behind them were gargantuan homes with long driveways and gated entrances. Amanda marveled at the beautiful houses and their landscaping.

"Who lives in these homes?"

"They are attractive, aren't they? Mostly entertainers, producers, and authors. They're good neighbors. It's quiet here, I like it."

"And near these bigshots, eh?"

"What, money surely can't buy you happiness, can it?"

Amanda averted her eyes, crossing another line in the sand. She didn't know if a response was required based on how dark his face had become. *Geez, I sure am racking up 'good points'. First, the eggs and now my stupid assumption about money and happiness. I need to get right with Mr. Huckfinn fast.*

"I'm sorry, did I say something wrong?"

Harvey exhaled, "No. I happen to know some of my neighbors and famous as they may be, there is a lot of trouble within their homes."

Amanda mulled over what he said. "You're right, things don't always seem as they do." She thought of the situation she was in, masking family pain from Ryan and denying it herself with her drinking.

"What made you become a pastor?"

He grinned sheepishly at her, "It's not like I received a spiritual calling, per se. It was something I needed to devote time to, cultivate my spirituality that is, which led me to embark on the vocation."

"How long have you been a pastor?"

"Four years, my egg farm definitely came first."

They stayed on the same road for a while. With the mansions behind them, farms began popping up—cows, horses and goats came into view.

Twenty minutes of driving in silence, Harvey asked, "What are the ages of your kids again?"

She was staring at a red barn, mesmerized by its beauty, when the question startled her. "I'm sorry for being distracted but that barn is gorgeous."

Harvey glanced at the farm. "Yep, that is one of the beautiful Roberts' farms; they own at least thirty-five farms in Tennessee. They produce butter, milk and pork chops. You can't see behind the structure but it sits on at least a hundred acres of land."

Amanda gaped as they passed by. Turning, she answered his question, "Emily is seven; Rose is four. They're great kids."

"You love them?"

She looked at him squarely, "Why wouldn't I?"

"I don't mean to judge, but someone who has small kids usually talks about them more. You haven't told me nothing except their ages, facts only."

Tears suddenly pooled at the corners of Amanda's eyes. "Are you kidding? Of course I love my children. But, I've let my addictions take control over my life, so much so that it's not easy for my family to live with me."

"Interesting, do you think you have an addiction to alcohol?"

Amanda nodded solemnly, "I do, a dependency for sure." *I can't be in denial anymore.* Harvey gave her a reassuring smile. She continued, "When I got married, I thought I was happy. In a secure relationship with someone who loved me, Ryan wanted kids from the get-go. I thought I did too." She bit at her hangnail. "When Emily was born, she was colicky and cried all the time. I strained my lower back during labor and had been taking prescription drugs for the pain. When my back healed, I still had my pills. To deal with Emily's colic, I'd take them and sometimes mix it with alcohol. Ryan was working late nights and I was home alone trying to deal with the baby. It was difficult for me but easy to get into drinking because I had drunk liquor before. You understand?"

"I get it."

Amanda took a tissue from her purse and dabbed at her eyes. "When Rose came along, my back felt better so I didn't need any meds, but I didn't stop drinking; it was what I knew, especially seeing my mother drunk all the time when I was a teenager. Secondly, it was my 'go to' stress relief to help me cope, raising two small children. Ryan did a lot of traveling, I drank to relax. I love them, I do, Harvey. But I know I've wasted many years, not being the mom I should be to them. Hopefully, I can rebuild a stronger relationship with my girls when this is over, but I'm also anxious because I know I lost their trust. I feel like a yo-yo lately. Does that make sense?" She moaned. *That was hard. I've never admitted to anyone how my addictions have gotten out of control.*

Harvey nodded, "You're not a bad mom. You have to get some things straightened out. You're doing the right thing being here. One day you will tell them your story. Your girls will come around."

"What about you? Do you have any children?"

"I have twenty. My ex-wife, Sandy, and I couldn't have kids. I think it's what drove us to divorce. I threw myself into the rodeo and it was more than she wanted to handle, so she left me." He lifted a forefinger, "I'm not entirely by myself. I have my chickens, my church and great kids at the detention center."

"Do you have any regrets about your marriage?"

"Not anymore. I believe I've made my peace with the Lord. He helps me give it back in everything I do."

They came to a winding road. Harvey expertly took to the curves. The road straightened as soaring trees lined both sides. In the distance, to the left, she saw a large wooden mailbox. Harvey pulled up to it and removed a stash of letters and magazines. Throwing them in the backseat he said, "The detention centers' mail." Five minutes later, the forest stopped at a dead-end. The entire place was enclosed in black-linked fencing with barbed wiring.

Harvey stopped at a gate and a guard came out. They said a few words, and the gates opened. Looking around, Amanda remarked, "This prison looks ominous."

"Detention center, not prison. These kids aren't murderers; they're a little messed up, that's all."

Harvey pulled to a stop in a reserved spot in front of a large gray building with colossal columns. He nudged her. "Don't go saying anything. This space is reserved because I'm a pastor. See, it says, *Pastor Harvey Huckfinn.*"

"What a privilege."

"It is, but well worth everything I take away from here, even if I didn't have my own parking space." He turned off the engine and made a call. In the meantime, Amanda looked at the building. *What kind of kids are in there?* She thought of Emily and Rose being in a place like this and shuddered.

Harvey hung up. "I have two boys taking the eggs to the kitchen. I will get you set up with a visitor's badge at the front desk and then we have a round table with my kids; I'll introduce you to them."

Amanda nodded, doubtful she'd be of use to a bunch of teenagers, "Sure."

He patted her on the arm, "You'll do fine. Not to worry, it will be rewarding for them to have a woman to talk to."

"Terrific, I can deal with more pressure."

Inside the building, Amanda studied the paintings on the walls surrounding a rectangular information desk. It was a circular layout with brown leather couches and magazine-topped glass coffee tables. There were no uniformed guards, only well-dressed men and women, like accountants or lawyers, bustling around. The woman behind the desk had Harvey fill out Amanda's information, and then she took her picture.

He whispered, "All visitors have to have their photo taken for security purposes."

After getting processed, Harvey and Amanda walked down a long corridor with a woman dressed in a black pantsuit neither talking nor looking at them.

On the walls were different canvases of artwork Amanda noticed; she ooed and ahhed at each one. Harvey commented, "Yes, they are beautiful, aren't they? Many of the kids that have come through these doors since 1979 have created cool artwork prior to their discharge."

Amanda stopped, "What do you mean by 'discharge'?"

"Every kid is given the tools and a new vocation and reentry once an extensive evaluation deems them fit. We can boast an eighty percent success rate. Whether they follow through with what they've learned and applied is up to them. The center does what it can for them."

"I see." *This is pretty intense.*

The woman stared at both of them, "Please, we need to continue." They went left and then took another left until they came to a large, gated entryway. Two young men in matching tan jumpsuits asked them to swipe their badges on an electronic device on the wall. The gates opened and they entered an area that was a cross between a mall and a YMCA, with glass window boutiques, classrooms, a food court, even a gym area. There were teens studying, playing basketball and eating there.

"Welcome to my life's work."

"What is this place? It's beautiful."

Her mentor shook his head, "Don't let the surroundings distort your perception. There are many troubled kids here. They wanted to make this detention center a place for rehab, recharge and rebirth."

Their female chaperone closed the gates behind them and disappeared. Harvey and Amanda strolled through the area. He told her most of the kids were victims of family abuse, domestic violence and/or drug and alcohol addiction. The average age was sixteen, with a few exceptions, and if treatment didn't work the first two times, they stayed until their twenty-first birthday.

There were dorms and each dorm room was occupied by two teens. Each teen was expected to be working so there was a program in place for that, as well as online courses to help them finish their studies and get their GED's. As Harvey brought her up to date on the facility, kids and employees alike greeted him.

One young man gave him a bear-hug and continued on his way. "Nice shirt, Mr. Huckfinn."

Harvey lunged to poke him, but missed. "Thanks, I'll get you later, Jerod."

Another girl with long blonde hair and big-brown eyes stopped him. "Mr. Hucky, my parents are coming by tonight to see me, I'm so excited."

The man embraced the girl. "What fantastic news! Keep doing what you're doing, kiddo."

People kept coming by. It was obvious he was a well-respected member of the center. One trim man close to Amanda's age stopped and introduced himself as the gym teacher, commenting on an upcoming event. "Harvey, I'm gonna need you next Friday night. It's the basketball war game. You are coming, right?"

"You betcha."

Amanda and Harvey approached a room with doors ajar. Amanda presumed it was a meeting room. A bell chimed from somewhere. Soon, kids started filing out of other rooms and the food court. A dozen came right away, said their hellos to Harvey as they filed into the room and sat down at the round tables. Another fifteen came in as Harvey asked Amanda to take a seat in the front of the room facing the crowd. Closing the doors, Harvey sauntered to his seat and turned on his mic.

"Hi everyone, good morning."

Replies rippled through the crowd. Meanwhile, Amanda observed the kids. Some were clean-cut Harvard types, some jock-like, some studious-looking and some looked rebellious and unkempt. It had been a good many years since her high school days, but one thing she noticed, the kids never changed. They were typical teenagers but these teens were bruised and scarred.

Harvey asked the kids to introduce themselves, then it was Amanda's turn. Harvey told her quietly she should be honest about her journey to rebuild her life.

Nervous at first, she spoke about her addictions stemming from when she was a teenager and the current neglect to herself, to her children, and her husband. When Amanda got around to sharing her experience about detoxing and eating right with Gretchen, and learning that her addictions have been a band-aide to bigger demons, she relaxed.

Laughing to herself, Amanda concluded, "The truth is, I'm not perfect, and neither is anyone else. I may not know the answers to all your questions, but I'll be honest enough to tell you so."

They spent the rest of the morning going through Harvey's lesson plan, a compilation of games centering on what a person could do to avoid temptations and what guilt can do to anyone if not tamed and treated. He read from the Bible and they prayed. Harvey and Amanda split up, circling the room, talking to the teens about issues they were dealing with.

Before Amanda knew it, it was lunchtime, they went to the food court. Harvey directed her attention to a troubled fifteen-year-old, Lacy, she had two children under the age of three.

"You mind sitting with her? She's been hard to talk to and spent the last year in and out of the detention center recovering from drug abuse. Her children are in foster care."

"Ah, sure." *What am I supposed to do?* Standing in line behind Lacy, Amanda followed her to an empty table. The girl had black stringy hair, a lot of dark makeup on and piercings on her forehead and her ears. She looked intimidating.

With tray in tow, Amanda asked, "May I join you?"

Lacy didn't answer; instead, she unfolded the wrapping of her sandwich and opened her soda.

"Um, hi, I'm Amanda."

"I heard."

"What's your name?" She unwrapped her sandwich as well.

"Does it matter?"

"For me it does. I'm trying to make small talk."

Between bites, Lacy sneered, "There are plenty of other people here who don't mind 'small talk'. Go talk to them, not me."

Amanda was crushed. *This girl is hard to get through to.* She scanned the room and caught Harvey's eye. He signaled for her to take her time.

Contemplating her next move, Amanda replied, "You're right. I don't want to talk, either. Silence is good, unless ... unless *you* want to talk."

Lacy stared at her with dark eyes. "I don't have anything to say to you."

"Fine by me."

They ate in silence. Amanda watched as the other kids were animated, joking around and conversing with one another. *At least they are trying.* Lacy, however, wasn't. Mother of two, abandoned and shoved in a center where everyone pushed her to get help, the last thing this young girl needed was another psychiatrist trying to solve her.

Amanda got up from her seat. "I'll be back in a minute." Lacy didn't budge. Strolling over to Harvey, she asked him what the rest of the day looked like. He told her they would be doing some projects, going outside for exercise and then the kids would spend the rest of the afternoon writing in their journals.

Amanda tried to put herself in Lacy's shoes. If it was her, and these group activities weren't cutting it, what would she want to do? An idea popped into her head. "Could I take her outside after lunch? Maybe get some fresh air instead?" There was a small creek she'd seen on the way in; the trees and gardens might help Lacy to open up.

Harvey snapped his fingers. "Great idea, regroup with me afterwards." Amanda nodded, excited.

Walking up to Lacy, she announced, "Why don't we blow this place and hang out outside?" A big grin appeared on the teen's face.

Finally, a little progress.

Chapter 25

They strolled silently through the hallways. The girl was a few inches taller than Amanda's five-feet-five-inches. Checking out with the receptionist and going through security, they exited the building. It was sunny with a slight breeze; the temperature hovered at eighty degrees.

Stepping through the parking lot, emerging onto a grassy field, Amanda steered Lacy toward the creek. There were giant trees everywhere with humongous trunks and flowering branches. They looked like mushroom tops. Together they approached the curvy, shallow creek. It had enough water in it to keep a few ducks happy as they paddled by. Sitting side-by-side on the lawn, Amanda studied her surroundings; the sky was blue, not a single cloud above. Beyond the creek were more towering trees lining the property and the barb-wire fencing.

Amanda commented, "Humph. Has anyone ever tried to climb that fence?"

Lacy cracked up, "I don't know. The building has been nicknamed the 'Spa Retreat for the Rich'."

"Why?"

The girl leaned over, sun beating down on her raven mane, "You really don't know? This place isn't for the average kid. This is where wealthy parents send their children when they don't want to deal with them anymore."

It was the most the girl had said. Amanda was shocked. She composed herself and asked, "Do you think that's what happened to you?"

Somberly, Lacy replied, "My mom and dad don't want anything to do with me."

"Why is that?"

"Just cause."

"Don't you have children?"

"Two in foster care, my parents don't want them, either."

"Will you ever see your kids again?"

Lacy shrugged. "Don't know really. I can't even finish regular high school, been taking classes here."

Amanda decided to share more on her addiction problems with Lacy hoping to help her open up more. "My dad died when I was seven. My mom got into abusive relationships, became a drunk and eventually neglected me and my older brother. Things got really bad, so we ran away to Chicago when I was fourteen. Long story short, my brother, Joshua, took care of me until he died twelve years ago of cancer. It's been a lonely road, alcohol has *always* been my friend, if you know what I mean?"

"Bummer. Is that why you drank?"

Amanda nodded, "I learned that from my dear old mom. Watched her drink and did it myself. I got addicted and couldn't stop for many years. I bottomed out and attended AA, staying away from the booze until recently. I relapsed again because I've been holding a lot of things in. I'm still craving to drink, I just can't do it anymore. Hurt my family too much."

Lacy made an effort to smile. "Wow, you've got big problems."

"Yes, I do. It will be okay for you too. You are still very young, resilient, and can jump back into a decent life. Make peace with yourself and move on."

"Have you made your peace?"

"I'm working on it. Getting help and getting healthy at the same time."

"Good for you. Never be no daddy's for my kids, though. Who knows where they are. My parents hate me and don't want to deal with my issues. They wanted so much more out of me and I screwed it all up. They dumped me here."

Amanda hugged Lacy. They had a connection. *I need to help this child.* Rising to her feet, she said, "Let's walk a little more. We'll join the others soon."

When they united with the teens, Harvey had them in groups of four, and they were playing charades. Lacy went to a group who wanted her with them and Harvey met up Amanda.

"So?"

"Better than I expected, the outside air was a good conversation starter, she actually talked to me a little bit."

Her mentor smiled, "That makes me very happy."

"I'm worried for her though and I want to help her. She has no love or support from her parents and on top of that she has two children she can't see or take care of."

"I'm grateful she opened up to you. Let's talk more about Lacy later. For now, we need to finish this game. Then, we're going to talk about basic socialization strategies. I have two of my kids over there," Harvey looked at sixteen-year-old, Devon, and nineteen-year-old, Tim, "who are graduating in a week or two. Can you take on the other ten kids?"

"I think so."

Amanda and Harvey stayed with the kids into the early evening hours. They brainstormed, trying to come up with ways to help Lacy. They informed the teens they'd be back the next morning. Even Lacy seemed interested.

It had been a fruitful day for both of them. Back at the ranch, Amanda bid Harvey good night after dinner and went to her room, her head bursting with ideas. *This could be my Emily and Rose if I don't get well and set an example for them. I want to make a difference here, and at home with my daughters. I've wasted my life wallowing in the past, keeping it inside and drinking to cover the damage. I need to change. I don't want to continue to be like my mother and I certainly don't want my girls to end up here. I have to help Lacy come around.*

Chapter 26

"Wake up. Wake up."

Amanda thought she was dreaming until she felt someone shaking her, "What? What's the matter?"

"We need to leave right away."

Groggily she answered, "Leave? Where are we going?"

"It's Lacy, she's dead."

She blinked. "What do you mean, 'she's dead'?"

Wearing round gold-rimmed eyeglasses she'd never seen before and the strong stench of cigarettes on his breath, he said in a faint voice, "They said she committed suicide."

"No ... No ... I don't believe that."

"We need to go to the center. The police want to talk to you."

Amanda turned over and looked at the clock. It was barely 5:30. "Now, what for?"

He grabbed her, his eyes moist. "I ... I don't know, maybe she said something to you."

What happened Lacy? Why? They'd had such a good conversation yesterday afternoon. Amanda was confident that with her help Lacy would get better. *Now she was gone.*

Fifteen minutes later, she and Harvey were on their way to the center. When they arrived, the place was surrounded by police cars, an ambulance and a firetruck.

"Whole damn police and fire department is here," Harvey muttered.

Less than twenty-four hours prior, Amanda was feeling proud, making positive steps toward helping Lacy. *Did I miss anything?*

They parked and got out of the car. Harvey lit a cigarette, took a few drags and put it out on the pavement. "You're going to be grilled, try to remember everything about your conversation with Lacy."

"Okay, but I can't think of anything out of the ordinary. I told you everything she told me."

He put his hand on her shoulder, "I know you did."

Amanda saw the devastating hurt in his eyes. She suspected this had never happened to him; here he was supposed to be helping her, only to lose one of his kids in the process.

A detective and two uniformed policemen approached them. The detective, wearing a crumpled beige suit with a coffee stain on his blue tie, greeted Harvey. "Hi Mr. Huckfinn, I take it this is Mrs. Amanda Reynolds?"

"Yes, Amanda this is Detective Bingham." She nodded.

With a curt nod, Bingham marched toward the entrance of the building. She followed him with the two officers right behind. Walking past the information desk, they turned down another corridor Amanda hadn't gone down the day before. They entered an empty conference room. The room contained a small rectangle table with two chairs. A plastic bottle of water was situated across from a chair, Bingham directed Amanda to sit. He did the same, flipping a notepad open, while the two officers stood by the door.

This is weird. Am I being held responsible for Lacy's death? "Um, excuse me, Detective?"

He held up his hand while reading notes. "I'll ask the questions."

Amanda pursed her lips, "Am I being singled out for something here?"

Detective Bingham stared at her with beady eyes. "You tell me, are you responsible for Lacy's death?"

Amanda jolted up from the table; the officers were at her side in a flash. "This is insane. Harvey asked me to talk to her. I was just helping her, providing some counsel and conversation. The poor girl hadn't spoken to anyone about her underlying issues, but she opened up with me. We talked for twenty minutes outside, that's it."

Bingham waved the officers away. "I'm sorry, Mrs. Reynolds. Please sit. Let's start from the beginning; tell me exactly what happened because we *don't* know why Lacy committed suicide."

Chapter 27

For the next hour and a half, Amanda recounted her conversation with Lacy. From what she gathered during their afternoon conversation the day before, the girl was suffering because she had been placed in this facility by parents who didn't care for her, she wasn't able to go to school like a normal teen and was missing her two young children.

Bingham's cellular phone buzzed and he excused himself. Looking through a rectangular barred window, she stared outside. Amanda could make out the towering trees and the creek beyond them. She kept going over their conversation in her mind. Her eyes stung. *What went wrong? What if I was able to dissuade her just a little bit longer? I needed more time.* She stood and grabbed the table as sharp pains shot through her stomach. She pictured herself as a grape being squished between her forefinger and thumb, all the anger and resentment bleeding out of the grape. *I need a drink. Damnit, this isn't a good confidence builder for me. If I can't help someone else, how am I supposed to heal me? Lacy, I'm so sorry.* Amanda sank in the chair, exhausted. A minute later Detective Bingham returned.

Perspiring, the man stood before her, "Thank you Mrs. Reynolds, I appreciate your time. We found additional clues that may shed light on Lacy's suicide."

"Anything you can share?"

He coughed. "Not at the moment." The man tugged at his stained tie. "I'm sorry, but I've gotta go."

She watched him leave, shaking off anymore images of smashed grapes. Amanda then composed herself and left the conference room, searching for Harvey.

Amanda found him in one of the classrooms with some of his kids. They were scattered about and wore solemn faces.

Harvey greeted her with an embrace. "I was worried for you. How did it go?"

She sighed, "It was a rough conversation. Nothing I told him gave any more clarity as why she did it. He left after getting some new information; he wouldn't share it with me." Harvey kneaded his temples in disbelief. "How are the kids taking it?"

"They are saddened, confused and devastated."

Loud cries came from the hallway. They both turned in the direction of the noise. Teens jumped out of their seats; Mr. Huckfinn shushed them, motioning them to stay in the room while he and Amanda went out to see what happened.

Two police officers were escorting a woman through the building, she resembled Lacy, except she had burgundy-colored hair. A salt-and-pepper-haired man followed, cursing at the officers.

Harvey flagged down the detective, "Excuse me, Detective Bingham. Is that Lacy's mother?"

Bingham stepped forward and closed his notepad. "Apparently, Mrs. Parker is terribly shaken up."

Amanda thought of her precious daughters. "Gosh, I can't imagine her grief."

Her mentor inquired further, "Detective, can you tell us how she died? We haven't been told anything. Was it drugs or what? You have to understand, these teens are battling abuse, anything from drugs to domestic violence. We need to know because here at the detention center, we work really hard equipping, encouraging and educating the kids to start fresh, giving them the tools to grow and change." Harvey stuttered, "La … Lacy's suicide is a terrible loss to say the least."

The Detective nodded. "I don't doubt it and I'm glad there is a place like this for kids who are suffering. Having said that, I'm sorry to say it, but Lacy hung herself."

"Ah, Jesus!" Harvey scowled.

"We will get to the bottom of this. I promise." The detective held up a smartphone. "Lacy may not have had any friends, but she talked into her recorder, confessing the abuse she endured from her mother while at home. It's obvious she couldn't take the pain anymore, a real shame; she had her whole life ahead of her." Bingham's cell buzzed again, "I need to take this. You can go. I've got it covered. Thank you both for all your help."

He departed, leaving them with the bad news hanging in the air like an oppressive fog. *I tried God. I really tried. Why wasn't I able to help her? Why didn't YOU stop it?*

In the classroom, Harvey gathered the kids around in front of the room and asked them to sit in a circle and hold hands, Amanda included. Most of the students were angry, some were even sobbing. He bowed his head and prayed, "Dear God, we have lost one of our sisters to a painful death. We don't know why it happened this way. We will miss her terribly." He paused and glanced up at her, "The hard part is forgiveness. I know you are all bravely working on it."

The kids protested.

"Cut it out," Harvey said, "let's stop blaming others. This isn't how we are supposed to respond. Hear me out. Only God can take your life. We must still forgive her," he eyed each one of them. "I am asking you to find forgiveness in your heart for Lacy and her parents. Now, we need to pray and then you are all dismissed for the day." He bowed his head again. "Lord, we ask you to surround the Parker family with your grace and help them seek You. We ask that you help us to be understanding and forgiving. In your name, Jesus. Amen."

Dropping hands, the clergyman stepped out of the room. Some of the teenagers remained seated, others gathered their things and filed out into the hall. Amanda hurried, following him out the door to the truck.

They were silent for most of the ride back to Harvey's house until her cell phone jingled. It was Ryan. In that split second Amanda realized he was wondering when she'd return home. She hit the ignore button and gazed out the window. *I'll call him later.*

Harvey broke the silence. "I know it's Friday, but I'd love nothing more than for you to stay through the weekend. I want to do a community rally service on Sunday morning for the Parker family at my church."

Amanda was baffled and upset. She couldn't envision staying two more days, let alone attend church. *What? Is he nuts?* "I don't know if I can ever forgive Lacy's mother; whatever she did to that poor girl led her to kill herself. Dammit, Harvey, I couldn't save her!" Her heart was bursting with grief. She was also feeling homesick.

"If you want to be forgiven, you better learn to forgive others," he said flatly, as the truck slowed to a stop on the gravel drive.

Speechless, Amanda spilled out of the vehicle and slammed the door. Marching into the house, tears flowing, she threw herself on the bed in her room.

Chapter 28

Amanda's arms and legs were stiff from sleeping on her stomach. The smell of onions and barbequed meat floated into the bedroom. Her stomach growled. She rose and stretched. After washing her face and putting on a fresh shirt, she entered the kitchen.

Martha was cooking, "Mr. Harvey with chickens."

Amanda walked out into the late afternoon sun. She lifted her head, soaking in some Vitamin D. As she neared the chicken coops, clucking resonated. Harvey was sitting on a yellow lawn chair with his jeaned legs propped up on a heavy-duty cardboard box. An open Bible and a notebook filled with scribbled notes sat on his lap.

He glanced up, cigarette dangling from his lips, "There she is. How was your nap?"

Amanda smiled, "Um, it's been a long while since I've taken an actual nap without being liquored up."

"Take a seat." He motioned for her to sit on an empty lawn chair next to him. "I have to confession." She sat and waited, uneasy of what his confession could be about. "My wife and I divorced because of me, not because she couldn't have kids, but because I didn't want them. I was the one. I ruined her dream of having a family." He closed his notebook and his Bible. "It was because of my selfishness."

"Why?"

"I know what I told you. It was a lie. I'm sorry. As a pastor I am expected to be a righteous man. Jesus was, after all. His shoes are hard to fill, but I know I must try every single day. I am more broken than that piece of splintered wood lying on the ground over yonder and I was an asshole to her. It took years for my ex-wife to forgive me. She finally did, I'm thankful for that. I wouldn't be where I am today, serving others especially those kids, if it wasn't for her." Harvey paused, puffing out a ringlet of smoke. "I'm happy she remarried and adopted two children from China years ago. She fulfilled her dream. But most importantly, Amanda, we all need forgiveness, each one of us. I'm sorry for not being honest with you. I often forget I'm human and have my share of failures, many that I hate to dredge up, if you know what I mean?"

Amanda saw genuine grief in the man's eyes. She thought about how Louise abandoned her and Joshua. Wondering why she continued to hold this unyielding grudge toward her. *I feel chained to my fury. Will I ever be able to forgive her?*

Harvey's eyes bore into hers. It was making her uncomfortable. "Why the look?"

"You know what you need to do for yourself and your mother?"

Several hens clucked, as if listening in. Frightened by the sound, Amanda sprang upward. "No, I'm not ready."

"You are. Let it go. You haven't indulged in any alcohol, any caffeine or chewed a thousand pieces of gum. I know you are disciplining yourself. You've made strides. But your road isn't clear of debris yet. Being sober is a lot of work."

Amanda felt better, stronger and in more control. Her clothes were loose due to her change in diet but her heart was still hardened. She'd forgotten many happy memories of her young childhood because she only remembered troubled ones, like the way Louise treated her and Joshua, how she neglected herself later in life living at the trailer park; a vision that would never go away.

Sitting down again, she said, "My childhood was robbed. All I remember is the way we left her and what she'd become when I went to see her from afar after my brother died."

Harvey threw the butt and stubbed it out. "Clothes don't define a person. People can change, you know. Is your mom still alive?"

Amanda shook her head "I don't know." It was true. She had no idea if Louise was alive or if she even lived in Mount Pleasant. *I should find out. Do I even want to?* Sighing, she added, "Do you think Mrs. Parker warrants forgiveness from the community for abusing her daughter and leading her to take her own life?"

"I do, you shouldn't condemn the sinner, only the sinful act."

Amanda weighed the statement, attempting to make sense of it. "This is hard to digest. I mean I understand it; I don't want to believe it should be that way. There are so many evil people who are evil through-and-through and consistently hurt others. Like my mother and Mrs. Parker. And yes, there are *some* good people too. Don't they deserve a break in life?"

The preacher rose from the lawn chair. "Life is hard anyway you cut it. Evil or not, we all deserve second chances and forgiveness. That's why it's important you understand what I'm trying to teach you."

Amanda slumped forward. *I don't want to forgive evil people, let alone my mom.*

"Want to help me snag some eggs?"

Relieved, Amanda nodded and followed Harvey into the coops. They spent an hour going in and out of coops with baskets, collecting eggs. It was loud in the coops, the hens didn't want to be disturbed. But it was a good diversion from her thoughts about the event at the center, Harvey's confession and her own issues with Louise. Afterwards, she excused herself and walked to the little girl statue at the front of the house.

Amanda felt a tug to stay. *I should be at home. What should I do?* No one answered her silent plea for help. "Got nothing to say, eh? Hello? Anybody? Joshua? God? I'll just handle it on my own then." She dialed her home number.

"Hey."

"Hi, how are you and the girls?"

"They hate my cooking."

Amanda laughed, knowing only two things Ryan did well, grill steaks and burgers and make pancakes. "That's not true; you're great at the grill. There might be frozen dinners in the freezer still."

"We're out. I've accepted way too many offers from Cecilia and I don't want to bother her anymore. I figure we can survive until you come home. Tomorrow right, what time?"

"There's been a change of plans."

"Where are you, Dubai?"

"No, silly, there was a suicide at the teen detention center, Mr. Huckfinn is a counselor there. I was with this girl yesterday. What a terrible tragedy. Harvey wants me to stay for his church service on Sunday. I think I really should stay—"

"Argh—"

"What did you say? Ryan, are you still there?"

"I'm here. Listen, I'm sorry about the girl, but tomorrow *is* Saturday. Your thirty-day retreat is over."

"You are right, honey. It's my forgiveness I need to work on."

"Terrific, work on it at home. I'm busting my ass and you're parading around counseling teens. Damnit, Amanda! We have our own kids. They need you now."

She massaged her temples. "I can't, Ryan, I have a serious issue and I need closure."

"I hope you get what you need. This, this disease, or whatever you have." The line went dead.

Amanda sobbed. *I pissed off my whole family again. They'll never forgive me for this.* Wiping her eyes, she looked at the statue of the girl closely. Its eyes glared back at her. Goosebumps prickled her neck. Harvey was right; the statue had human-like eyes.

Yep, I'm a jerk! She needs to be here. Ryan slumped in the brown leather recliner. It was going to be a busy weekend with the girls. Emily had dance practice for two hours every Saturday, a twenty minute ride from home; Rose had swimming lessons every other Saturday. Two events at the same time, tomorrow morning. He wondered how he was going to juggle his daughters' activities.

He loved spending time with his kids. They were his pride and joy but it was overwhelming with his wife gallivanting across the southern states, him working sixty-hour work weeks, and trucking the girls to their extra-curricular activities.

Ryan wandered to the kitchen. Opening one of the cabinets, he reached for the Scotch hidden behind the cups and glasses. He poured himself a shot, drank it, returned the bottle to its place, only to take the bottle out again and pour another shot. *This is not right.* He poured the remaining booze into the sink. *If she's stopped drinking, I'm gonna have to. I'm supposed to be supporting her, not knocking her down.*

Leaning on the counter, letting the liquor soothe him, Ryan stared at the coffeemaker in the corner. *That damn coffee maker!* He missed his wife. Amanda was the center of their family. He knew she was broken, but to what extent he wasn't sure. She handled a lot of the domestic chores in the household. *I wonder if she had gotten too overloaded and that made her spiral.* He made the sign of the cross over his chest and prayed she was healing, remembering her visits to rehab years earlier.

It happened on a Thursday. It had been a long week, but a productive one. Ryan was doing fantastic. In the top three of his sales group nationwide, he was on the fast-track making a name for himself. A little after two in the afternoon, his boss had told him to go home and get ready, they were going to celebrate his accomplishments at an exclusive steak house in downtown Chicago followed by a comedy show. Reservations were in for six, spouses included.

Ryan phoned to tell Amanda the great news and for her to put on a sexy dress. After a couple of attempts with no answer he left and went home.

When he got there, he found Rose sleeping in the playpen and Emily sitting on the floor in front of the television. Amanda's car was gone, her cell phone was on the counter, and the front door was unlocked. There was a bottle of vodka on the kitchen counter, bone dry.

She's left the girls home all alone! A half-hour later, he received a call from the police, Amanda had crashed her car. Her alcohol level was two times the legal limit. The car was totaled, but miraculously nobody was hurt; his wife had walked away with just a few bruises.

Ryan cried as he held his two children. They could have been hurt or worse, in the car with their mother. He knew the drinking and partying was partly his fault. Their lifestyle surely contributed to his wife's constant abuse.

His thoughts were interrupted by giggling and laughter coming from upstairs. Cecilia was playing with his daughters. Ryan was grateful for their wonderful neighbor. He needed to talk to her about tomorrow. *I could sure use her help.* Starting up the stairs, his cell phone pulsed, it was his boss.

"This is Ryan."

"It's Pat, Sam Mumford has a problem with the proposal you put together. You need to come in and redo this right away."

Chapter 29

That evening, after Amanda informed Harvey about her call with Ryan, he decided to take her out to dinner instead of eating in. They arrived at a small barbeque joint twelve miles from Harvey's residence. It was Friday night and the place was crowded. While waiting to be seated, Amanda's pulse raced eyeballing the large bar right in the middle of the dining area.

"Harvey, I can't eat here."

Her mentor encouraged her, "You got this. This is a good test to control your temptations. Remember the reason you're doing this."

Once they were seated, Amanda calmed her nerves and perused the menu. Set on ordering a spinach salad, he insisted she try the ribs. They ordered a half slab of ribs each with a baked potato, a side of collard greens, a corn muffin and two sweet teas. Licking her fingers, she said, "Gretchen wouldn't approve of these ribs. This isn't healthy."

The man snorted, "Who cares, Gretchen doesn't need to know. These are the best ribs ever." They both chuckled and continued eating, neither of them conversing. In between bites, Amanda people-watched. She saw patrons drinking at the bar. *Look at those people enjoying cocktails. I have to ...* Harvey finished her thoughts, "Hang in there?"

"Yeah, with liquor only a few feet away, not to mention the shock of Lacy's death, I guess I'll be okay."

He nodded, "I know, right. Those kids are suffering from a million different issues and demons. I wish she would have opened up to me. I wish ..." he hesitated, "Lacy had gotten to know you earlier."

"I feel the same way, I'm sorry I couldn't do more."

"Don't beat yourself up."

Amanda stabbed at her baked potato, feeling vulnerable. *Gosh, I'm thirsty for one right now. It's been so long.*

"Are you okay? What's the matter?"

She hung her head, "I have a tremendous urge to drink."

Harvey touched her across the table. "Look at me. Take a couple of deep breaths. It will pass." Amanda did as she was instructed. *I can do this.* "There you go. Good job."

She attempted to smile back. "This is so very hard."

"At least you're not following through. Gretchen will be happy to hear you've progressed."

Finishing off a bite of broccoli, Amanda answered, "You guys talk a lot?"

"She does like my eggs, so I make sure she has plenty of them. Plus," Harvey winked, "I promised her I'd take special care of you."

"Thank you."

A veil of warmth hugged her heart. Joshua had made her feel cared for; Ryan was her rock and her soul-mate; and Harvey had become a father-figure to her, even though he is a man with issues. She admired how he made it right with his wife and his life, by serving God with the kids at the detention center and at his church.

Harvey stood up slowly, "Let's get you home. We need to look for flights. You should leave tomorrow."

"I'm sorry I won't be able to stay until Sunday. I do need to go."

"It's okay, really."

While paying for the bill, Harvey received a call and he excused himself. Amanda walked to the front entrance rubbing her belly. A few minutes later, he returned, looking serious. "What happened? Is everything all right?"

"No. That was Pastor Feldman. We have a parishioner who is dealing with her teenage daughter's drug overdose."

Amanda perked up, "I'm sorry. If you need help, perhaps I could do something?"

"I'd like that, we need to go now."

"Does she live far from here?"

Harvey paused, "Less than two hours away, in a small town called Decaturville."

"Oh, okay." *It's far from here.*

Patrons came between them exiting the restaurant and she and Mr. Huckfinn moved out of the way. "So, Kate Weber and her daughter,

Patricia, were long-time parishioners until recently. Her daughter got into trouble with drugs and has been in and out of rehab for the past year. Kate is a single mom struggling to make ends meet by working as a yoga instructor. The rehab center contacted her during one of her sessions to tell her what happened. I'm sorry but I need to go and see Patricia right away."

"Tonight?"

"Yes."

What about my flight? "Don't you have to prep for your Sunday service?"

"I have the sermon ready; Pastor Feldman can cover if need be. Besides, I could use your help. What do *you* want to do?"

Amanda didn't know what to do. She wanted to help, but what about Ryan and the girls? She needed to get home soon or else she might lose them. "I need to use the restroom."

She went to the bathroom to wash up and think about what to tell Ryan. She splashed cold water on her face several times. *I have to call him. What is the right thing to do?*

"Stay here, tell Ryan nothing."

Amanda jumped away from the sink, "Oh my God! Why the hell do you have to scare the crap out of me?"

Joshua smirked leaning on the counter next to her, "It wasn't my intention."

"What do you want?"

"You had a couple of questions I know I can answer. Should you go help Patricia and her mother? Yes. Go. It's is a short trip, what's a few more hours?"

"That's not the point. I'm needed at home!"

"Don't worry, it will all work out okay. Ryan can get Cecilia to help him."

She wiped her face and threw away the paper towel in the waste basket. "You're not just saying that so I will go?"

"No, Emily and Rose will be taken care of, I promise."

Hearing the names of her daughters, Amanda gasped. *What am I doing?* She pushed her brother away from her. "Forget it. I can't go. I have to get home. I need to be with them now."

Joshua grabbed her, "No, this is still part of your journey."

Loosening from his grip, Amanda wept, "I'm losing my kids, don't you realize that? They must hate me for what I've done to them. I want to go home."

He blocked her from the entryway. "You have to go with Harvey."

Dabbing her eyes with a tissue, Amanda was furious. From the moment she awoke this morning, everything had gone wrong. A girl died; her husband was angry at her, and now she was taking a trip to help a mother deal with a drug addicted teenage girl when she should be home tending to her two daughters.

"After this, I'm going home." Gathering her purse, Amanda walked toward the exit door when she stopped and turned, "What did you mean by I had a couple of questions?"

Joshua's voice oozed into her, "Well, didn't you?"

"I don't remember what my other question was." Exasperated, Amanda started for the door again.

"Mom passed away five years ago. She's buried in Mount Pleasant, Iowa."

She whirled around. *Wait! What did he say? Mom never left Mount Pleasant after I saw her last.* There was no one in the lavatory. Amanda stood by door letting the information sink in, an image of Louise came to her, the time when she and her mom played hide-seek in the backyard between the bed sheets hanging on the line. Her mother was wearing a red and black short-sleeve sundress. They were laughing. Amanda could still remember the smell of the woodsy pine soap her mother used for the washing. And then, her mother was gone and so was the warm thought of her.

Walking out, she met Harvey waiting by the entrance door. "Are you coming?"

"Yes."

He gingerly held her arm and escorted her out. "Let's get our things and leave as soon as we can."

Amanda stopped, "By the way, my mom is not around anymore. She died five years ago."

Harvey's brow furrowed, "I thought—never mind. We need to hustle." They slid into the truck without another word. Her feelings of resentment suddenly didn't matter anymore.

Chapter 30

By the time Harvey and Amanda got home, he had spoken to Kate Weber twice about Patricia's condition. Kate was a wreck. Patricia was her only child. Only sixteen, she had suffered quite a bit in the last few years, getting arrested for shoplifting, using drugs and being molested by her father who was currently behind bars in Denver. Kate wanted to make a fresh start by moving away from Nashville, heading to Decaturville to open her own yoga business. She had prayed this change would do both of them a world of good.

Unfortunately, the new life wasn't going well for Patricia. Grateful for Harvey's congregation, Kate Weber knew where to go to get help. That's why Harvey wanted to get to Patricia before it was too late.

Borrowing an oversized knapsack from Harvey, Amanda packed another outfit and toiletries in case they stayed overnight. In less than an hour, Harvey made arrangements for coverage at the church and connected with his workers regarding the chickens and eggs. It was after nine-forty when they jumped in the truck and got on I-65 North to I-840 West and I-40 West headed toward Memphis.

During the ride, the pastor filled Amanda in on the situation with Kate and her ex-husband, Timothy. He'd had an affair and it had been complicated and ugly, and then the Weber's marriage had crumbled. Timothy molested his daughter and two other girls, thereafter. Timothy went to jail and Kate had hit a new low until she joined a new church, giving herself to Christ. She'd been living among her community and neighbors since, doing quite well. Harvey's parish, *The Chosen Saints*, had taken her into their congregation the last four years and helped her get back on her feet. Rescuing her daughter from a life of drugs hadn't been easy.

Amanda mostly listened during the ride. They came up with a plan; as soon as they arrived in Decaturville, Harvey would head to the Quarium Mental Health Center where Patricia was staying, and Amanda would stay with Kate at their apartment.

This situation is similar to mine, especially with Louise's boyfriends. If it hadn't been for Joshua taking me away, I don't know where we'd end up. Amanda thought about her mother. *I can't believe she died five years ago. What was I doing then?*

Five years ago Amanda was thirty-one, Emily was two and Rose had not been born yet. She and Ryan had moved out of their Naperville residence into their new home in Schaumburg, a cute four-bedroom, three bath, burgundy brick house in a cul-de-sac. It was a surefire move; he had received a terrific job offer at another company in the same town. The job came with a lot of entertaining though; they had to attend many galas where alcohol was easily accessible. Her drinking had been over the top, fueled by many temptations.

Dozing off to a twangy beat coming from the radio, Amanda dreamed about her first booze bash. She was thirteen at the time, she and Joshua were still living at home with Louise.

It was a Saturday afternoon. Amanda had visited her big brother at his job, a pizzeria, for lunch; she'd had a meatball sandwich with a side of cheesy fries. She walked home around three-thirty and found her mom getting dressed to go out. Nursing a glass of Jack Daniels with ice, Louise caked on her makeup. Amanda knew her Mom was going to have a long night.

When Louise's date arrived, she didn't kiss her daughter nor did she say goodbye. Amanda spent the rest of the evening in front of the television. Venturing into the liquor cabinet, she poured her first drink. There were shot glasses and regular drinking glasses to choose from but she wasn't sure which to use, so she grabbed a bigger glass and poured the whiskey to the top. *If Mom can do it, so can I.*

The amber-colored liquid was bitter, it burned her throat. Amanda spit it out on the first sip, drinking water to dilute the yucky taste in her mouth. The second sip was the same, but after the third and fourth, it didn't burn anymore. By then her head was spinning and her stomach started feeling queasy.

At one-fifteen in the morning, Amanda was startled by the front door slamming. Awake and feeling woozy, she tip-toed out of her room to find Louise on the couch. She was crying. It was only the second time she'd ever seen her mother cry. The first time was when her father died six years earlier. Amanda was scared. Sitting down next to her, she noticed blood on her mother's cream-colored skirt. When she asked her about it, her mother blubbered even more. Thoroughly frightened, Amanda reached over to give her mom a hug, but the woman shoved her away and kept crying. Moved by emotion, she joined her.

When the crying stopped, the two of them hugged from an awkward position. Amanda could smell liquor on her breath. She couldn't recall what happened next but they both awoke in the morning with their arms wrapped around each other.

That one time had been the only affection Amanda had received from Louise in a long time. But that ended abruptly when her mom realized they'd slept together. Louise pushed her daughter to the floor and stomped out of the room. Humiliated and rejected, she felt like a mangy dog left to die in a ditch. From that day on, Amanda started binging on alcohol, never knowing why her mother was crying that night.

Feeling a chill, Amanda shivered in her seat and opened her eyes in time to see Harvey turn into a long driveway. He looked over, "Are you okay?"

Shaking her head, she answered, "No, I mean, yes."

Chapter 31

Harvey parked behind a silver minivan next to an old, two-story dark-wood home. There was a balcony on the top floor built over a front porch. The house sat on an acre of grassy land in need of a good mowing.

Walking up the stairs, Amanda admired Ms. Weber's sitting area, a wicker loveseat, a chair and a coffee table. It was inviting, just right for dozing to the sounds of the crickets, frogs and beetles.

It was close to midnight. Harvey pressed the doorbell and Kate Weber opened it, letting them in. She sported black yoga knickers and a fluorescent green V-neck racerback tank-top. Her blonde hair was up in a pony-tail, accenting a lined face that revealed the stresses of the last forty-eight hours.

"Thank you for coming on such short notice, and … so late at night," Kate said sinking into Harvey's arms.

"No worries, we're supposed to help each other out." He introduced his pupil. "This is my friend, Amanda Reynolds. She's here to help." Kate nodded a greeting.

Entering a long, narrow corridor of hardwood flooring with various planters and table-tops holding elegant vases, Kate led them to a cream-colored leather couch across a mirrored wall with a fireplace. She had a kettle whistling in the kitchen and offered chamomile tea. Obliging, Harvey and Amanda took a seat and waited for the woman to return.

She came in and placed a tray with black mugs containing the steaming liquid. They spent the next several minutes discussing the details of Patricia's drug overdose, possible clues which Kate might have noticed, and any other indications like an Instagram post or a diary entry. In the end, they came up with nothing.

Patricia's new rehab was a decent place, she had already been there two months. The doctors claimed to have well documented notes on her progress.

The woman fidgeted with her ponytail, "This is so stressful. I don't know why this happened? I took her away from Nashville because of her drug contacts and now this is what I get? The rehab staff told me they were taking full responsibility, and they had started an internal investigation."

Harvey played with his watch. "It's almost twelve-thirty. I need to head to Quarium to see Patricia. I'll be doing my own investigation, see what I can dig up. I'll call you soon. Mind if I leave Amanda here to keep you company?"

"Okay, she is more than welcomed to stay."

Harvey stood and squeezed Kate's shoulders, and then proceeded out the door. Amanda followed, uncertain of what to do next. "Harvey, wait up." He stopped. "What do you want me to do here with Kate? I don't know what to say."

"Comfort her. Sometimes not saying anything is the best comfort anyone can give. And, wish me luck."

Amanda shrugged, "Sure."

The door closed behind him and she stepped softly on the creaky hardwood floor, heading back to the couch where Kate was resting with her eyes closed. Taking up her mug, Amanda sipped her tea trying to stay awake.

Kate sat up but didn't say anything at first. As soon as their tea was empty, the women casually started conversing, mostly about living in Decaturville as it compares to Nashville.

Decaturville was a small town, less than a thousand people. It was expanding to include a new shopping center with plenty of farmer's markets and organic farms. Kate believed this town could benefit from having a yoga/health facility. It was risky, but she was positive things would work out, and would do anything to be away from her past.

The conversation became more personal, Kate wanted to learn about Amanda's relationship to Harvey. So, she gave the woman a recount of her alcoholism and journey thus far, confessing the hardest part was having her two daughters witness her alcohol poisoning episode.

Ms. Weber's blue eyes teared up, "Thank you for coming with Harvey. I don't have any family nearby. I'm thankful for him and the parish. I can't help feeling it was a mistake uprooting Patricia and coming here to rebuild my life."

"You've done what you believe was the right thing to do."

The woman cupped her hands over her mouth. "I've hurt my daughter. Look where she is."

"*You* haven't done anything to harm Patricia."

"That's exactly my point! I haven't done anything. I put her in a rehab center and threw myself into my job."

Amanda grabbed her, "You can't keep beating yourself up for this. At least you've placed Patricia in a rehab to get treatment. You had a business to establish so you could put food on the table, as well as make sure your daughter is being provided for. What more could you have done?"

Kate rose from the couch. "I could have listened to her when she begged me not to leave Nashville. We left because I didn't like her friends, what they did to her and what she did to herself. But mostly, I left because I wanted to remove myself from the memories of my ex-husband, whom, I might add, was horrible to me and especially to Patricia."

Amanda stood too. "Again, you did what you thought was best for your family. You have to forgive yourself." *There it was. I said it, forgiveness.* She had said it and explained it to another person. *This is what Harvey had been trying to tell me, what he received from his ex-wife.* The next sentence she shared with the suffering woman made sense to the both of them. "You've been given a second opportunity to start over. Patricia is alive." Kate buried her face in her hands, sobbing. *I can feel this woman's pain. I wish Mom would have taken better care of us and been more involved in our lives.*

Her cell whistled, breaking up their private moment. She ran to get it from her purse. It was Harvey. "What's going on with Patricia?"

"She's been transferred to a hospital. You and Kate need to come to the Francis Memorial Hospital."

Amanda started shaking with worry, "What's happened?"

Her mentor's voice sounded calm. "Hurry, I'll fill you both in when you get here." He paused, "Don't alarm Kate. Be calm. See you soon."

Harvey clicked off, leaving Amanda in a state of bewilderment. She heard Kate calling. Taking a deep breath, not knowing what condition Patricia was in, she walked over to the distraught lady.

Kate was hugging herself, a look of concern across her face. "Well?"

"We need to drive to a Francis Memorial Hospital. Do you know where it is?"

"Yeah, I do."

Amanda reassured her. "Harvey said he will explain everything when we get there."

Chapter 32

Seventeen minutes later, Kate and Amanda were rushing to room 3311. Harvey was standing outside the door as the two women approached.

"Where is my daughter? I want to see her!" Kate wrestled with the older man trying to push him away from the doorway. "What's happened to my child?"

He held her at arm's length. "Please relax, she's okay." Kate slumped toward him. Harvey coaxed her. "Let's sit in the waiting area so I can explain the situation."

Amanda followed behind, wondering what he was going to say to Kate. They moved some chairs together to form a semi-circle. Harvey tented his fingers over his lap. "There is no easy way to put this. I'm sorry but your daughter just lost her baby. She was six months along."

"Pregnant!" Kate blurted, "by whom?"

"She'd been raped. Unfortunately, no medical staff knew of her pregnancy. She'd kept it hidden."

Amanda's mouth dropped at hearing this news. *Rape? How did this young woman endure this violation to her body and not say anything to her mother or to anybody?*

Kate started to cry. "Why didn't she tell me?"

"I can't answer that for her."

"But she lost the baby."

"I know and I'm sorry."

The woman raised her arms in the air, "How could I have missed it? I'm so angry with myself."

"It's not your fault. She secretly got hold of some drugs and overdosed. The rehab center thinks a staff member gave them to her."

Wiping her tears, Kate replied, "This is shocking! What kind of rehab center have I placed her in?"

"The police are involved, and will get to the bottom of this," Harvey assured her.

Hearing this news and seeing Kate's anguish, Amanda felt sorry for her. *What more can happen to this woman?*

"Now what?" Kate asked.

"I've made a few calls. Patricia will be transferred to Bridgeford Health Services in Memphis after she recuperates from her surgery. She needs your love, support, strength, and plenty of rest."

The woman bolted from her seat. "Another rehab treatment center? In Memphis! That's a couple of hours from here. No, no, no. I can't afford another place. It's too far."

"The parish will help you."

"No way Harvey, I can't take money from the church. Come on! I'm not helpless. I still have my dignity."

He took her in his arms, "Then help Patricia by finding her a more hands-on-facility, with more monitoring, more supervision. I promise you, she will get better. She's asking for help. She needs love, your love." Kate sniffled.

Amanda watched the whole conversation unfold. The older gentleman was perspiring; he gave her a 'one more thing' look. *Here it comes.* Taking the cue, she moved closer.

"Kate," he whispered, "there's something else."

She looked over at him. "What else is there?"

"Patricia won't be able to have any more children. There were complications when she lost the baby. I'm sorry."

Kate shrieked. "I want to see my daughter. Now!"

"Of course."

Amanda felt helpless. *I don't know what to say to Kate!* The three of them walked back to room 3311. Kate opened the door and went in.

Harvey nodded to her. "Our work here is done. They need time alone." He turned on his heels and left. She watched her friend shuffle his feet on the tiled floor, his gait slow but determined, shoulders hunched. She could sense the fatigue and burden he must be feeling, dealing with Kate and Patricia. It was the middle of the night and no one was around. Sobbing could be heard through the door, but a sense of peace was coming over Amanda as she lingered a bit, hoping this family would make a commitment to work things out. *At least they have each other.*

A middle-aged couple passed her. From their innocent smiles and nods, they looked like any other couple. She followed them with her gaze. They stopped at the end of the passageway; the man held the woman and he looked like he was whispering something in her ear, and then they staggered through a hallway door marked *ICU. Such irony! A reunion is happening through a door in front of me while another tragic incident happens elsewhere.*

Amanda sighed, feeling sentimental. "I've been covering up my burdens for too long. Look where it has gotten me. I wish Mom would have given me more than disappointing memories." *I will not do the same to Emily and Rose.*

Chapter 33

Amanda found Harvey with his back against the wall outside the hospital's main entrance smoking a cigarette. His eyes were bloodshot and he appeared overwhelmed. "I'm sorry for leaving so abruptly. Going through a suicide and losing a baby all in one weekend, it's a little hard to take in."

Amanda lifted her head up to a star-lit sky. "You're telling me. I'm used to catfights and jealousy over clothes and shoes at my house, surely not this."

"Gosh, I'm so sorry. I haven't been the best mentor either. I'm supposed to be healing you, instead of asking to you tag along taking care of others."

"It's been quite an experience, but I am learning a lot."

Her mentor grinned and dropped his cigarette to the ground. "You're a trooper for sticking around and helping me out."

Amanda hugged him, "You're an amazing gentleman, Harvey Huckfinn. Your parish and God are lucky to have you."

"Thank you. Shall we go home?"

"Will you be okay driving?"

"Honestly, I'm pretty wired up and could use the drive to think. Plus, I prefer not to stay overnight at a hotel if I don't have to. I always come prepared, just in case."

They rode in silence, it was almost four when they arrived back at the ranch. Harvey excused himself and went to bed. Amanda drifted to her room, tired from the night's events.

As she lay in bed, she tossed and shifted thinking of Kate and Patricia's futures. The urge for a drink made her agitated when she remembered the flask she had stowed in her suitcase before the trip.

One sip and I'll be good, just to settle the nerves with so much going on. Amanda jumped out of the bed and rummaged through her bag. *Where is it? I know it's here.* "Where the hell is my flask?"

A knock on the door scared her.

"Yes."

"It's me, Harvey. Can I come in?"

Not a good time. "Sure."

Her mentor had dark circles under his eyes and his hair was disheveled. The smell of cigarette smoke lingered around him. "Sorry, I couldn't sleep. I heard some commotion." He produced a silver and black flask. "Is this is what you are looking for?"

Her eyes ablaze, she lunged for it. "How did you—give it back to me."

"No!" Harvey steered away from her grasp.

Amanda plopped to the floor, "What the heck!"

Harvey stooped next to her and sat down. "Not this time, you got this. You're doing great. Don't ruin the momentum. Breathe with me."

"I'm saddened, Lacy's gone and Patricia overdosed, even losing her baby! The girl is barely sixteen, she'll never be able to conceive."

"I know, it's unfair. Life is unfair sometimes."

Amanda squeezed his arm. "Ryan is in Chicago, pissed off at me and so are my children. What am I doing? I need to go home."

Harvey nodded. "I understand."

Amanda shivered. She wanted to leave, but was also afraid she'd go on another binge if she did. Her own mother had been warm and loving, but after her dad passed on, Louise had become like a ghost. "Sometimes I feel like my mother, unemotional, not caring. Kate is a parent. I don't know if I am a good one. I miss my family, but I'm scared; what lies ahead for me?"

The man hugged her, "You are a good mother. Forgive yourself."

"Forgive? Does everything revolve around forgiveness?"

"Yes and no. Love should come first."

"My mom never loved me."

"I'm sure she did. Distractions filled her life. Forgive yourself and grow in love."

Amanda pondered his statement. Feeling the sting of missing her family, she said, "I need to call Ryan. He's so mad at me."

Harvey glanced at the clock on the dresser while getting up. "Not now. It's only five-thirty. Get some rest and call him later. See you soon."

With the door shut again, she climbed into bed and closed her eyes. *He's right. Let me sleep and then I'll call.*

She awoke to her phone ringing. "Hello," she answered groggily. It was ten-fifteen.

"Are you at O'Hare?"

"Not exactly."

Ryan shouted, "What the hell, Amanda!"

She cringed as his voice growled through the line.

"Is that Mommy on the phone?"

Amanda heard Emily's voice. "Emily, Emily … Hey girl—"

"You can't talk to her right now?"

Amanda sat up in bed, "Please! Why are you doing this to me? Let me talk to her."

"When you get home."

She heard the line go dead. "Ryan, Ryan!"

Ryan clicked off. He had an urge to punch the wall in front of him, but couldn't. Emily's eyes bore into him like a flame at the end of a match. *I can't believe she's still in freaking Tennessee!*

His daughter's lips quivered. "I wanted to talk to Mommy. Why didn't you let me talk to her? Don't you love her anymore, Daddy?"

I'm such a selfish asshole. I should be more supportive. Ryan tried making light of the conversation. "I'm sorry, honey. It was wrong of me. I love Mommy. We are going through important grown-up stuff, nothing else."

"Are you mad at me and Rose?"

Ryan crouched to be at her level and embraced his daughter. "No, sweetheart, we love you and your sister very much. Don't think we are upset with you because we're not."

Emily looked reassured. Ryan brushed a strand of hair from her eyes. "Go get ready. You have dance class and Rose has swimming today." Emily hugged him again.

Once she was out of sight, Ryan shadow-boxed the wall. *I want to bust this wall.*

Amanda met Harvey fifteen minutes later in the kitchen, still reeling over Ryan's abruptness.

Harvey set down his knife and fork, his pancakes almost gone. "Uh oh, I see a look of frustration on your face. Is it your husband again?"

She nodded, "I'll need to book a flight for tomorrow. I've had enough excitement to last me a lifetime."

Taking a sip of orange juice, he said, "You and me both. Let's go see what flights are available to Chicago."

Amanda hated leaving Harvey. "I'm sorry for doing this to you, but I've been gone for too long and I can't stay for your church service tomorrow."

The craving came over her again. She needed one drink to take the edge off, feeling hurt from Ryan and experiencing two family tragedies in one weekend. *One little drink will do the trick. If only I could?*

"Don't stress, Amanda. We'll get you home. You have been doing a phenomenal job. Eat now."

Amanda grabbed a dish off the counter and joined Harvey. "I don't have a choice. It's this or nothing."

He waved her off. "I've been there, I know."

A few minutes later, they convened in Harvey's office. He fired up his laptop and searched for flights the following morning from Nashville to Chicago. Within a half-hour, they had narrowed it to a direct flight that left at 10:10 a.m. It was an extra hundred and fifty dollars for the flight, but Amanda wasn't bothered by the additional cost. She was going home tomorrow no matter what happened.

Chapter 34

Amanda fidgeted while driving to the airport with Harvey the next morning. She'd spent three-and-a-half weeks detoxing, eating healthy and controlling her temptations. The last few days she had even witnessed the power of forgiveness and what love could do. *Do I have the courage to apply forgiveness to my own life? Will I be successful at it? I have to be. I want to change.*

Amanda made a mental note to call Ryan when she got to the airport to let him know she was on her way. *Will he forgive me?* Maybe this time they could work on forgiveness together, supporting one another and keeping each other accountable. Grinning, she caught Harvey looking at her, "What?"

The dark circles under his eyes were still there, but his face radiated an unwavering affection toward her. "Wondering what you're thinking?"

She bit her lip, "... My family."

"What about them?"

"I want my life to have a purpose."

"You will. I'm glad I've been part of your journey. I will pray for you, Mrs. Amanda Reynolds. Remain diligent."

Amanda sighed, thankful for his thoughtfulness. "Are you going to make your morning service?"

"Yes, I'm scheduled for 11' o'clock."

"What will happen to Kate and Patricia, you think?"

"I have one of our newer pastors working with them, getting Patricia into the other rehab with round-the-clock support and treatment. I'll follow up with Kate in a few days. I'm confident her daughter will be in good hands."

Amanda was in awe of Harvey. He was involved in so many people's lives. It was getting close to eight-fifteen as they neared the airport. "I appreciate the time you spent with me. I wish you tremendous success with your egg farm, your involvement with the kids and pastoring at your church. But, I wish I had the chance to hear one of your services too."

"I understand, family first. If you ever come back to Spring Hill with your family," he nudged her arm, "you better attend our church."

Amanda put her hand on her chest, "I promise."

The truck slowed to a stop at Terminal 3. She had two hours until her United Airlines flight departed.

Harvey and Amanda got out. He squeezed her tightly. His skin smelled of Old Spice, a fragrance she clearly remembered her dad using when she was younger.

"Good luck to you." He spoke softly reaching in his pocket to pull out a couple of business cards, "Call me anytime."

Her voice shaken with emotion, she squeaked, "Thank you."

Amanda took her suitcase from Harvey and waved goodbye. Watching his vehicle roll away, she relaxed. "Time to go home."

Checking in and going through security, she wandered to Gate 72 and found a seat facing the window. The plane to Chicago coming in from Atlanta wasn't there yet, so she telephoned her husband.

"Hi, it's me."

Ryan's voice sounded tired, "Hey."

"I'm coming home today."

"Good."

She sighed, "Flight arrives in Chicago at eleven-forty-five."

"You want me to pick you up?"

"No, I'll take an Uber. Where are the children?"

"At Cecilia's for breakfast. I have work to do."

"What are you doing working on a Sunday morning?"

"It's complicated. A deal I worked on last month, had some issues."

"I'm sorry, hon. Have you had anything to eat?"

"Nah, not yet."

Amanda closed her eyes. She missed weekend breakfast time with him, Emily, and Rose. She was grateful Cecilia was pitching in. She owed that woman so much for taking care of her daughters.

"Tell them, I'll see—"

Several shots echoed through the air sounding like fireworks. Amanda bolted from her chair, bracing herself against the window, seeing the reflection of people fleeing, ducking, and screaming.

"My God!" She screamed, spinning around to watch the frenzy in front of her.

"Amanda, Amanda, what's happening? Do I hear gunfire?"

"I don't know! It sounds like it could be fireworks."

She heard someone yell to get down because someone had a gun. *Oh, no!* Suddenly, about eight men in uniform converged near Amanda's terminal. They were barking orders to passengers. One big, muscular black man holding a rifle charged toward Amanda and two other patrons. "You there, move it," he pointed at her and toward an open doorway leading onto a ramp.

"What the hell is going on?" Ryan's voice thundered. Amanda ducked not sure where the shots were coming from.

"Move it. You are in danger," the man said as he shoved her through the aisles until she was standing in line with twenty other frantic people.

"Ryan, turn on the news, something is happening."

"Amanda? Amanda? Talk to me."

The same black man with thick beads of sweat on his brow ripped her phone away. "Excuse me!" she scowled at him. Turning it off, he threw it back to her. He pointed to another man in military attire giving instructions to the people in line. "That's your lifeline!"

He brushed past her trying to help other passengers. Amanda was pushed through the doorway along with two dozen others. Women were crying, children were hysterical, along with the military personnel herding them through an underground corridor. When they couldn't go any farther, she was pushed to the floor next to a woman with her head wrapped in a flowery scarf holding a rosary, praying.

Amanda looked at a male attendant nearby. "What's happened?"

He was a short, stocky, and balding, his nametag read *Ricardo*. "I don't have any details. There's been a shooting. Don't move please."

Amanda jumped to her feet, "Terrorists?" Chaos erupted. People screamed louder.

Four more shots exploded through the terminal. Ricardo grabbed her arm and jerked her to the floor. "Lady, I don't have time for chit-chat. I need your cooperation. Shut up!" He marched away, yelling for the confused passengers to settle down.

Rubbing her bruised arm, Amanda thought about the enormity of the situation she was in. The woman next to her coughed. Turning, their eyes met. *Oh, my! This lady doesn't have any eyebrows!*

"God be with you. God be with us." The woman began reciting The Lord's Prayer.

Tears trickled down Amanda's face. *How are we going to get out of here?*

A door opened and then slammed shut. A brazen-faced man with a medal-laden military jacket marched in. His voice was loud and gruff, "Attention please, my name is Sergeant Fields. There has been a civilian attack on the south side of the airport." Grumbling sounded through the vestibule. "The entire airport is under security lockdown."

Wiping her face, Amanda uttered, "Oh, my Lord."

Grumbling and gasps echoed by the passengers.

"We've been instructed to stay here until it is safe to leave. I am also asking that you not make any calls. We are in a localized state of emergency. This is for your own protection. I appreciate your undivided cooperation and patience. Thank you."

There was more grumbling, and then an abrupt silence followed as the sergeant left the area. Amanda's mind spun. *Did Harvey make it out of the airport?* Pulling out her phone again, she dialed as the woman with the flowery scarf watched her.

"I'll let you know if someone is coming," the woman spoke in a low tone, keeping an eye out.

She heard a piercing ringing like the line was disconnected. Amanda redialed several times and received the same tone. She leaned against the wall. "Damn, my friend was leaving the airport. I can't get hold of him. I'm worried for him."

Amanda tried to get through to her husband. After three unsuccessful attempts, it was useless, the line was busy. She texted him: … Airport under lockdown. … An attack. … I'm safe. … I can't get through the line. I love you. … Will call ASAP … Pressing *Send*, she hoped her message went through. It didn't. Amanda shut off the phone and threw it in her purse.

The woman coughed loudly and offered her hand, "Would you mind praying with me?"

Amanda looked at her. *No time for God right now.* "No thanks. I'm good."

"I'm not asking if you want a soda, I'm asking you to pray. If you haven't noticed, we're in pretty dire straits." Amanda reluctantly took the woman's hand. "Thank you, I'm Jane Weaver."

"Amanda Reynolds."

Chapter 35

An hour had passed from the time passengers were corralled into an oversized room, similar to a storage room. The smell of engine oil and dust filled the air; they were surrounded by worn airline seats, beverage carts and other interior plane-related equipment. Sergeant Fields spoke to them two more times. The police and FBI were working feverishly to apprehend three other gunmen still at large; two had already been caught.

Amanda and Jane talked quietly. She learned the woman had Stage 4 breast cancer and was only given six months to a year to live. Returning from San Francisco after seeing another doctor to get a fourth opinion, Jane was instructed to go home and be with her family in Tennessee. On multiple medications, Jane was optimistic, hopeful that by God's grace she'd defeat the cancer that was killing her slowly.

A mother to two children, Leslie eight and Marcia six, Jane believed she had to fight to the end. Her family depended on it. Amanda was amazed by the woman's story and her heroic efforts to live for her family.

Jane twirled her Rosary, coughed constantly and murmured words under her breath. Curious, Amanda asked, "I don't mean to pry, but what are you saying so softly?"

"No bother, I'm reciting the Psalms."

"You know all the Psalms by heart? There must be hundreds in the Bible."

"Actually, there are one hundred and fifty, if you're interested in knowing."

"How do you do it?" *That's crazy.*

"Do what?"

"Live life to the fullest knowing you might die any day?" *This woman is incredible. I have to know.*

Jane shifted crossing her legs on the floor. She was bony and frail-looking and her eyes were bright. Settling her cough, she replied, "I surround myself with loved ones. I don't take anything personally and I give it my best every day. Most importantly, I give all my fears up to God. He has taught me to be worthy of myself because I am worthy in the Lord's eyes." She paused, "I also spend time in the Bible every day, by reading His word, praying and reflecting."

"Wow, honestly, Jane, I don't know how or what to pray, let alone what to read in the Bible. Where would I start?"

"Praying is the easy part. Talk to God like you're having a conversation with a girlfriend. You could pray in gratitude, thank Him for things in your life or ask Him to help you with a burden. I'd recommend you start by reading any of the four gospels: Mark, Mathew, Luke or John. Most people start with John. Here," she pulled a frayed maroon-colored, leather-bound Bible out of her bag, "take mine. I have another at home."

"No, I couldn't."

"I insist. Read this book," Jane pointed to it, "even for just fifteen minutes a day. You are worth it."

Amanda took the Bible from the woman's ice-cold hands and held it, thumbing through the book. There were over a thousand pages, content perhaps too complicated to digest for such a short time each day. Placing it in her purse, she replied, "Thank you."

"You're welcome."

Time trickled by. Amanda watched Jane as she dozed periodically. She'd wake, cough, say a few words and doze for another few minutes, wincing at times. *How much pain is this woman in? Is she married? She's not wearing any rings.*

Amanda began to recognize the parallels in her own situation with Jane's. She had traveled to New Mexico and Tennessee when she could have easily found her own counsel, treatment and remedies in Chicago. Ryan pleaded with her to stay home but she was grateful she'd left. It had been a good experience. She wanted to get home and be with her loved ones, and live a new lifestyle, hopefully a controlled, healthier one, one without alcohol. Feeling homesick, she thought of Emily finding her passed out on the bed. *I was such a fool.*

There was a noise next to her. Surprised, her thoughts interrupted, Amanda glanced at Jane who was sleeping sitting up against the wall. White, bubbly foam had formed at the corners of her mouth. "Oh my God! Jane, Jane!" She elbowed the woman. Amanda scrambled to her feet. "Help, help, I need help here."

Two attendants hurried over, one was Ricardo and the other, a younger man with blondish hair. Many of the detained passengers stood up, looking on. There was a ton of commotion, neither one of the attendants had any medical experience; they started asking if any of the passengers were doctors.

A man, around forty, fit and tan, sprinted to her side. He said he was a nurse as he checked Jane's vitals. He spoke fast with a New York accent, asking for a mat, a blanket, anything to lay the woman on because she wasn't responding. Another attendant hurrying to their aide yelled that he had a blanket. Hastily, the nurse and Ricardo moved Jane into a prone position on the blanket. The woman coughed, spitting up blood. Amanda staggered backwards, feeling uneasy. Ricardo grabbed a roll of paper towels, pulling sheets off and wiping Jane's mouth. "Shit!" he hollered, "she needs to get to a hospital fast."

Chapter 36

Amanda helplessly watched as the attendants took Jane out of the room to a nearby hospital; the airport was still under lockdown. She couldn't believe she'd been involved in a suicide counseling, a mother's anguish over her daughter's fatal drug addiction and an attempt to comfort a terminally ill woman. The journey was wearing on her psyche. *Why is this happening to me, God? What is the meaning of all this?*

Holding Jane's Bible, thoughts of uncertainty wrestled within her head. *Did Harvey make it safely home?* She thought of Gretchen in Taos sweeping the porch. She thought about Ryan checking the news for any information on what was happening at the airport. She thought of her daughters missing her. She thought of their generous-hearted neighbor, Cecilia, helping with their family, her dead brother, Joshua, his bizarre appearances and Jane. *Did she make it to the hospital in time?* A headache was coming on. *I can feel it.*

Exactly one year before Joshua's death, her brother had been stationed in Germany for four months. Amanda was home from work, she remembered. Not having grocery-shopped in days, she was making macaroni and cheese for the second night in a row. Joshua wasn't expected home for another two weeks. His absence made her lonely for his company. She'd had been dating a research assistant at DePaul University, Roger, but the guy was too busy with work to see her.

For fun, Amanda grabbed a photo of her brother and taped it to the chair across from her, doing a little role-playing with Joshua's picture. "Don't overcook the elbows. It should be 'al dente'," she said in a deep voice.

Tasting a few elbows, Amanda said, "Relax, brother, it's perfect. Just the way you like it." Taking a small silver colander, she drained the pasta in the sink. "What's next, Sis? Hurry up. Get the butter and milk." *He always said that.* "I know." *Now I am talking to myself, I miss him so much.* Amanda cut half a stick of butter and tossed it in the pan. Then, she poured one-fourth of a cup of milk in the pan. "Wait. Is that two percent milk you're pouring in the pot?" Amanda chuckled watching the butter melt in with the milk. "No sis, you have to use whole milk." Holding the wooden spoon up and looking back at her brother's picture, she answered, "Two percent is better for you. Zip it for a minute." Tossing the pasta and throwing in the cheese powder packet, Amanda worked the wooden spoon around the pan, coating the elbows with the cheesy mixture. She filled two small bowls and placed them on the table, one for her and the other in front of her brother's photo. "Here," she mocked sticking her tongue out at his face, "eat this." Sitting down, Amanda's eyes teared up, "I wish you were here." She tried a spoonful, "Yuck, this is disgusting."

A few minutes later, the front door burst open. Joshua's face was ashen, and his body thinner than before he left. They embraced.

"What the heck are you doing here?"

He removed his jacket, "I've been sick. They sent me home to see a doctor in the States."

She scrutinized her brother, "What happened to you? Why are you so thin?"

"I'm fine. Stop your worrying." Entering the kitchen, Josh noticed two bowls on the table and his picture taped onto the chair. He burst out laughing. "What the hell are you doing?"

Her cheeks burned, "I've missed you. I made your favorite."

"I see that." Peeking in the fridge, he glanced back at his sister. "Don't tell me you used two percent milk?"

"What do you think?" They both cracked up over it. It was a great evening. But days later, their reunion was met with somber news when Joshua was diagnosed with leukemia.

A loud noise dragged Amanda out of a dreamy state. *Gosh, I miss you, Josh.* She'd been put to the test, physically and emotionally, even fending off urges to drink, *like right now*; no matter how many times her stomach did flip-flops. She was taking a courageous step to better her health with new eating habits and even using her own inner wisdom to help others in times of need. One thing was certain, she'd have to earn her trust with Ryan again. Prior to getting married, he often asked her about her past, but she had never been truthful to him until recently. Her mother's abandonment and Josh's premature death had been hard to talk about. *New beginnings this time.*

Amanda meandered through the crowd of stranded tired passengers. When she returned to her spot, there was a small lavender-colored box wrapped in a yellow ribbon with a little card sitting next to her purse. Squatting, she opened the envelope. It read, *Almost home.*

She looked around. *Where did this box come from?* The travelers near her seemed preoccupied with their own things. Nothing seemed out of the ordinary. Putting the envelope aside, Amanda opened the box. Inside was a large chocolate-covered strawberry. Pulling it out, she ran her fingers across the smooth coating. It was cold. She searched the crowd to see if anyone else had a similar box near them. Her mouth watered just holding the strawberry.

A female attendant walked by. "Looks delicious."

Ready to bite into the fruit, Amanda stopped. "Wait."

The attendant hurried back, "Yes."

Pointing at the strawberry, Amanda asked, "Did you guys pass these out?"

"I wish we had. I'd like one myself."

"Okay, thanks." Amanda studied the box. On the bottom of the box, in the far right corner, there was a cursive letter *J* written in fancy script.

Could it be from Joshua? The little hairs on her arms stood up on end. "Thanks, big brother." Looking at the strawberry, she plunged her teeth into the chocolatey fruit.

Chapter 37

Amanda thumbed through the Bible. Many of the pages were highlighted and dog-eared. She couldn't believe Jane had memorized the entire book of Psalms. Her fingers stopped at a page and her eyes were drawn to a scripture highlighted in pink. It read, *"His work is honorable and glorious, and His righteousness endures forever. He has made His wonderful works to be remembered; The Lord is gracious and full of compassion." Psalm 111: 3-4.*

Amanda prayed to God to be gracious and compassionate to Jane, for her to be well enough, at least for a little while longer to continue to honor Him through her life's passion.

Another flight attendant passed by. Amanda asked her if they'd heard anything about Jane, but the woman hadn't.

Sergeant Fields returned sometime later, informing the passengers that police and the FBI had caught the three remaining gunmen. Cheers erupted with the good news. The Sergeant went on to tell them they'd soon be escorted out and given an opportunity to speak with airline representatives about rescheduling flights. Mr. Fields cautioned, with the backup, it could be as early as tomorrow or even a couple of days before anyone could fly out. *Wow, I can't believe this.*

Later on, it was clear to move. There was chaos as people bumped and pushed to get out into the terminal. Amanda squeezed by and was directed by an airline representative to follow the signs to Baggage Claims; she would pick up her luggage for the time being.

There were two missed calls and a text from Ryan and one voicemail from Harvey. She called her husband first. "Amanda, are you okay? I have been so worried."

"Yes, thankfully I'm fine. What a scary mess. There were at least forty or fifty of us plus passengers that had exited a different plane hiding in a storage room. They were pretty strict, and I can appreciate it for all our safety. I did try and text you though."

"The news has been reporting an attack, several casualties, but they're not saying whether it was terrorist-related or disgruntled employees. Trying to be PC. What bullshit, though!"

"I know, they weren't specific with us either. But I've been hearing rumblings from some of the passengers that this looks like an isolated incident."

"Where are you right now?"

Amanda bustled passed crowds of people, "Getting my luggage. Hopefully, I will be able to *get* my luggage. I know for sure I won't be getting out of here today. It's so crazy."

"That's what the news said."

All she saw was crowds in front of her. "It's a mess here." Amanda veered from people as she talked.

"Can you go back to the pastor's house, if you can't leave today?"

She checked her watch for the time. It was past two-thirty. "Good idea, he left a voicemail for me. I know he had a sermon this morning. I need to call him right away, he dropped me off and I have no idea if he is alright."

"Hurry and call him. Let me know as soon as you know more. This was such a scare. I'm so thankful you're safe."

"Ryan, I—" Amanda struggled with her words, fatigue was setting in. She was also homesick. *I need a fresh start.*

Chapter 38

An airport courtesy car made a left turn into *The Chosen Saints* church parking lot. It was just past six-thirty. The sun was still high overhead, but inside the car the air was on full blast. A round light-pink brick building with a manicured lawn and trimmed shrubs outlined the perimeter. There were big ceramic vases with an array of colorful flowers in front of the sliding-door entrance.

Amanda gathered her things while the car parked. Harvey had been concerned for her safety according to the voicemail. They had connected; the older gentleman was relieved to hear from her and said he'd left the airport and was driving to the church when he heard there were gunshots fired.

Amanda notified Ryan on the way to the church that she was staying at Harvey's place for the night, and that her mentor called in a few favors and was able to get her on a flight to Chicago the very next morning. Her husband had been so thrilled to hear the news, astonished that Harvey had been able to arrange a flight so quickly, even before she got to the church.

The door of the church opened and Harvey rushed out with another gentleman at his side. Harvey snatched her in a tight hug. "Praise the Lord, you're safe." Filled with emotion, she stayed longer in his arms, feeling a warm love surround her.

Amanda exhaled loudly, "You have no idea."

The preacher moved aside and introduced the man next to him. "This is Pastor Richard Feldman." They shook hands.

The man looked to be about her age, medium-height, freckle-faced with crooked teeth. "It's a pleasure, ma'am." His voice was low with a southern accent. "Harvey has told me about your journey of self-healing to a sober beginning. Even with the shooting at the airport, which was so frightening to hear, I applaud you for your courage."

"Come on in. Let's have some sweet tea. The sun is burning my head. Richard and I are wrapping things up. Then we'll head on home to rest."

Weariness seeping into her bones, Amanda's shoulders sagged. "Thank you for taking me in for another night, Harvey."

They entered the church foyer. Dark brown carpeting, egg-shell colored walls and large potted ferns decorated the sparsely furnished entryway. Everything smelled new and there were no pictures of Jesus, crosses or statues of saints. It was modern-looking.

As they walked, Amanda filled them in on the attack at the airport. The two men confirmed that the identified gunmen were in fact disgruntled union workers let go over a recent theft. She also talked to them about Jane Weaver, choking up at the thought of her.

They entered Harvey's office, it was cluttered with books and papers. "Please make yourself comfortable." The man moved several folders off his desk and leaned up against it while Pastor Feldman excused himself to get their tea.

Sitting on a squishy sofa, Amanda retrieved the Bible from her purse. "Jane gave this to me. She recommended I start reading the New Testament. This whole experience has been dreamlike for me, *with Joshua materializing*. I'm just speechless."

Harvey joined her, "I'd offer you a drink, but I know you can't have one."

She snorted, "Ha ... I'd need something really strong."

"You're an overcomer, Amanda. Recovery is a life-style change, stick to it. You have to believe you are worthy of this grand new life you've been given." His eyes were misty, his words genuine.

She regarded her new friend. *Am I worthy of God's love? Do I deserve His forgiveness?* "Being worthy in God's eyes, that's what Jane told me too."

"She's right. You've been fighting past demons that have blocked you from being healthy, forgiven and worthy. You used alcohol and harmful foods to mask the pain. Let the goodness come in and surrender to Him."

Feeling dizzy, she responded, "You are a 'demon squasher'."

"I guess I am," Harvey's belly jiggled. The two continued their discussion. Amanda brought her mentor up to speed on Ryan's workload and her children's behavior. Richard joined them after a while and they took sips of the refreshing drink. "Ah, finally, our tea, where have you been? Did you make it from scratch?"

The younger man chuckled at his colleagues' whimsy, "You said your friend's name was Jane Weaver?"

"That's right."

"I have several family members who work at hospitals around here, and you piqued my interest, on such a Godly woman. So, I made a few calls."

Amanda stood, "My goodness, what did you find out?"

"She's at Vanderbilt University Medical Center. My brother-in-law is a nurse there. Jane is in ICU but only family can see her. If you like, give me your number and I'll pass it on to him, he can get a message to her. That way you can both keep in touch."

Appreciative of Pastor Feldman's nice gesture, Amanda hugged him. "Thank you. You didn't have to do that. I'm relieved she's at a hospital where there is medical staff monitoring her."

Harvey bowed toward his partner. "I'll forgive you for taking so long for our drinks, this one time." They laughed and sipped their tea.

Amanda remembered the community rally regarding Lacy's suicide. "Before I forget, how did the rally go for the Parker family? And your sermon?"

"Good, we had an incredible turnout. Lacy's funeral is tomorrow and I'll be presiding," Richard said.

Harvey piped in, "It was a positively charged supportive rally. Mrs. Parker is getting help. She's dealing with a lot of anger issues."

She thought of Kate and Patricia Weber. "What about the Webers?"

A big smile lit up Harvey's face, "Healing together, I talked to Kate earlier. She and her daughter have made amends and Patricia wants to get better. The girl is going to Bridgeford Health Services later this week."

Amanda regarded each of the men. "This is such good news. You've both made my day and after what I've been through at the airport."

The older man held out a piece of paper. "I have something else for you."

Pastor Feldman grabbed his tea and exited through the door. "My cue to leave. Nice to meet you, Mrs. Reynolds."

Amanda waved, "Likewise."

She considered her mentor, "You, sir, have done plenty. I could never pay you enough."

The older man grinned, "It's no big deal. Besides, I had some time before you arrived."

Amanda took the offering. There was a name, number and address, and an email inscribed on it. "What's this?"

"A friend of a friend knows a good alcohol sponsor in a town just outside of Chicago. El. Gin. Or something like that."

"Elgin. I know it. Not far from Schaumburg where I live."

"Good." Harvey leaned on his desk. "When you feel yourself slipping into temptation, feeling withdrawals, or want someone to talk to, you can call this wonderful lady, Claire Summerfeld. She's super nice. I've spoken to her and she *will* hold you accountable if your husband is unable to or if you need more than one person to keep you on track."

"Geez, Harvey Huckfinn." Amanda reflected on her journey. Her heart was overflowing. Despite all that had transpired in her life, the setbacks, the pains, and the constant struggle with her temptations, she was blessed to go through this rehabilitation and meet so many wonderful people.

She was going home. There were many questions spinning around in her head. Would she ever be able to drink liquor again? Will her family give her another chance? Does Louise deserve to be forgiven after abandoning her and Joshua? Had she been deemed worthy by God to start all over? Could she be a better wife and mother to her family? She'd have to try it in order to gain their forgiveness.

Part III: WHERE TO FROM HERE — THE SUN IS RISING

"Don't just chase after the wind, but be the wind that people chase after."

Musical Inspiration for this Section

"The Sun is Rising" by Britt Nicole

"Coming Up to Breathe" by MercyMe

Chapter 39

August. Monday Morning.

Ryan watched the clock; it was close to five-thirty and his mind was in awhirl from his work screw-up to Amanda's relapse. If all the documentation was approved, and he needed to tweak them first, he'd get a huge bonus from the six-million-dollar Mumford deal. Emily and Rose were still torn apart by the uncertainty of their mother's disease. *Yes, it was a disease.* And, the one person that held them all altogether was not altogether as he had believed, his beloved wife of twelve years, his alcoholic wife.

Turning over, Ryan rubbed his forehead. *Amanda's coming home today. What'll happen when she's into her motherly routines? Will she relapse again?* Ryan decided he wasn't angry for not knowing her past, he was wondering who he actually married—a woman full of secrets? *This isn't a good marriage if things are kept from me. Why did she keep her addictions from me? Why didn't she come to me with her problems? I contributed to her abuse, the late night drinking and the fancy parties. I've been a jerk to her while she's been away. Worrying her with the kids, not even letting her talk to them, all because I'm such a coward and have made this about me instead of her.* Ryan was exhausted from worrying all night long. He shut off the alarm set for six, slithered out of bed and groggily staggered to the bathroom. *Another workday, another week.*

The plane landed at O'Hare at approximately 10:25 a.m.; Amanda stared out the window as the plane taxied to the gate. She thought about the brief telephone conversation she'd had with Jane before getting on the aircraft. Jane was still in ICU. The woman had a lung infection and would be staying in the hospital for a few days. Her condition didn't look promising, but she was glad to be home surrounded by family. Amanda was saddened when the two spoke; hearing Jane's voice made their encounter bittersweet even though her new acquaintance sounded upbeat.

Before hanging up, Jane recited a scripture from the *Book of Psalms*. "Listen, my friend, I'll be okay because I know where I'm going. Life has a way of making a lot of noise, but if you quiet your soul you can actually hear God's voice. I want to leave you with this as you continue on your healing journey, *'Be still and know that I am God.'* It's from *Psalm 46:10*."

Recalling those words comforted Amanda. She moved her neck from side to side. A businessman sitting next to her commented, "Welcome home, eh?"

"It's been quite a trip."

"Hope it works out for you."

"That makes two of us."

Antsy, Amanda couldn't believe it was already the last few weeks of summer. From the jet window, she observed the rising heat generated by the silver-colored planes sitting nearby. She figured the humidity-level was high, where one's skin felt sticky. This kind of weather didn't bother her. This was her city.

At the gate, Amanda followed the rest of the passengers to the baggage claim. Standing to the side, she paused long enough to call the house. The phone rang and rang at least a dozen times, but no answer. *What happened to the answering machine?* It was close to 11:30 on a Monday morning. *Emily should be in dance class and Cecilia must have taken Rose to the library.* At least that was the schedule. She'd call again in a few minutes.

Amanda headed to the restroom to freshen up. Upon exiting, she collided into someone. "Oh, my! I'm so sorry."

"Are you sure you're ready to go home?"

It was her brother. *AGAIN! Yikes!* "What the hell are you doing here, Josh? Go away. I have to get home."

"Not yet." He pushed her into the bathroom.

She wiggled from his grip. "Let go of me. Get out. Women will be coming in here any minute."

"Don't worry; it's not open to the public at the moment." Joshua winked. Outside was a yellow stand noting the lavatory was being cleaned. Leaning against the counter, Amanda looked intently at her brother. He folded his arms, "So, I've been thinking."

"Make it quick. I'm anxious to see my family."

Her brother smiled. "They left for Wisconsin Dells this morning. It's Emily's dance tournament."

Shocked, Amanda said, "No. No. It can't be. I totally forgot. Why didn't Ryan tell me?"

"He didn't know either apparently."

"Shit!" she shrieked, kicking her bag. *I'm sure Ryan is not going to be happy having to drive the girls to Wisconsin. Add that to my hate list.* Taking a breath, Amanda turned and faced the mirror, studying her features. In the last few weeks, she'd regained her youthful look, lost some weight and had more energy than before. *How will they react when they see me?* She spun around, faced her brother, and punched him. "You knew they'd be gone, didn't you?"

Grinning, Josh flinched, rubbing his elbow, "Ouch. That's not nice."

"What's going on?" He laughed and danced in a circle, giving himself a high-five. She couldn't hold it in and giggled along with him, missing the quirky moments they'd often shared. "Enough. Tell me already."

"Do you remember my last words to you at the hospital?"

It had been over twelve years; a lot had happened since then. "Not exactly."

There was a noise outside and her brother went to take a look. He came back. "We don't have a lot of time. Let me remind you. The one thing I told you was to make your life matter. The second thing, the most important thing, was that I wanted you to visit mom and forgive her."

"I did see her, so don't start. I don't want to remember her that way."

"I understand. It's disappointing, but she is still our mom."

"So what? Now you forgive her?" Amanda asked, shifting from side to side.

"Yes, a piece of me was never complete and I thank God for giving me that opportunity to see her one last time."

"See her, how?"

"Before mom died I visited her in the hospital. She had liver cancer."

"How, you were dead."

"That's correct. God gave Mom and me closure."

"Great. How was that experience?"

"Liberating, she didn't know I … I died. We cried a lot. The best part, we prayed and Mom accepted Christ."

"Was she sorry?"

Josh jumped onto the counter. "Yes, she felt burdened all the way to the end. There are other issues that I don't have permission to explain."

"Like what?"

"It's not the right time, okay."

She slinked to the floor. "You forgave her?"

"I did."

"Good for you, anything else?"

"I need a tiny favor from you. Here." He passed her a piece of paper and a paid train ticket.

On the paper was an address for a cemetery in Iowa. Looking at her brother, she said, "I won't go."

"You have to. That's where Mom is buried. Make peace once and for all," Joshua said sternly.

"This is insane. I don't know. I'm already in deep shit with Ryan."

"You have the time to do this. Go and get on the Amtrak heading to Mount Pleasant. The train leaves in two-and-a-half hours. A taxi will take you to the cemetery. Sis, make it right; make it matter." Joshua kissed his sister and waltzed out.

Amanda faced the mirror again speaking to no one in particular. "Oh, Lord! Please don't prompt me to do anything else."

Chapter 40

Once outside the terminal, humid air wrapped around Amanda like a blanket. She hailed a taxi and climbed in. "Union Station, please. Hurry, I have a train to catch."

A young Asian man with a dimpled smile peered through the rearview mirror, turning on his meter. It was twelve; the ride to the city was slow on Interstate 90 from O'Hare. Amanda relaxed against the worn gray leather seat. She couldn't believe Josh had visited their mom five years ago and actually forgave her.

Amanda had no desire to travel back to Iowa. *Will I be able to stand at the grave and forgive my mother for not being there for us when we needed her most?* All she wanted was to get home to her husband and daughters, to be forgiven and start over again.

Amanda understood what her brother was doing; in order to be forgiven, she must forgive her mother first. Harvey Huckfinn preached to her about the same thing. Even though she was determined to get it over with, a veil of sadness shrouded her. She wished Louise had been there for her marriage to Ryan and the birth of her grandchildren. *Can I do this?*

When the cab pulled up to Wacker and Adams, Amanda paid, opened the door, and sprinted through the station with twenty-five minutes to spare. She boarded Amtrak, finding an empty seat next to a middle-aged woman reading a copy of *Good Housekeeping*. They exchanged hellos as she made herself comfortable, while memories of years past came unbidden to her mind.

"Want vanilla ice cream, honey? It will make everything better," Louise said, gently kissing five-year-old Amanda.

Amanda gingerly rubbed her bandaged knee as rivulets of tears blanketed her cheeks. The thought of vanilla ice cream though, put a smile on her face. "Okay, Mommy. Can we get a little chocolate fudge on it too, with nuts?"

Her mom lifted Amanda in her arms. "You bet kiddo, anything for you. Let's go inside and get some ice cream with all the fixings."

Joshua had been standing at the curb; he came jogging behind them. "Don't I get ice cream, too?"

Amanda stuck her tongue out. "Nope, just me, I'm the one who fell."

Joshua stuck his hands in his pockets. "Not fair."

Louise swung her around as she approached the front door of the ice cream parlor. "Sweetie, of course your big brother gets ice cream. He's your hero and will always be your hero. I wouldn't have known you fell if it wasn't for your brother watching over you."

She looked over her mom's shoulders. "No nuts for Josh, though."

"Mom!"

Amanda stirred, a smile crossed her face. Opening her eyes, the smile vanished thinking of a trip to a city she didn't want to go to and a cemetery she had no desire to visit. Turning to the woman next to her, she asked, "Excuse me, do you know when we'll arrive in Mount Pleasant?"

"We should be getting to the station soon."

Amanda looked at her watch, six-twenty-five. She knew most cemeteries closed at sundown, which didn't leave her a lot of time. Before she left Chicago, Joshua had told her there'd be a taxi waiting for her at the station to take her to the cemetery. *Gosh, I hope this is a painless visit.*

Ryan stepped out of the auditorium and into the foyer of McCullen Arena in Wisconsin Dells; Emily was there for her final summer dance recital. His oldest was favored to win second place. He was so proud of her; she'd been working all season to qualify.

With many projects going on at work and Amanda's relapse, he had forgotten the girls were scheduled for this trip. Luckily, Cecilia had called in the morning to remind him where to find Emily's pink leotards.

He checked his phone for any messages from Amanda. The plane landed hours ago. She should have called. I hope nothing serious has happened to her.

Ryan sent her a text. … Where are you? … We had to leave early to get to Wisconsin Dells for Emily's dance recital. I told the girls you're coming home. … They are thrilled. Call me or text. Be back late tonight. … Love you.

The doors opened, Cecilia and Rose popped their heads out of the auditorium. "Emily is up soon."

Rose ran to him, "Hurry, Daddy. Emily is next."

Ryan put the phone in his pocket, picked up his youngest and followed Cecilia inside. "Okay, let's go see your big sister break a leg."

Chapter 41

The train glided into the Mount Pleasant train station at 6:47 p.m. A lot had changed in twelve years, the station was modern-looking, no longer a one-room building. There was a food court/seating area, tons of vending machines and two restrooms on both ends of the building. It was strange seeing a lot of people bustling through the station of the small town at this hour.

After noticing a large poster board, Amanda understood why there were so many people traveling from Chicago to Mount Pleasant. It was the tenth annual three-day-long "Dog-n-Brat" festival, a bratwurst and hot dog eating competition just a few blocks over. She sniggled as she freshened up in the restroom. *I'm never eating another hot dog or brat now that I've learned about organic foods from Gretchen.*

Exiting the station, she couldn't believe Mount Pleasant had become so popular. The wind picked up, ruffling her hair. There were several cabs alongside the curb. *Which one is my cab?* She dug into her pocket for the address to the cemetery when a stocky man with a scruffy face approached her.

"Amanda Reynolds?"

"Yes."

"I'm your ride to Riverdale Saints Cemetery."

"Thank you." Amanda took her suitcase and followed the man to his taxicab, a rusted out yellow and white car without any hubcaps. She opened the door and slid in.

The driver got in, "It will take us roughly thirty minutes to get there. The streets are closed due to the festival. Given that, you have a short time before the cemetery closes."

"I understand. I don't plan on staying long." *I'll look for the grave of a woman who didn't care about us and say, 'I forgive you.' Then I'm getting the hell out of here.*

The cabbie sped off. There were a lot of detours as they wove through many neighborhoods to get to a cemetery only eleven miles from the station.

When they arrived forty-minutes later, one side of the gates was already closed. A wiry-framed security guard with a lined face was straddled on a stool while looking at his watch. When the cab approached, he motioned for them to stop. Ambling over to the driver's side, he said. "We're closing in a half-hour. What do you need?"

Amanda rolled down her window, "I have to pay my respects to a family member. It should be enough time."

The man picked at his tooth with a toothpick. "Where is he or she located? This place is huge. It could take you a half-hour to find your family member, and then I'd have to close you in," he snarled. "Wouldn't want to be stuck in a cemetery overnight, eh?"

Amanda was exasperated and wanted to be done with everything. She was not planning on coming back the next day, and had already reserved one night at the motel, the same one from years earlier with a mid-morning train ride back to Chicago. She presented the sheet of paper with the location of the grave to the guard. "This is all I have."

Her phone buzzed in her purse. Taking it out, she read Ryan's text, cringing from his sharp words. *I'm missing Emily's recital! I have to call him after this.*

Amanda texted back, I'm in Mount Pleasant, Iowa. ... I know about my mom. She died five years ago and is buried here. ... I'm visiting the grave site now. ... Coming home tomorrow. I'm so sorry. Again! ... Will call you later.

The security guard coughed. "You're in luck, lady. I'm familiar with that area. You can find your family member up that way to your right, behind that white granite mausoleum. I'll let you in, you have twenty-five minutes before the gates close. Here, take this." He supplied her with a flashlight.

"Thank you, sir." She motioned for the cabby to go.

The driver said, "Twenty-five minutes okay, ma'am, no longer. I don't like being here."

"Don't worry, I feel the same way."

The taxi moved through the gate. It was starting to get dark. When they spotted the white mausoleum, the car stopped. With the flashlight provided by the grouchy security guard, Amanda weaved through the grass in search of her mother's grave. She found it quickly. A gray slab marked her grave. It read: *Louise Jackson Lenger: Rest in Peace. 1954 – 2007*. She was fifty-three-years-old when she passed.

The area around the headstone was overgrown. There was one drying burgundy-colored mum wrapped in foil sitting in a glass cup on the side of the stone. Amanda bent to feel it, wondering who had put it there in the first place. There was no picture of Louise, she flinched remembering her mother at the trailer park.

"I still hate you. You gave up on Joshua and me when Dad died. I don't know if I can ever forgive you, but coming here at least gives me closure. Josh was right about that." Amanda looked back at her cab. It hadn't moved. She resumed her venting, "I have two daughters of my own. I have never told them about you. Frankly, I won't. You were beautiful Mom, but you threw it away for alcohol and abusive men. I screwed up, but I'm clean now. I feel great and have learned to eat healthy. I can't wait to get home to my husband and family and live again. I will not live in the past. I'm a new person, understand, a new person!"

Tears pooled in Amanda's eyes. She made an effort to wipe them away but they wouldn't stop. Kicking a rock away with her foot, she heard a sneeze and glanced over her shoulder. A young man wearing a Chicago Cubs baseball cap stood nearby. He was lanky. He carried a cane and hobbled over to her. "She wasn't that terrible."

"Who are you?"

"She drank, and her temperament wasn't great at times. Geez, it was even worse when the damn cancer took over. Couldn't blame her after that, the pain was unbearable." Amanda scrutinized the man, a younger version of Joshua. "Name's Peter Mitchell, and you are?"

"Amanda Lenger, her daughter."

Peter removed his hat, his wavy hair stuck out. "I was wondering when you'd come, been waiting for you and Joshua."

Amanda grew uncomfortable and looked past the man for the taxi. "Hey, where did the cab go?"

"Oh, him," Peter shrugged, "I sent him on his way."

She brushed past him. "Why? Okay, then. Well, I don't know who you are and I don't want any trouble. I'll be on my way."

Peter followed her. "The gate is already locked. Ed is pretty punctual. I have the other set." He dangled the keys from his hand.

Holy cow, I'm locked in a cemetery with a crazy person. Amanda took off, side-stepping other graves in her path.

"Wait, I'm not going to hurt you," Peter hobbled behind her. "I'm your brother."

Amanda stopped before the curb and twisted around, "What did you say?"

Breathing heavy and bending over, he responded, "Damn, you can sure run." He caught his breath. "Half-brother, my dad is Jacob Mitchell. He and our mom married and had me. Or, was it the other way around? Conceived me and then married. Never quite knew the truth between those two. Co-conspirators, I used to call them. I'm the grounds-keeper here. I'll call you another taxicab. Your things are there," he pointed toward the street.

Amanda glared at Peter. She didn't know what to say. Joshua never told her they had a brother. She found her voice and aimed the flashlight toward his right leg. "What happened to your leg?"

He coughed. "I was hit by a car while riding my bike when I was eighteen, shattered the thing in twelve places. It never healed properly. Frankly, haven't gotten on a bike since. I have this limp to show for it. It's a character-builder and a good conversation starter with the ladies."

Though the situation was awkward, Amanda chuckled. She recognized the same humor and honesty Peter shared with their big brother. The wind whirled around them and Amanda hugged her arms. "You live nearby?"

Peter put his cap back on. "Yep, right on the grounds. My house is around that curve."

"You live in the cemetery?"

"Better than on the streets. This has been my home with my dad the last ten years after he lost our house to foreclosure. He died of heart failure three years ago. Since his death, I've lived alone." Peter coughed and composed himself. "Ed Favor and his wife, Helen, are third generation owners of this cemetery. His great-grandfather opened it in the 1800s. They've taken me in. My dad worked for him for over twenty years. Good people. By the way, there are some cool graves here."

"No thanks, I'm not a cemetery-kind of girl."

"I suppose it creeps people out, but I have my dad on the other side and mom over there. I get to visit with them every day."

Amanda shifted on her feet. She couldn't stop staring at Peter. There were so many questions. She wanted to know more about Louise. "What did you mean by 'when I'd come'?"

Peter looked up toward the stars and then back at her. "Mom was a pretty honest person, always said what was on her mind. When I was younger I used to question her about why I was an only child. One time, I can't remember the conversation exactly, she mentioned having more children. Later when she got sick with the cancer, Mom told me the whole story about you and Joshua leaving her."

Putting her hands on her hips, Amanda grew defensive. "Did she tell you why we left? It wasn't of our own accord. I was fourteen! She practically abandoned us! She didn't even go to Joshua's high school graduation."

Peter said, "Hold up a minute. She told me it was her fault, and she tried to be a good mom to me. Humans do err and we fall back to our own demise."

"Sheez, you sound just like Josh."

"Goes to show you, genes go a long way."

Amanda remembered her own battles with alcohol and addictive foods. "Was she sorry at least?"

"Up until her last day, she always hoped you and Josh might find her again and forgive her."

There it was again. *Forgiveness.*

"Joshua told me he visited Mom and he forgave her."

Peter shrugged, "Really? I don't know anything about that. Then, you're the one I'm supposed to be waiting for."

This is very strange. Gosh, it's pitch-black out already.

"You drink coffee?"

"Used to, herbal tea is my drink of choice now."

"I have plenty of that. Want a cup?"

What am I doing? I've seen the grave, Josh. Ah, okay. I guess I'm going to do this. Hesitantly, Amanda accepted. Peter directed her; together they retrieved her belongings and trekked to his home.

Chapter 42

The property was surrounded by a black-chained-link fencing. Peter's home was once a large woodshed that contained lawn mowers and snow removal equipment. The structure was rebuilt complete with dark-blue vinyl siding and a black oak door. A septic tank was situated directly behind the house across from a small patio.

From the front door, Amanda made a slight turn and entered a den area. A large-screen TV with surround-sound and video display occupied one side of the room. Across from there was a brown-leather two-seater couch. The den connected to the kitchen, a small round table occupied most of the area. Peter had black and white appliances mixed in with a small set of natural oak cabinetry. A short hallway off the kitchen led to a bathroom and two bedrooms. The place smelled of aftershave and sweaty socks. It was homey, masculine and orderly. She estimated it to be no more than twelve hundred square feet of living space.

Peter explained that ten years earlier, Ed Favor, the owner, had asked Jacob, his dad, to remodel the shed and turn it into a house. Ed's nephew was moving from New Hampshire to work with Jacob on the cemetery grounds. Carpenter by trade, Jacob rebuilt the inside to include a kitchen area, a den, two modest-sized bedrooms and one full-bath. When Ed's nephew's circumstances changed, the man never moved in, the home stood empty for seven months. Due to financial issues and losing their home, Ed bequeathed the shed to Jacob and Louise.

While her brother got the kettle going, Amanda went to look at two pictures hanging on the wall in the hallway. One was a picture of Louise, an old picture before she had any children. She sported a light teal dress with a gold sash across her waist. *I remember that picture. It was on our coffee table when Dad was alive.* Louise's hair was in an Updo. Her skin was creaseless and her eyes were alive and bright. The second picture was a picture of a man, a younger version of Peter, and Peter around six or seven-years-old. The two looked identical, with fair skin, light eyes and wavy brown hair.

Peter joined her. "Gosh, I remember taking that picture. Dad wanted to do a father and son photo shoot. I'm so embarrassed."

"It's cute."

"Mom looked great, didn't she? She liked taking pictures of others but she was never in pictures herself. We found this in one of her boxes she'd packed up in the attic. I wish I'd known her when she looked like that."

"She was so vibrant. I wish she could have stayed that way. My father's death changed her."

The kettle whistled and they returned to the kitchen. Peter poured hot water into two mugs and set them on the table next to a plate of lemon cookies. They sat across from one another.

"I have to apologize; I thought I had tea bags. I must have run out. I'm sorry. Hot water is all I have."

"It's fine, really." *My head is exploding with this new revelation of a half-brother. I have to know more.* "Can I ask you something because it's weighing on my heart?"

"Shoot."

"How old are you, anyway?"

Peter took a sip of his water, "I turned twenty-five on July 7th."

What if? "Did you ever live at the Grand Heritage Trailer Park?"

"Why do you want to know?"

"Twelve years ago, I visited Mom. You said you rode a bike. Did you have one when you were younger?"

The man leaned forward, "What are you getting at?"

Amanda massaged her temples, remembering the ride to the trailer park. *Coincidental? It just can't be?* She took a sip of hot water, "Was it a black and yellow racer?"

"I had one like that, how did you know?"

"I took a taxi and saw our mother standing on the steps, and you— oh, my goodness! That was you riding your bike."

Peter placed his hands over his head. "Huh, I think I remember that. It was weird seeing a cab sitting there with its engine running, not picking anyone up."

"That was me. I left soon after."

"Why did you leave?"

Because that wasn't my mother. "I don't know, I was afraid."

Peter rested over his chair. "I wish you'd have stopped in. Who knows how things would have turned out?"

A burning ache coursed through her stomach as Amanda pondered her brother's statement. She hated regrets. This one was difficult to take in stride. Uncomfortable with this reality, she changed the subject. Avoidance of the current situation was what she was good at doing. "Do you miss Mom and your dad?"

"You bet. I envy people that still have their parents around. Sure, I'm an adult. One day I'd like to meet a girl and get married. What breaks me up is the fact that I won't have parents to experience my wedding because they're gone."

Amanda's eyes watered. *That's what happened to me. Mom wasn't around for my wedding or the birth of Emily and Rose.* She realized she'd spent most of her adult life hating the woman who brought her into this world. She hoped her girls would never hate her like that. She was sorry, but also glad she'd met Peter. It was past eight-thirty. *Oh, no! I'm supposed to check in at the motel and I have to call Ryan.* Her train was leaving at eleven-thirty the next morning. Feeling a wee bit awkward, she got up and placed her mug in the sink.

"It's getting late, I should go."

Peter coughed, "What? Where are you going?"

"I don't want to inconvenience you anymore than I already have plus I have a reservation at a motel near the train station."

"Inconvenience me? Give me a break. Can you cancel your reservation and stay here with me?"

Amanda went over to Peter, "Stay here?" *I hardly know this man but I feel a strong kinship toward him, like I've known him all my life.*

"Yes, stay here *please, you're* my only family. I want to know more about you." A tear rolled down his cheek.

"You have someplace for me to sleep? Otherwise, I have to go. I leave for Chicago in the morning."

Peter poked her in the arm. "I have a guest room but I've never had a guest stay in it. You'll be my first."

What are the chances of me meeting my half-brother? She'd spent the last twelve years in denial, until that Memorial Day parade. *Could this be a chance for me to get the closure I need to kick my dependency on alcohol? I should stay and find out more about my mother.* "Thank you. I'm honored. Give me a few minutes; I have to call my husband. Can I use one of your rooms for a little privacy?"

"Sure, the second room on the right."

"Thanks." She excused herself, entered the room and turned on the light. "Hi there," she whispered when the line clicked through.

"Amanda?" Ryan blurted.

Sensing his impatience, Amanda said, "I'm leaving tomorrow mid-morning from here. I'll arrive in Chicago before five. I have so much to tell you. Guess what?"

"Gee, what is it this time?"

She took a deep breath before answering, "I found out I have a younger half-brother. He's only twenty-five."

"Say again?"

Amanda paced back-and-forth in front of the mirror. "I rode the train to Mount Pleasant to visit my mom's grave and I met Peter, that's his name. He works at the cemetery. He has pictures of my mom and—"

"Whoa, are you kidding me? How did you find out she died? This is unreal, Amanda. I was ready to punch the wall when I read your text."

She bounced on the heels of her sneakers. "I'm so sorry, Ryan."

"This Peter guy, you are with him now? He's really your half-brother and not just some whack job?"

"Yes, he lives on the cemetery grounds." She laughed at her husband's accusation. She felt so giddy like she'd just opened a chest full of toys. "And no, he's not crazy. He's got a portrait of my mother hanging in his hallway. It used to be in our house when I was growing up."

"Right, living in a cemetery, huh?"

Amanda felt ecstatic. "I'll tell you more later. Forget me. What happened at the tournament in the Dells? How is Emily?"

"It was terrific," Ryan responded with an edge. "Your daughter placed second. She was awesome." His voice grew soft, "You missed a great tournament. The next one is in October in St. Louis."

She studied her reflection in the mirror. *Emily's first competition!* Choking up, Amanda replied, "Please, please tell her I'm so sorry. I won't miss the next one, I promise."

"You better not. Come home. No dilly-dallying. Be careful."

"I will. Thank you. Give the girls hugs for me. Love you. Talk soon."

I have so much to explain and actions to make up to them. Oh God, if you're up there, help me to be strong. Make it right. Canceling the motel room and futzing with her hair, she walked out of the room.

A half-brother? Who lives on a freaking cemetery, anyway? My wife went from being an only child with deceased parents, to living with a drunken mother who abandoned her children, to taking care of a sick older brother discharged from the military, to having a half-brother who lives in a cemetery. This is bizarre.

Putting the receiver down, Ryan entered the kitchen. There on the counter was Emily's second-place gold statue. He picked it up. She'd done such a great job; he couldn't believe how well his eldest danced. In the three years that his daughter was in dance class, he never attended any of her practices or quarterly events. Amanda took care of all those things, attending them without him because he was busy working. *I have tried hard to be successful, but to what end; I've missed so much, until now.*

Massaging his brow, Ryan felt the fatigue of the day. *A night cap sounds great.* Putting the trophy back on the counter, he opened one of the cabinets searching for his Scotch. *Shit.* He remembered he'd dumped all the liquor down the drain.

He chuckled. *This is a good experience for me. If I hadn't been working all the time, Amanda wouldn't be where she is.* Ryan heard crying coming from one of the bedrooms upstairs. *It must be Rose.* "I'm coming," he muttered, taking two steps at a time.

Amanda found her brother in the den. He was sitting down, adjusting his cane on the side of the couch. "So, what have you been up to all these years?"

"Gosh, where do I start?" She sat next to him and took her sneakers off, recounting her life with Ryan, Emily and Rose, her alcohol addictions and the current journey she was on. Peter shifted his attention on her, expressing his sympathy and admiration for her courage. When she was finished, her mouth was dry. "You don't happen to have any cold water, do you?"

"I do." Peter inched his way off the couch and fetched a glass from the fridge. "Sounds like you have learned a lot about yourself. Your family will appreciate the new you, I'm sure."

Amanda took a large gulp of water. "I hope so. I've been gone a month, renewing and refueling myself. I miss my family."

"I'd miss them too, if I had what you had."

Amanda got up and grabbed her purse from the kitchen counter. When she came back, she showed Peter two pictures: one was just of the girls, and the other was their family picture together.

"What a beautiful family."

Amanda stuffed the photographs in her purse. "They're your family now, too. You have two nieces and a brother-in-law."

They were silent until Peter said, "Tell me about Joshua."

Folding her arms over her chest and closing her eyes, she smiled, "Joshua was my guardian angel. He took care for me. There was nothing he couldn't do. He was a marine. Even when he was in stationed in Germany, he'd call and check on me and had the rent paid months and months ahead of time. Unfortunately, he died way before his time. I miss him terribly."

"What did he die from?"

"Leukemia."

"What a shame."

"It is a shame. Ever since he passed, I've been very diligent, getting my yearly checkups and blood tests done. You never know, right?"

"I know what you mean. I wish I'd had a chance to meet him."

"You two look a lot alike."

The phone jingled. Startled, Peter leaped from the couch but fell back.

Amanda rose to help, "What's wrong?"

He winced, "This darn leg, it gives me pain from time to time. I'll be okay." Peter hobbled to the kitchen. It was Ed, making sure Amanda was off the property. She could hear him reassuring the old gentleman that everything was fine and that he had the man's flashlight.

Limping back, her brother had a wide smile across his face. "I have a surprise for you." With that, he shuffled through the short hall and brought out a box marked *old things*.

Sinking slowly to the floor, he lifted the lid off the box. Inside, were photos of Amanda and Joshua from when they were babies and up through their teenage years. Astonished, she joined him and together they scoured through dozens of pictures.

Picking up different pictures she held them next to Peter. "Yep, you two look so much alike."

"See," he grinned, "I've been waiting for this day. Mom shared these photos with me and promised one day we'd connect again. She was right. One day, I will meet the grown-up Joshua, and reunite with Mom and Dad."

Amanda searched through pictures of her and Joshua, pictures of their mother when she was young. She realized her brother and Louise were up in Heaven conspiring, waiting for this great meeting to occur. They continued going through the photos and reminiscing about their youth.

Later, a little chime sounded in the background, "What's that?"

Peter started coughing erratically. "It's my clock in my bedroom."

"Are you okay?"

Peter waved her off, coughing harder. "It rings every three hours. It must be eleven. Excuse me a moment."

He staggered to his feet still coughing, as blood trickled from his lips and dripped onto the carpet.

Amanda rose to her feet. "Oh my, are you alright?"

"I'm fine, don't worry." He pushed her away and tottered off.

Amanda grabbed a napkin, and after putting water on it, went to dab the beige carpet to get the blood out.

When Peter returned, he looked himself again. "Sorry, I have allergies. I have spot remover somewhere."

Amanda was unsure what to say next. She stretched and glanced at her watch. Her brother was right. It was eleven. Time had flown by. She yawned. "We should get some sleep."

"Of course."

Amanda looked at him closely, something was off. "Oh no! Your nose is bleeding."

Peter touched his nose as he entered the kitchen to retrieve another napkin.

"What's happening?" she asked, following him.

"No big deal." He twisted a piece of napkin and stuck it up one nostril.

"Is it better?"

"Yes, thanks."

"Have you eaten?"

"I have. Quit it."

Amanda wasn't satisfied with his answer. She'd been there a few hours. She saw him drink only hot water. *That was it! He hadn't even munched on his tea cookies.*

Looking over to the couch the pictures were still strewn on the floor, Amanda went to put them in the box.

"What are you doing? I'll get them."

"It's fine. I'm already here." After filling the box up she set them in a corner and rearranged the pillows on the couch.

Amanda went back into the kitchen, thinking of her next move. *This feels good, being with Peter. I have more family. This might be a long shot, but what if I asked him to accompany me to Chicago? He could meet the family. It'll reinforce my commitment to start new without liquor. Will he go for it? I have to ask. This is impulsive.* "Do you have any time off?"

Peter pulled the napkin out of his nose. "What do you mean?"

This is crazy, but I'm taking a leap here. "I was wondering if you had any vacation time, maybe you'd want to come to Chicago and meet the family."

A smile spread across Peter's face, "Really, I thought you'd never ask."

Chapter 43

Amanda awoke and stretched to the whistling of the tea kettle. The second bedroom was surrounded in maple-colored paneling and a dark shade covering an oval window over the twin-sized bed she slept in.

Rubbing her eyes, she searched the room looking for a clock, but found none. Getting up, Amanda grabbed a robe from her bag and opened the door. Walking into the kitchen she saw Peter dragging his leg as he prepared a breakfast for her, rice crispy cereal with a banana, a cup of hot water and two pieces of white toast.

"How thoughtful. Thank you. How's the leg pain?"

Peter leaned on the chair opposite his sister. "Forget about that, it will go away. You're welcome. Come on," he waved, "sit down and eat."

"What are you having?"

"I'm good. I ate already." He pulled out a chair.

Scooting in she looked for a clock, "What time is it anyway?"

"A little past eight."

"Call the station and see if there are seats available to Chicago."

Peter watched her. "Done, I've already reserved my seat."

"Awesome," Amanda said between bites. She saw a small knapsack on the floor near the den. "What's in there?"

"My things, what else?"

"What can you carry in that? It's so small."

"It's all I have. I'm a pretty simple guy."

Amanda stopped eating, taking in the kitchen again. There weren't any pots or pans lying around, no plants of any sort and she didn't remember seeing cereal boxes anywhere. The kitchen was bare and so was the rest of the house. Going to the sink, Amanda discovered there were no dirty dishes. She turned and faced him. "Peter, did you really eat?"

"Yes but that's for you."

"You're already so thin. Please, have some."

Peter stood up, "You're my guest."

Sitting again, she took a bite of her plain toast. *Needs butter.* Amanda went to the refrigerator and opened the door. Inside she only found a chunk of cheese, one egg, and a small carton of half-and-half which he'd used for her cereal. "Where's your butter?"

"I don't have any."

"Peter, you hardly have anything in here."

"What can I say? Bachelor's life."

"Do you eat? Ever?"

"Of course, mostly out. Not a cook per se. Boiling water is my forte`."

Unconvinced, but not willing to pry further, Amanda sat back down. "Have you told your boss you're taking a few days off?"

"Ed is good with it."

"Will he watch the house while you're gone?"

"Yes, it's Ed Favor's house anyway. The twin bed you slept on and the blankets, my clothes and the pictures are mine. Like I said before, it's a home and it is sufficient for me."

Amanda had no idea her brother didn't own the house or that some of the furniture wasn't his, either. She wondered if he had any money. She hoped they could talk about his financial situation on the train. Losing her appetite, she washed her dishes and went to her room to get ready.

Amanda heard Peter coughing again. He had gone outside. She peeked through the window. She reminded herself to get cough syrup at the station, but her thoughts were interrupted by him calling her. A cab had arrived to take them to the station.

They got to the station before ten-forty-five. Peter got his ticket and they sat side-by-side awkwardly waiting to board. They hardly spoke on the way over. *Was this a good idea for him to tag along? It might help break the ice, with me being gone for so long.*

As if reading her mind, he asked, "Are you sure your family will accept me? Your husband might kill me."

Amanda giggled, "No, he'd kill me first." *This isn't the first time I've surprised him. Oh, shoot, I should have texted Ryan to tell him I'm on my way.*

Peter smiled, "If you say so."

She patted his good leg. "No worries."

They boarded the train, found their seats and settled in. For the second time in Amanda's life, she was leaving Mount Pleasant, Iowa. For as much as she had learned about Louise's resting place, she didn't want to return to this small town. *Not ever.* Thrilled by meeting Peter, Amanda sensed her journey was coming to an end. Soon she'd be home again with her family and they'd start over. *A second chance to do it right this time. No drinking.*

It was gorgeous out, the sun was shining. Looking through the window as the train travelled out of the station, Amanda observed a cloudless sky. Questions consumed her, thoughts of Louise. Turning, she asked, "What kind of cancer did Mom have again?"

Peter crossed his arms. "Liver cancer, she smoked like a chimney, but her main addiction was drinking. She even told me she smoked and drank while carrying me. Heck, I still came out okay."

Amanda squeezed her eyes in disfavor. She remembered, it was several months after her father passed that Louise began smoking. At first, it was here and there with an occasional drink, but when she started having men staying overnight at the house, it became constant. To this day, the stench of cigarettes made Amanda's stomach turn.

"It was a bad habit of hers," Peter commented, "my dad tried getting her to quit but she wouldn't give up cigarettes or alcohol, even when she was so sick at the end."

"I will admit to acquiring one of her appalling habits. I've been battling alcohol addiction for a long time. But I believe I've finally broken the cycle. A burdensome weight has been lifted from my shoulders and I'm finally feeling free."

Her brother nudged her. "That's wonderful news. I don't drink. Dad did in the beginning, before he had problems with his kidney and pancreas. He once admitted he could chug an eighteen-pack in three hours. He was a heavy drinker."

"Wow."

"Mom loved hard liquor, Bacardi, Jack Daniels, and Wild Turkey."

"I remember her drinking them."

Peter hung his head. "We had our share of tough years. Not as hard as when she was diagnosed with cancer. It spread so fast. She lasted less than a year from start to finish."

"It was like that with Josh, too."

"I'm sorry."

Amanda studied him. His skin was white, no sunburn or tan. *Two family members have died from this terrible disease. What are the odds of me or Peter being diagnosed with it?* Her brother caught her staring, "What?"

Should I ask him about his health? "You have your physicals done regularly, right? I mean, with Joshua and our mom, and I suppose with your dad's history?"

Peter rolled his eyes. "Well that's a stupid question. Of course I do." There was a quiet time between them, and it became awkward again. The train coasted along.

Another memory sprang to Amanda's head. She recalled the times her mother read books to her, the trips to the park, playing in the bathtub. They were good times. *Did Peter have the same experiences?* "What are some of your fondest memories of Mom?"

Peter relaxed, "When she was sober she was a bitch, cranky and irritable. But when she had liquor in her, she was a superstar. We had a lot of fun then. She loved to be outside. We'd get the hose and she'd run around me with it. We went to the zoo a lot, took long walks in forest preserves."

"Mom liked to be outdoors. She read a lot of books outside."

Peter made an O with his mouth. "Mom read? I never saw her pick up a book. She read stupid gossip magazines. What kind of books did she read?"

"They were thick books with pictures of half-naked men on the cover, you know, romance novels."

"Huh, I learned something about our Mom today."

"Me too, ever been to Chicago?"

"Never, you might say I'm a small town kind of guy." He grinned, "I do love the Cubs though."

She cringed, "Yuck."

"What?" Peter gawked, "You don't like the Cubs?"

"We're a White Sox family." Shrugging, Amanda added, "You and Ryan are going to butt heads for sure."

He puffed out his chest. "I can handle it. I'm a big boy." They both laughed.

"I think you'll like Chicago. We live in the burbs, so it's not so exciting."

"I can't see how living in the burbs with two cute daughters could be anything but boring."

Amanda snorted, "Eh, you're right, my days are never boring."

It had been an hour into the ride, Amanda and Peter agreed that the rhythmic movement of the train was making them sleepy. They decided to take a catnap and resume discussions later. Before Amanda closed her eyes, she checked her phone. There was a text from Ryan asking her to call him. *What will Ryan think of Peter? This is like a dream. From Gretchen, to Harvey, to Joshua in the flesh!*

She texted Ryan from the train. … On the way, I'll call you when I arrive at Union Station. … Peter is with me. … Gonna stay with us for a few days. Wants to meet you and the girls. … I love you.

Laying her head back, she soon dozed off, her mind overloaded. When Amanda awoke afterwards, Peter wasn't seated next to her. His jacket was on the chair but he was nowhere to be found. She scanned the aisle. The entire cabin was full of passengers. *Maybe he went to the restroom. I hope he's okay.*

Glancing out the window, fields of corn, soybeans, and wheat in full season were flying by. Her heart ached, Emily and Rose loved farms. Soon enough, Amanda spotted Peter hobbling through the cabin with his cane; she waved and picked up her brother's jacket to move it. A prescription bottle fell from his pocket onto the floor. Bending over to avoid letting the bottle roll, she snatched it. It was for Vicodin. Frantically, Amanda jammed it back into Peter's pocket. He was carrying two paper bags.

"What's in there?"

"I was hungry so I bought some candy. I know you can't have gum or candy, so I bought you a bag of mixed nuts and dried cranberries."

"That was sweet of you."

Peter gave Amanda her bag as he opened his own snack. She watched him. First, her brother crunched all the chips, then he sucked on several sour candies, and lastly he devoured a foot-long candy bar, all within a few minutes. The way Peter was eating wasn't like someone who had a full breakfast a couple of hours before. *I bet he didn't even eat. He was pretty slim for a guy over six feet. Why is he taking Vicodin, for his leg? They are addictive pain killers.*

Amanda pondered whether she should ask him about them. *It's none of my business.* She opened her bag and munched on her snacks.

"How long have you been married to Ryan?"

"On November tenth it will be twelve years."

"Congratulations, tell me your story?"

Amanda loved answering that question because Ryan couldn't have come into her life any sooner. She'd dated many guys, but none were as warm, loving and patient as Ryan. He had put up with a lot from her. Being away for so long, she questioned their marriage's future success, even her relationship with her daughters. She had let them down but was determined not to do it again. "You want the long story or the short concise one?"

"Whichever one you want to tell me."

Okay, I'll answer his question and then I need to talk to him. "I'll give you the short version. Let's see, it was a few months after Joshua passed, living back in Chicago, after the trailer incident; I was working temporarily as a waitress at an organic eatery. Ryan and his buddies from the investment firm came in one morning for breakfast and honestly," Amanda blushed, "I think I fell in love with him that day."

Peter lightly punched her in the arm. "Come on? Are you pulling my *good* leg?"

Amanda giggled, "No, I think I did. We ogled each other the whole time I served them their food. I was awestruck by him. Not to mention, he was kind. They left a generous tip." Smiling, she continued, "The next day he came by again, alone, and again, until the third day when he asked me out and we started dating."

"Sounds like a dream romance."

Amanda crumpled her empty bag. "I was lonely without Joshua, Ryan rescued me. We married six months later."

Peter finished his snacks and took Amanda's empty bag. "Thank you for sharing." He got up and threw them in the trash. Rummaging through his jacket, he pulled out his prescription bottle and popped a pill.

Amanda braced herself, but knew she had to broach the question carefully, "Why are you taking Vicodin?"

Peter bore into her, "Who told you it was Vicodin?"

"I read the label."

"What the hell are you doing looking through my jacket?"

Amanda sensed some defensiveness in her brother's voice. "The bottle fell on the floor when I moved your jacket. Sorry, I didn't mean to peek."

Peter softened, "Never mind, I get these pains in my leg, they can be unbearable."

She looked him over, "Have you considered physical therapy? Or surgery."

"I don't have insurance and I can't afford therapy, let alone surgery."

Amanda crossed her arms, "How do you get prescription medication without insurance?"

"A friend of mine works at a pharmacy. He made the phony label."

"That's not good. Vicodin is addictive."

"I've been on it a little while, and no, I'm not addicted." He waved her off, starting to cough again, "it helps with the pain." Amanda cursed herself. "What is it?" Peter coughed.

"I forgot to get you cough syrup."

His cough quieted, "I had some at home before we left, doing better as a matter of fact."

Amanda wanted to know more about his work at the cemetery but was interrupted by an announcement; they would be arriving at Union Station in less than a half-hour. Peter collected his jacket, sat in his seat and closed his eyes.

Amanda stared out the window again. *I'm not the only one with issues and pains.* She'd been able to remove a lot of junk from her life. It was important for her to try to help Peter do the same.

Twenty minutes later the Amtrak entered Union Station. Even before the train stopped, Peter was standing and opening the overhead to grab her luggage and his knapsack. Amanda leaned over, "Take a seat; you're going to fall over."

Peter flopped down in the seat, bumping his leg against his cane. He swore under his breath. "Are you hurt?"

He grimaced. "Peachy."

Inside the station, Amanda approached a Garrett popcorn stand; the smell of fresh popped corn reminded her of movie nights with her daughters. She stopped, "Do you mind if I get popcorn for my girls?"

Peter shook his head, "Give me your stuff and I'll hail a cab."

She bought two small bags of popcorn, cheddar cheese and the Chicago mix, and cheddar cheese mixed with caramel popcorn.

Hurrying toward the exit door, her phone buzzed. "Amanda?" It was Ryan.

"Yes, I've arrived a bit ago."

She heard her husband sigh through the line. "I'm glad you're in town finally, let me pick you up."

"Peter is getting a cab. Hey, I also bought some of the famous Garrett popcorn."

"Yum. What time do you think you'll get here? Should I cook pasta or order pizza?"

"Pizza sounds good, order from Nick and Vito's."

"Okay."

"I'll call you fifteen minutes out."

"Sounds good."

She hung up just as Peter approached her. "Thought you were getting us a cab?"

He coughed again. "It's out there, waiting, a yellow cab number 237."

His nose started bleeding again. "Oh no! Here." Amanda handed him a tissue from her purse.

As he wiped the blood off, he said, "Thanks, let me go to the men's room and get this taken care of. I'll be right out."

I'm so excited. We are going to have a family reunion. Finally, good stuff happening. Overwhelmed with joy, Amanda stared into her brother's eyes. "I'm so glad you're here with me. Thank you for coming along." She thought of the Veteran's Memorial building where the military had put a plaque for her brother. It had been years since she'd visited. *I should take Peter there since we are downtown.* "There's a special place, I want to stop by before we go home." Her brother's face grew pale.

Amanda laughed. "Don't worry, you can trust me."

He wiped his nose again. Balancing with his cane, Peter headed to the restroom. "Sure, let me clean up. I'll meet you at the cab."

A soft breeze was coming off Lake Michigan. She crossed Dearborn and hopped in the cab. She noted the traffic on the street.

It's so busy. What if his nose is still bleeding? He's going to have to walk across this traffic-laden street again? I should go and get him. Amanda told the driver to wait and ran across to the station.

Once inside, she marched toward the men's bathroom when she heard someone screaming for help. A crowd had gathered, two teenagers came scurrying out, one vomiting and the other looking distraught.

"Help, we need help! There's a guy shaking on the floor." Fear washed over Amanda. She ran inside and saw her brother on the floor. Blood was spurting from his mouth and his body was wracked with spasms.

"Peter, Peter, what's wrong? Help, someone, help!" She blubbered. *Why is he shaking like this? Is he having a seizure?*

His eyes fluttered, he exhaled softly and then his body went limp. "Peter!"

The paramedics arrived, attempting to resuscitate Peter, but it was too late. While the medics put her brother on a stretcher, everything around Amanda seemed to move in slow motion.

An hour later, Amanda was sitting in the waiting area of the emergency room at the county hospital in downtown Chicago. Her phone buzzed several times, but she couldn't answer it. Shock consumed her whole being. She had known Peter for twenty-four hours, had learned something about him and her mother, and had planned on showing him Joshua's military plaque at the *Veterans Memorial Building.*

A doctor approached her, "Mrs. Reynolds?"

Amanda stumbled out of the chair, "Yes."

"I'm Dr. Burns, walk with me, will you?" They were silent until they reached the hospital morgue. "Mr. Mitchell suffered a seizure. You said he was taking Vicodin, is that correct?"

"Yes, he told me he was taking it for his leg pain. That's all I know. Like I told the paramedics, we just reconnected yesterday."

"You didn't know that Peter was terminally ill, either?"

Amanda's mouth opened, "Impossible."

"We found a medical ID card in his wallet. He had cancer. We contacted his doctor in Mount Pleasant, they've confirmed it. He also had a number in there for his legal guardians, Ed and Helen Favor. We contacted them as well."

"What did they say?"

"They confirmed his illness. They said Peter wished to be buried at Riverdale Saints Cemetery."

Amanda felt dizzy. *He said he was healthy.* "What happens next?"

The doctor flipped his chart open, "We need a release from you. His body will be transported to Iowa in the morning."

"And his things?"

"You may take them if you like."

"Thank you, do you have the number for the Favor family?" With stiff fingers, Amanda signed her name on the release form. *Why do I feel like I've gone back in time, first Joshua, now Peter?*

The man scribbled numbers on a sticky. "I'm sorry for your loss, here's their number."

"Yeah, um, can I see him?"

"Yes, of course."

The doctor escorted her to ROOM 3. A nurse uncovered the sheet from Peter's face and waited outside the door as she viewed the body.

The room smelled like bleach and other heavy-duty disinfectants. Even with his eyes closed Peter's features reminded her of Joshua, except Peter had a full head of hair and Josh's had fallen out due to the chemo. There were still a lot of questions she wanted answered, but Amanda knew she'd never get that opportunity. She touched his face and blew him a kiss. "You're with Momma, your dad and our big brother. I'm so glad we met even for a short time, Peter Mitchell."

Chapter 44

Amanda sat on the curb. She needed to make a couple of calls: to her husband and then to Ed Favor, owner of the cemetery. Ryan barked, "I've been calling! Tell me you're fifteen minutes out?"

"Not exactly," Amanda stuttered, "something serious has come up."

"Right," he growled.

"No, this isn't a joke." She held back tears, swallowing hard, "Peter is dead." There was a long pause through the line. Amanda sniveled, "Just before we were going to get into a cab, he … he had a seizure at the train station."

"Oh my God! I'm sorry, Amanda."

"He had terminal cancer. I had no clue, Ryan. This is devastating."

"What the hell, honey?"

She was sobbing, "It's crazy. My mother had cancer, Joshua had cancer and now Peter. Am I next?"

His voice softened. "Don't say that, please. Jesus, this has been quite a rehab experience for you."

"Tell me about it," Amanda whispered.

"Where are you?"

"Cook County Hospital."

"It's not safe there."

"I know it's not a safe neighborhood, but he had no insurance."

"Don't move, I'm coming to get you."

"No, stay with the girls please." A few people passed Amanda as she hugged her short-sleeve covered arms.

"Stop being ridiculous, what are they going to do with Peter?"

"They're transporting him to Iowa. He has guardians there."

"Enough already let me come get you."

"No."

"Why not?"

The years had come and gone and she'd never visited the *Veterans Memorial Building* even though she had memorized the address and promised herself she'd go someday. This was the one place she'd never wanted to see, until now. *It popped into my head with Peter; I will never know what triggered it. If this is where I need to be, then so be it. I must fulfill this one last small piece of my recovery.* Amanda straightened, "Because I have to make a stop. Last one, honey."

Her husband sighed, "Come home, for God's sake."

"This is important for my closure." The line went quiet. "Ryan? I'm sorry to have put you through this. I'm a hot mess right now. I couldn't have done it without your support."

"Yes—"

"Trust me please, I gotta go." Amanda clicked off before she had to explain further. She hated to be so abrupt with him, but she had to finish what she'd started.

Reaching into her purse, she withdrew Ed Favor's number. *What should I say to him?* Sorry seemed so cliché. A tear slipped down her cheek. Amanda wanted to scream with weariness and pain. In her thirty-six years, she had witnessed the passing of both siblings. *Why me?*

"Damnit! Damn you, Joshua! Damn you, Peter! Damn you, Mother! Damn you, Father!" Her entire family was gone. *I need a drink. I need a drink! Breathe, breathe.* A car drove by and Amanda imagined what the driver might be thinking seeing a woman shaking her fists at the sky. Grabbing a tissue, she wiped her eyes and plopped to the ground, tapping the numbers on her cell.

A scratchy voice came through the line, "Ed Favor here."

"Hello, this is Amanda Reynolds."

"We were expecting your call."

Her lips quivered, "I'm so sorry, Mr. Favor. I don't know what else to say."

"Thank you. There are no words."

"The doctor informed me they were taking Peter's body to Iowa tomorrow."

"Yes."

"Mr. Favor, can I ask you a question?"

"Feel free."

"How long did he have?"

"Well ..." As the man recounted the facts, Amanda listened with her head hung low. Peter had been terminal for months. His body was deteriorating fast, he couldn't do any work or travel. It was just a matter of time. Mr. Favor had begged him to not go with her when he talked to him in the morning, but the young man wouldn't listen. Peter told Ed he was so happy to finally meet his sister. The older gentleman started crying and Amanda joined in his sorrow. They stayed on the phone for a few minutes, weeping.

"Peter had pictures of our family. May I have them?"

"I can mail them to you."

"Thank you." Amanda shared her address with him.

"It's the least we can do."

She wiped her eyes, "Where will he be buried?"

"He picked a plot next to his mother."

"I see."

"This is where he lived and worked. This was his *home*."

Amanda wanted to say more, anything to express her grief, but no words came out. Ed asked if she wanted to attend the service with them, Amanda declined. She'd already paid her respects in the hospital morgue. She didn't feel comfortable going back to Mount Pleasant again. That was for the Favors, they had known him longer. She wished him well. Ed assured her she'd have the pictures in a few days and they ended the call.

From the curb, Amanda stared a while at the cars in the hospital parking lot, when she remembered Peter's knapsack lying next to her.

Taking it and putting it on her lap, she carefully unzipped it. Inside were a pair of jeans, a red short-sleeve t-shirt, a couple of pairs of boxer shorts, two pairs of black socks, a shaver, deodorant, toothpaste and toothbrush and a Ziploc bag containing prescription pills. As she perused the contents, Amanda couldn't imagine living so simply. She chuckled, recalling Peter saying he was a "Midwest kind of guy with an uncomplicated lifestyle." Her forefinger slid across something smooth but pointy at the bottom of the bag, "Ouch!"

It was an envelope, it had her name scribbled in pencil on the front. The wind started picking up, Amanda grabbed the bag and wandered into the hospital waiting area. Putting her things on the floor, she sat on a chair across from an elderly man. Opening the envelope, she took out two handwritten pieces of paper and began reading.

Dearest Amanda,

By the time you read this letter, you will know the full extent of my illness. First, I want to apologize for not being upfront with you. Seeing you filled my heart with the little joy I still have, and selfishly, I didn't want to ruin it. The cancer has been a blessing. Both my parents are gone and I have longed to be with them. There have been many years of sadness in my life, especially the years I watched them suffer.

I am thankful to Ed and Helen Favor for taking care of me all these years. They've done their best to fill a parentless void; but it has never been the same.

You coming here gave me a new hope for normalcy. God had other plans, right? He, at least, answered my prayers and I had the chance to meet you. I wish I could have met Joshua.

I'm sorry for the pain I've caused you. It was not my intent. I've been sick as of late and my doctors told me time was not on my side.

Amanda's eyes watered. Blinking to focus, she read the other sheet.

I want you to have the pictures. Call Ed, he'll gather them and ship them off to you. I don't own much, nor have I any extra money. Know that in the short time we've known one another; you've given me a special peace. I didn't want you to see or experience this, but this was meant to be.

Be strong, get healthy, live again. Don't miss the moments. Risk it all. It's worth it.

Love, Your Newfound Brother,

Peter

Grumbling with sadness, Amanda folded the pieces and stuffed them into the envelope. *He should have been upfront with his condition. Why did he agree to travel with me when he knew full well it might impact his health?* Amanda swore again and held her stomach, guarding it to calm her nerves. The elderly man across from her stirred and glared at her, "Sorry."

Forty-five minutes. That is all the time I have left. Inserting the envelope into the knapsack, Amanda collected her suitcase, her purse, Peter's things, the popcorn bags and raced out of the hospital to the curb, hailing a cab. *One more stop and I'm done.*

Chapter 45

"Michigan and Ohio, the Veterans Memorial Building, please," Amanda blurted, sliding into the car.

The cabby, a middle-aged man with wavy silver hair nodded and sped off. But soon they were caught in rush-hour traffic.

A nice glass of Vodka on the rocks would help me deal with the pain of losing another family member. But she couldn't and wouldn't do that. Her family depended on her getting better.

The cab was at a stoplight, two blocks shy of the building. Amanda's watch read 7:30. She huffed while staring out the window. "Can you hurry? The building closes in a half-hour."

"Doing my best, ma'am. Always bumper-to-bumper around this time."

The driver pressed on the gas and jumped a sidewalk causing the patrons to rush out of the way. "What the hell are you doing?" Amanda barked, holding on to the peeling reddish-purple leather seat.

The car made it to the front of the line at the light on Ohio and Michigan. As soon as the light changed, the driver made a U-turn into oncoming traffic. Half a block away, a car was leaving a space, the taxi glided in, then halted abruptly.

Amanda smoothed strands of hair out of her face. Her heart beat fast. Leaning over to pay the driver she noticed the meter was off. "Wait, what do I owe you?"

"Just get in there before they close."

"You saved me a ton of time even though you almost got us killed. Please ... let me pay you something."

The driver turned. He had a line-free face and sported a trim mustache. He was obviously older by the color of his hair but his face was youthful-looking. "Go."

She hesitated, "Um … Okay. Thanks."

"You're welcome, Amanda."

"What? How do you know my name?" *Have I seen him before?* She opened the car door.

"Jacob Mitchell." Amanda did a double-take. "Time's ticking away, Cinderella."

Oh, my! He was the spitting image of Peter's Dad? "Are you—?"

The man tapped his wrist again, "Ticking …"

Flabbergasted, Amanda hurried, carrying her luggage, Peter's bag, her purse and popcorn, waving to Jacob as his cab disappeared around the corner. Charging to the elevator, she pressed the sixth floor button. I hope it's the sixth floor.

When the elevator stopped and the doors opened, she spotted the reception desk, rushing to it. A middle-aged woman with bifocals, the ones with the lines on the lenses was sitting looking down at her wristwatch. Peering over her glasses she said, "Closing time soon. Perhaps you'd rather come back tomorrow?"

"I can't come tomorrow. I need to be here now." Amanda fumbled with a small sheet of paper, unfolding it to reveal a set of numbers, "Wall 27, section 41, space 21."

The woman, Kiera, moved her People Magazine out of the way and stared at her.

"Please, just give me five minutes."

Kiera pointed the way, "Down the hall, make a right, past a utility door, make another right, the wall is on your left side. We close at eight. You have less than ten minutes; I'm coming to get you if you're not back in time."

Amanda tapped the counter, "I appreciate it. Can I leave my things here?"

The woman nodded and Amanda scurried away holding her purse. *Turn right, turn right, wall on the left.* She was out of breath when she arrived at the appropriate section. Searching for her brother's name plate, Amanda located it a third of the way down from the ceiling. Neatly inscribed Memorial plates hung from the wall with the names of men and women lost in battle or due to an illness.

Ceiling to floor windows lined the corridors. It was dusk outside, and some of the city lights were coming on. She could see the traffic on Michigan Avenue. *I really hate traffic.* Collapsing on a bench against the window, she stared at the wall of names and focused on one, *Joshua Lenger.*

"I'm here. This is real to me, unlike your strange appearances." Amanda sighed. "This is where I wanted to take Peter, to see your name, to realize the sacrifice you gave for our country. Oh, my sweet big brother, I will always honor and cherish your love."

"Thank you."

Amanda glanced sideways. "Josh! It's really you!" Leaning over, she embraced him. He wore his Marine Corps dress blues, his head was shaved. Amanda felt his uniform. It was spotless and clean. Even his shoes were polished. She remembered when he'd get ready to go off for duty, how she enjoyed watching him iron his clothes and shine his black shoes.

"Hey, hey. Hi there," he squirmed out of her grasp. "Someone's finally happy to see me."

Amanda's shoulders sagged, "So much has happened."

Her brother nodded, "I know. I'm sorry, Sis."

"Thanks." She peered closely at him. "What's with the uniform?"

"You don't like it?"

"No. You look handsome."

Josh beamed, "Mom asked me to wear this for you."

Amanda scrunched her face. "Mom, huh? How is Mommy?"

"Happy that Peter is with her."

"Sounds like fun."

Joshua touched her nose, "Not your time, Sis. You have two beautiful girls at home who need a mom, a healthy mom. You also have a loving husband who adores you."

"I know, Ryan has been my 'Saint Francis of Assisi'."

Joshua drew her close. A sense of peace washed over her. The circle was coming to a close, the last line of one chapter and a new sentence in another.

"You've come almost full-circle. Your journey will end soon. Don't come here again. I thank you for the visit, but this isn't where I belong."

"What do you mean by 'full-circle'? I'm done. No more."

He cocked his head, "Don't fret. You've done what you were supposed to do."

"I feel like Scrooge. Anymore ghosts I'm going to meet?" She remembered Jacob. "You know the man who drove me here, Jacob? Is he Peter's—?" Joshua nodded his head. Of course he knew. He orchestrated it. An involuntary whimper escaped her lips. "Are … Are you letting me go?"

"I'm letting you be you. To follow through on what you've learned. I will always be with you whenever you need me."

"But if you're not there, who can I turn to?" Amanda said the words softly.

Joshua lifted her chin, "You have my pendant, right, the emerald green one with the cross?"

"Yes, why?" she nodded, pulling a small plastic bag from her purse.

Joshua took it, unzipped it and pulled the chain out. "Because when you need me or want to talk to me," he unclasped it and put it around her neck, "hold onto the pendant."

Hot tears filled her eyes. *This is goodbye.* Holding onto the necklace she smiled, "Sure but before you leave me, I do need clarification on something."

He grinned, "Shoot."

"Where have you been all this time? It's been years and now you've materialized several times this last month. I've been fighting my battle alone."

"For one, you finally called on me to help you."

Amanda shook her head, "I don't know what that means."

"During your AA rehab and all that you went through, you never asked for my help. I promised I would be there, maybe not in human form," Josh touched her arm, "but in prayer and thought."

"I tried fixing myself on my own."

Josh stood, "Do you know the Bible story about Joseph and his brothers?" She nodded. "If you recall, Joseph's brothers sold him into slavery, years later while in prison, he experienced these remarkable dreams and he was freed because he won the trust of the Pharaoh and then rose through the ranks to become second in command."

She grew impatient, "Okay, what does that have to do with me?"

Joshua held up his hand. "There was famine all over Egypt and the brothers came to Egypt to beg for food. This was about twenty-two years later. Here they were face-to-face with Joseph and they didn't even recognize him. The story goes that it took all those years for the brothers to reunite. It was all God's doing. Joseph wasn't mad at them anymore. He ended up forgiving his brothers for their transgressions."

Standing up, Amanda looked at her brother. *This damn forgiveness thing!* "I'm sorry for being mad at you for leaving."

"It's not me you have to forgive. But, I'll accept it anyway. Timing is everything. Trust it."

She then snapped her fingers. "Ah-ha, can you explain this? Remember that day at the apartment when you were yelling at me to eat and you said something about accepting but then a train passed by. I never heard the rest of your sentence. What did you say?"

Joshua inclined his head, "Alright, I like that question and I do remember. Listen to my answer carefully this time. I knew you were drinking. I was explaining how you needed to accept what was given to you and suffer a bit because in the end you'd prosper. It was God's plan. Everything that happened to you was meant to be."

Amanda closed her eyes. *To go through all this hurt. What a stinky way to experience a revelation.* She was committed to making a new path to fulfill God's fate for her life. Seeing her brother's physical presence made her feel alive again, like when he was with her. Amanda was happy to be given another chance to move forward. They sat back down. Her brother drew a little gray envelope from his picket, "Remember this?"

At first nothing came to her mind. "The lockbox key! Where did you find it? I had no idea, whatever happened to it?"

He patted her on the shoulder, "You dropped it when you boarded the train on your trip to Chicago years ago. You'll need it now."

"I don't want it, whatever it is. If you think I'm going back to Mount Pleasant, you have another thing coming."

"Don't worry, I've since moved it to a lockbox at the Schaumburg Post Office."

"Are you kidding? Oh, never mind." Amanda folded her arms across her chest. "What's it for?"

Josh sighed, "It was money for you to continue your college education, which you never finished. At this point, you can use it for yourself or the girls."

"How much?"

"Fifty thousand dollars."

What? Amanda jumped from her seat, "Are you insane? I'm not taking that."

Her brother shoved the envelope into her hand, "I made a promise to take care of you, even though I couldn't be there for the rest of your life. You need to take it now."

Holding the envelope, she was unable to utter a word. *I was the one who got careless, was self-centered, thinking he'd abandoned me.*

Joshua grinned, "Okay?"

"Wow. Thank you."

Shaking his head, her brother said, "I'm glad. Now, I have one more surprise for you."

She raised her eyebrows. "Another one? What surprise? Quit it. I can't take any more surprises."

"Close your eyes."

"I won't, Josh."

"Please."

Amanda closed them just as her brother's lips brushed her forehead. When her eyes fluttered open again, she was alone.

Chapter 46

Forever.

There was a clatter down the corridor. Amanda straightened up remembering the security guard promised to come and get her. Taking a tissue out of her purse, she wiped at the corners of her eyes, stood and tossed the tissue into a garbage basket.

Squinting, she noticed a figure coming into view. It wasn't the security guard; the thin woman wore a red and black short-sleeve sundress, similar to the one her mom had worn during the time she and Joshua were playing hide-and-seek between the sheets as their mother was hanging them on the line to dry. Amanda loved that dress even though Louise always claimed it was her chore dress. As the lady came closer, Amanda knew the woman to be in her mid-thirties. She had auburn hair and was wearing red lipstick. Her face glowed. Instantly Amanda's jaw dropped. She recognized her. *This can't be. Mom?*

The woman stopped directly in front of her. "Amanda, look how grown up you are."

"Momma, is that you?" Louise smiled.

Amanda was seven-years-old. She saw her Barbie display on the floor in the corner, a tape player with two stacks of tapes laying on a dresser and her pink robe hanging on the hook behind the door. She wore princess pajamas and was sprawled over a pastel green comforter.

Her mother sat on the edge of her bed telling her a story about a little boy and his pet dog, Skippy. This little boy loved his dog, the two of them went everywhere together. They were best of friends for a long time.

Tragedy struck, Skippy had gotten sick. He was so ill, it ultimately left him blind and unable to do things he and the boy used to do. The boy was angry so he started treating Skippy harshly, hitting him and verbally abusing him. One day the dog ran away.

At first the boy didn't care, but he soon became lonely, missing his blind dog. He made a promise to himself, if he got another dog he'd never treat him cruelly ever again. One day his parents brought another dog home. This time, the boy treated the new dog well, loving him and caring for him. Years later, the boy contracted meningitis and was in the hospital. His dog stayed at his side until he passed away.

Amanda remembered it had been a sad story but with two important lessons her mom taught her. "... *First, never treat anyone meanly. Nobody deserves that kind of abuse. Secondly, if you love with all your heart, you can leave this Earth knowing your efforts haven't gone unnoticed.*"

Back at the Veteran's Memorial, Louise spoke, "Yes, it is me." Amanda, dazed by this vision of her mom in the flesh, stumbled backward.

The older woman reached for her hand. "My child, my heart has been hurting for a long time. I'm sorry for what I did to you and Joshua. I didn't mean to be like the little boy with the blind dog. I pushed you away. I wasn't willing to be courageous enough to raise you and your brother." Louise's eyes were crystal blue. Even in the low lights of the corridor, Amanda could see her mother held a reservoir of regret in her eyes.

"I hated you for so long."

"I know. I deserved it."

"And—" She wanted to say more but couldn't quite put them into words.

Louise stroked her daughter's face, "Sometimes adults do very stupid things. I was selfish and lonely when your Daddy died. I'd lost my best friend. He was everything to me, I should have honored him by taking more responsibility with you and your brother. I turned to liquor as a way to cope and I did the unimaginable. It took me so long to forgive myself for it."

She studied her mother, "What do you mean?"

The woman sighed, "Remember when I came home wasted and I was crying? We had fallen asleep on the couch. You were thirteen."

Amanda nodded recalling how her mother threw her to the floor.

"It was a horrible night. I'd had an abortion—killing a life within my womb."

The blood on her skirt?

"I'm sorry and feel ashamed for what I did. It was a sinful act."

She huffed, "You make me sick."

Her mother shrugged. She looked old. Years of holding regret inside outlined her face.

Amanda walked a few feet away from her mom and twirled around, "I endured many years of pain. Joshua had to be both mom and dad to me. You shattered my trust in you. It crushed me to see you living in that crappy trailer park wearing a raggedy old outfit with a cigarette hanging out of your mouth."

"Those weren't good times. I am not proud of those years. I hurt Peter too. But when God gave me cancer, a miracle happened. I gave my life to Christ and gave the best I had left for Peter. Time was not enough, but I made do with what I could. I'm so sorry, honey. I truly am."

Amanda paced the floor, her shoes click-clacking, echoing through the hall. "My life has been crazy, like a roller-coaster. I have lived with this feeling of unworthiness thanks to you. I became addicted to alcohol. I've been in rehab. I've been drunk and passed out in front of my kids, in front of my own kids!" She shook her finger at her mom. "No more, God willing I'll be sober for the rest of my life. I'm not going to wait for something bad to happen to me, I won't be like you. I'm seizing the moment while I still can."

Louise moved closer to her, "You should, I wasn't a good example to you, or for your brother."

Amanda stiffened, "What do you want from me now?"

"Your forgiveness."

"My *forgiveness*? Ha, that's real funny."

"Please, sweetheart."

Anger was beginning to boil over within Amanda. "What about all I've gone through? I can't erase what's happened."

"No, you can't erase the past, but you can pave a new future with your daughters because you know what it takes to be a loving mom."

"What if it backfires? What if I lapse into my old habits? What if my family hates me and can't forgive me for what I've done to them?"

"That could happen, but look at the wonderful people you've met. You're changing, getting stronger. You've said it yourself. Your family will see that. Give them time to warm up to you. They'll forgive you."

Amanda sank down on the bench. Peter was right. *My mom wasn't a rotten person, just someone who couldn't get out from under the trouble she created. And it took a disease to heal her heart. Mom is looking for closure, too.* She sighed. They were more alike than she'd ever thought or wanted to be.

Her mother joined her, "There's an old saying … *Make it right. Make it matter.*"

"I have heard that before."

Both women grinned and hugged each other. Louise released her first. "So?"

"You're not letting that go, are you?"

"I can't. I need your forgiveness."

She remembered Harvey had been forgiven by his wife. Amanda knew she had to do the right thing and finish her journey of self-forgiveness. "Alright, Mom, I'll forgive you. But, I'm not going to forgive you just to forgive you. I'm forgiving you to free myself."

Louise smiled, "Thank you for that. I love you."

"I love you—" Amanda jumped out of her seat, "Mom, Mom. Where did you go?"

The sound of soft sneakers thudded down the corridor. The security guard approached her. "Closing time young lady."

Amanda checked her watch. It was 7:59 p.m. "That time already? It can't be?" She was flabbergasted, the time had seemed longer.

"Yes, ma'am, eight o' clock."

"Thank you. It was worth every minute." She then grabbed her purse and blew a kiss toward her brother's nameplate. "Love you. See you on the other side."

Chapter 47

Standing on the curb in front of an Uber sign, Amanda waited on Michigan Avenue. The light changed at Ohio, a black four-door sedan made a right and slid into a space in front of her. A man wearing a silver trucker's baseball cap stepped out of the car. He greeted her, took her belongings, and placed them in the trunk before opening the passenger door. The inside smelled like jasmine.

"Schaumburg, please, Barrington and Schaumburg Road."

The man drove down Michigan Avenue and made a left on Ontario so they could merge onto I-90 West. Amanda settled in her seat taking in the sights of the city, towering buildings, fancy boutiques and the few remaining people wandering the streets. Anything on Michigan Avenue north of Ohio Street was known as the Gold Coast, very touristy.

Ten years ago, she and Josh lived on the North side, near Logan square, a diverse-historical community that has its own public square, hence the name, located at the three-way intersection of Milwaukee, Logan Boulevard and Kedzie. Early on when they had first arrived from Iowa, she and her brother would go to North Avenue beach, hang out near Grant Park and even go up to the Willis Tower, formerly the Sears Tower. Amanda smiled, those were fun times. She and Joshua enjoyed exploring the city, going to the Planetarium and visiting Navy Pier.

Sadly, other memories intruded, the day she witnessed her brother's passing and her departure from Chicago. *Who knew I'd end up here again, married and with a family.* Even though Iowa was her birth state, she considered Illinois her home state.

With her journey behind her, Amanda had a lot of mending to do with her family. *At least, my mind and heart are in the right place.* She closed her eyes and whispered to her family, "Thank you, Joshua. Love you Peter and Mom."

The highway was at a standstill. She knew it would be like that until Harlem Avenue, hopefully it would open up again for bit and get congested around O'Hare and then free up near Route 53 by the Woodfield Mall. Amanda called home.

"On my way."

"Are you sure this time?" Ryan's tone sounded bitter.

"Yes. Should be there in an hour."

"I'm glad."

"Did you guys eat?"

"The girls were tired of waiting. We have some left over pizza, but I also made you macaroni and cheese."

Amanda's heart bubbled, "Yummy. Thank you. I'll definitely have the mac and cheese. I've missed you."

"The same here."

"See you soon," she ended the call.

The driver had Jazz playing in the background. It sounded homey, like the times her father played the radio as he tinkered in the garage.

They passed the Harlem exit and traffic opened up. Amanda yawned. Having slept in different beds, she was looking forward to sleeping on her own mattress and snuggling up with her husband. They reached Route 53 and the Interstate 90 junction. Amanda's heart beat faster. Traffic lightened up. *Soon I'll be reunited with my babies, Emily and Rose—my God-given blessings.* She was lucky to have had them easily. She knew a lot of women that had problems getting pregnant. Her heart ached, she'd chosen to let alcohol consume her taking away precious time with her kids.

Taking their picture out of her purse, she held it to her chest, praying that she would be a good mom, not to let her family down. Her mistakes were in the past, but new opportunities lay ahead. She was going to focus on the future; a future with her family, *an alcohol-free future.*

Exiting Barrington Road, heading south, the car coasted along. Her children would have a lot of questions, Amanda fidgeted. This hadn't been a business trip. She'd have to be honest to let them form their own opinions.

Opening her purse out of habit, looking for a piece of gum, she closed it knowing there wouldn't be any in there ever again.

They were approaching Schaumburg Road. "Turn right here, after this strip mall make a left on Heather Lane."

"No problem."

Amanda watched the familiarity of her neighborhood come into view, Jewel Osco where she shopped, Nick and Vito's Pizza Depot, and the Kohl's where she often bought the girls their clothing.

She started rehearsing what she would say to her daughters. *Hi girls. I missed you. I love you. I'm terribly sorry for being away so long. Please forgive me.* Nothing sounded right. Amanda wanted to be genuine. Shaking her head, she couldn't think anymore. *I'm going to say whatever comes from my heart.*

"Go down two blocks and make a sharp right on Hemsley. It's 1417." She ran a Chapstick over her dry lips. "Third house from the corner on the right, the brown-brick two-story with the long driveway."

The vehicle slid in front of the driveway. Opening her wallet, Amanda began counting money to give to the drive when she heard an unusual voice. "Was my driving okay?"

She stopped and cautiously raised her eyes. The man turned, removing his hat to reveal short dark hair and long sideburns. He looked to be in his forties.

"Daddy?"

"Yes, it's me." He pointed to the house, "This it?"

"Yeah," Amanda mumbled, staring into his grey eyes.

"Are you ready?"

"Dad, I don't understand what's happening."

"What's there to understand courtesy of divine intervention?" John chuckled, a deep, hearty laugh.

She couldn't take her eyes off him, "Gosh, you haven't aged."

"You don't grow old in Heaven."

Amanda choked up. So many years had passed. She'd never been able to say goodbye to her father, to tell him she loved him.

As if reading her mind, John's eyes twinkled, "I know, I have felt exactly the same way myself. I'm grateful for your efforts toward recovery. There's a lot of work to do still. Don't stop. Temptation is everywhere. Live your life fully. Be happy with what you have, don't think about what you've missed."

She couldn't take it any longer letting all the emotion of the trip consume her. Her father reached over and wiped her tears with his hand. "May I have the honor of giving you back to your family?"

Amanda was moments away from making her life matter, making it right again, "Yes, Daddy."

Her father exited the car, popped the trunk and set her things on the curb. Getting out of the car, she saw the screen door open; Ryan stood in the doorway with Emily and Rose close behind him.

John came forward and looked at his daughter, "End of the line, girl."

"I know," her voice was soft and jittery.

John embraced her, "I love you."

"I love you too, Dad."

He handed her a medium-sized brown paper bag, "For you."

She carefully opened the bag and peered inside, *a box of macaroni and cheese!* Amanda squeaked, "What?"

With a big smile across his face, John answered, "From Joshua. He doesn't want you to ever be without it."

She snickered, "Whole milk, not two percent."

Amanda then gasped. Under the mac and cheese carton was her jewelry box! The one her mom had bought her. Opening the top, she looked at the figurine and her cheeks got wet.

"From Mom, she never got rid of it, share it with your daughters." She jumped into her father's arms again. John squeezed her back, "You don't have to chase after the wind anymore. You be the wind that people chase after. Stay sober. Be strong. Don't falter, please."

"Thank you so much, Daddy."

John waved to her family, got into the car and drove off. Amanda watched him go. She realized her past had just left her and her future was in front of her. Holding Joshua's pendant around her neck, thoughts and words from friends and family flashed in her mind:

Gretchen: "Your body is a temple. What you put into it fuels how you'll use that energy. What you don't need, you won't miss, believe me."

Harvey: "Life is hard anyway you cut it. Evil or not, we all need second chances. … Learn to forgive."

Jane: "I don't take anything personally and I give it my all every day. I give it to Him. I've learned how powerful God's love can be to make me into His image. He has taught me to be worthy of myself because I am worthy in the Lord's eyes."

Peter: "Don't miss the moments. Risk it all. It's worth it."

Joshua: "Whatever you do in life, make it right; make it matter, everything. ***Make it matter!***"

Amanda sprinted to her family, embracing and kissing her husband and scooping up her children. She held them tight. "I'm back … I'm home." *Going to do it right this time.*

Her daughters' shrieked with joy. "Mommy's home and for good this time…"

THE END

References

Alcoholism is an addictive disease. It consumes one's life and has destroyed many families. If YOU or anyone you know with an alcohol addiction, please do not hesitate and reach out for help.

Below are a few useful resources:

http://www.aa.org/
https://addictionresource.com/alcohol/treatment/hotlines/
https://recovery-world.com/National-Hotline-Phone-Numbers.html
http://www.alcoholic.org/research/the-stages-of-alcoholism/
http://www.addictioncampuses.com/resources/addiction-campuses-blog/the-4-stages-of-alcoholism-for-the-functioning-alcoholic/
https://alcoholrehab.com/alcoholism/recovering-alcoholic-or-recovered-alcoholic/
https://www.healthline.com/health/alcoholism/withdrawal
https://www.gotquestions.org/Joseph-brothers.html

Next Steps

Dear Reader,

If you've enjoyed *She Made It Matter*, I would love it if you would help others enjoy this book, too.

Here are some ways you can help spread the word:

A. **Recommend it.** Help other readers find this book by recommending it to friends, writing groups, reading groups, book clubs and discussion forums.
B. **Share it.** Let other readers know you've read the book by posting a note on your social media pages.
C. **Review it.** Very important. Good, bad or ugly, please tell others about this story. Review it on your favorite online retailer.

Your support of my writing endeavor is greatly appreciated.

Other Stories by the Author

"I'm not a bestselling author; I'm just a 'nobody' who uses stories as my communication tool to encourage others to find their purpose."

Please check out my other novels:

Love's Perfect Surrender. A Christian romance about a troubled married couple who lose the "us" part of their relationship after a failed miscarriage and still birth, until, the miraculous birth of their daughter, born with a congenital limb deficiency, who graces their lives shaking their core beliefs in hopes of making peace and letting love in.

Petrella, the Gillian Princess is a Middle-Grade fairy tale that interweaves themes similar to *The Little Mermaid, Cinderella, Tangled, Sleeping Beauty* and *Noah's Ark*. It's about a courageous young princess who defies rank and authority to follow her heart. A story of hope, bravery and triumph. It is meant to be enjoyed by all readers young at heart, but especially aimed at those children who read middle grade fiction: ages 8 –13.

A Tribute to Tulipia is a feel good story for all ages about a tulip and her family who live in an oasis of tangled vines, brush and shrubs. Bullied and picked on, the reader journeys with the alienated family who never backed down in their fight to unify a changing forest. It is a great lesson and reminder about what it takes to be a true friend, what sacrifice means to lay down one's life in order to save another, and to always, always **do the right thing** no matter what.

The Rekindler is a Dystopian short story about one man's vision for a revival, a return to God in the backdrop of a one-world government and one-world religion. It's about the persecution of believers in this day and age, colliding with nations wanting to have worldly power, a one-world religion, controlled by an elite few. It's a book on revival, evangelism, and the power of the Holy Spirit that lives within those who believe. It's also a tribute to all the past revivalists who have come before us to WAKE US UP and get right with God.

Acknowledgments

"Inspiration doesn't just happen on a whim; it takes persistent, focused inspiration."

I'm thankful to Jesus Christ, my Lord and Savior, for giving me the wisdom and discipline to write. For my husband and children, who continue to empower me to write stories about human complexities.

I couldn't have enhanced this tale from the very beginning (nine years ago) without the assistance of my beta-readers: Wendy Rue Sable, Lella Favia, Lawrence Konn, Alison Migala, and my wonderful editor and friend, Dennis De Rose from *Moneysaver Editing*. I truly appreciate their time and investment in helping my work shine.

To the musicians out there, I thank you. Your lyrics and melody have fueled my creativity in my all writings. I've found inspiration from your songs for each section.

Lastly, to all my reading fans, thank you for sticking with me, for your encouragement and positive words all these years.

Until next time …

Be well. Be safe. Be happy.

About the Author

"We are all vulnerable to stumbling like Amanda Reynolds who neglected to forgive her past; not believing that everything she desired had been in front of her all along. It takes a lot of courage to accept the things you can't control and take charge of those things you can control."

Chicago-born, a full-time mother and author, Chiara Talluto, is known as the Master Storyteller in her household. She writes Inspirational/Christian drama empowering women to discover their faith, use perseverance to overcome adversity, and become heroes of their own destinies. Chiara has also dabbled in writing middle-grade fantasy-fairy tales to encourage girls in developing strong morals and values, and to always stand up for what is right.

Currently, Chiara is hard at work penning other stories. Her motto is live, laugh and cry. To learn more about Chiara, visit www.chiaratalluto.com.